DATING FOR DECEMBER

LYNDSEY GALLAGHER

For Amber.

Full disclosure: your dad and I have every intention of becoming
Frank & Penny Jackson!
We love you xxx

Chapter One

AVA

Tuesday 28ᵗʰ November

Perving on the sexy stranger strutting by the frost-kissed sash window of my office is my favourite weekday past time. That broad frame swaggers past most mornings, radiating a presence so powerful it sucks the oxygen right out of my lungs.

I know nothing about him, except his cheekbones could cut glass, he possesses the ability to make my heart rate double in my chest, and he has exceptional and expensive taste in suits.

Every time my eyes land on his broad masculine shoulders, tapered waist, and the sculpted curves of his ass cheeks, I can't help but wonder who he is.

What he does.

And if he's single.

Though I'm way too preoccupied with other people's love lives to work on my own right now. Starting a brand-new exclusive dating agency has that effect.

HeartSync has a unique business model compared to other matchmaking services. It's the opposite of Tinder,

Grindr, Match.com or any of the other quick-fix fornication sites out there. Don't be fooled: I'm not frowning on fornication. I'm an avid advocate of affection, intimacy, and pleasure, as long as it's with the intention of developing into something meaningful.

My mission is to cultivate a community where people can find a partner with potential. To provide a safe service where women won't be preyed on. Won't be swiped past if they're not deemed attractive enough. Where the focus is on an emotional match before either party ever sees a photo of the other.

'Is that Mr Suave Suit Guy again?' Bonnie, my PA and childhood best friend, stands from behind the desk next to me, craning her neck to get a glimpse at the guy we insouciantly nicknamed months ago.

'How did you guess?' My gaze remains on those granite glutes cupped so perfectly by that indecently decent suit.

'I don't know ...' Her heart-shaped face angles upwards. 'Maybe it has something to do with the drool dripping from the side of your mouth.' She tucks her caramel highlighted hair behind her ears and wiggles her eyebrows. 'I'd hate to see the state of your panties.' She sniggers.

'Do you have to be so crude?' I toss a paperclip at her head.

'Oh, because you're not?' She scoffs.

My mobile phone buzzes on the maple-wood desk in front of me, stealing my attention from Mr Suave Suit Guy who strides purposefully into the distance.

He's sullen, serious, like he has the responsibility of the world on those powerful shoulders. He moves with meaning ... Does he save lives?

Is he on the verge of discovering a cure for cancer?

Or maybe that's just the romantic in me wanting to

believe this guy is some sort of suit-clad superhero. A man who looks that good has to be well ... good, right?

Using one claret painted finger I swipe the screen to answer the call.

'How's the dating scene going?' My brother's smug voice purrs through the phone.

I rock back on my ivory leather chair as my eyes return to Grafton Street again. Dublin is stunning this time of year, but the lavish twinkling Christmas decorations have taunted me since early November, a perpetual reminder that I'm facing into another festive season alone.

Nate, my aforementioned smug brother, on the other hand, is about to marry the woman of his dreams. He's also a hotshot Hollywood movie star, and if he wasn't my brother, his eternal teasing would be insufferable.

'Orgasm central. All night every night.' I lie, hoping the visual might deter my brother from asking any further questions. 'Things are absolutely randy. I mean dandy.'

Bonnie mouths, 'Liar' and shakes her head. Her nude-painted lips lift into a grin.

'Really?' Amusement gilds Nate's reply. 'Are you referring to the business? Or your own love life?'

'Both.' Another lie.

'Don't tell me you've actually got a date for my wedding?' A low chuckle of disbelief rumbles into my ear. Apparently the visual didn't work. I'll have to paint a more vivid description next time.

Nate's rented an entire island off the west coast of Ireland to enjoy his wedding without the fear of the pesky paparazzi who relentlessly pursue him, his fiancée, Holly, and their brand-new baby, Harriet.

So, I need more than a date. I need someone who's prepared to give up not just one, but several days of their life at one of the busiest times of the year. The wedding is set to be a lavish four-day celebration complete with before parties, after parties, and all-day parties.

'Of course I have.' My teeth nip the inside of my cheeks like they're punishing me for lying.

I haven't, but I'll find one if it kills me.

My taste in the opposite sex has always been questionable. Given my disastrous dating history, my brother and my four sisters consider my career choice hilarious. But my endless string of dreadful dates is the precise reason I *am* qualified to run a dating agency. I have experience. Mountains of it. If I don't use it for the greater good, all those dating disasters will have been for nothing.

I was so engrossed drowning in the dreamy eyes of my last boyfriend, Josh, I failed to spot the prison tag on his right ankle. Or the faint tell-tale pale band around the fourth finger on his left hand. It's hard to pinpoint exactly which of these omissions were worse, but ultimately the outcome was the same – I haven't dated since.

Instead, I've ploughed my time, energy, and every cent I possess into matchmaking others.

I'm a firm believer in true love. Hearts and flowers. Soulmates. Endless romance. Long, fulfilling, happy marriages. I might be a sucker for romance novels, but I've seen it in real life too in my parents, Penny and Frank 'zero-boundaries-let's-talk-about-our-sex-life-over-the-dinner-table' Jackson.

I just haven't experienced it myself yet.

And after Josh, the thought of putting myself out there again is one I've shied away from. Nate and my sisters might tease me for running a dating agency when I apparently can't get a date myself, but it's safer to focus on my business.

It's no secret that I'm looking for financial investors.

Set up was expensive.

The fancy website.

This slick city centre office.

The three wonderful women I employ.

The advertising.

I founded HeartSync knowing it would take a while to turn a profit, but I didn't factor in exactly how long. Though the secret appeal of having an investor is not just the financial security, it's having another grown adult to bounce ideas off. Someone to share the sometimes-terrifying responsibility of running a business with.

My hotshot brother agreed to invest, but with two staunch stipulations:

1. The business had to be up and running for a year before he would consider it. (I have a reputation for being impulsive when it comes to my career choices. I'm not flighty, just fussy. Life's too short to be anything but happy in a job that consumes more time than a husband, so I imagine).
2. I have to take a date to his wedding.

Not just any date either. One that looks promising for the future. Nate insists if my business is truly viable, finding a date for myself should be a walk in the park.

Luckily, next week marks HeartSync's one year anniversary. We're hosting an extravagant party in The Shelbourne hotel to celebrate and to generate a fresh wave of publicity. So that's one box ticked.

Unluckily, I don't have a date for my brother's wedding.

I sweep my wavy hair out of my eyes with the back of my hand. If I have to hire a goddamn male escort to attend my brother's wedding and fake it, then I'll do it. And if I'm ticking that box, I might get him to tick my own box too. Heaven knows, it's been a while.

Though hiring an escort won't do a lot to quash the niggling feeling in my stomach. The one that wonders if my siblings might be right. If I really am capable of running a successful dating agency, when I truly do have the worst taste in men. I'm a poor advertisement for my company's services. If I went to the dentist and his teeth were black and decaying in his head, I'd run out the door faster than a coyote on cocaine.

'So, who's the lucky man?' Nate pries, dragging my thoughts back to the conversation.

'You'll meet him soon enough.' I readjust my mobile to rest between my ear and my shoulder.

Thankfully, I still have five weeks until the wedding. I'm going to have to get over my apprehension and get back on the horse. Personally scour every single sign-up form ever submitted to HeartSync's database. There must be someone suitable in there.

'I'll meet him sooner than you think ...' Nate's deep voice penetrates my silent plotting.

'What?' My head snaps round, and I glance suspiciously round my open plan office like my famous movie-star brother might have snuck in, sending my employees' knees weak with desire.

The coast is clear for now. Cleo and Violet, my two loyal but lively admin assistants huddle together in front of Cleo's Mac, pouring over a sign-up form. The similar look of horror stretched across their faces piques my curiosity.

The extortionate registration fee usually deters applicants who aren't one hundred percent committed to finding true love, but occasionally we get the odd strange one slip through the net.

'You didn't think I was going to miss HeartSync's anniversary party, did you? I want to be a part of these things if I'm going to invest.' Nate's warm chuckle makes my blood run cold. 'I assume the guy you're dating will be there, right?'

Fuck.

I have work to do. And fast. On the plus side, I wanted publicity, and hot, happy A-List celebs generate that in spades.

'Of course he will. Got to go. He's on his way here now and he'll probably want to bend me over the desk before taking me for breakfast.' I hang up before Nate hears my groan. My forehead falls to my desk.

'What the fuck, Ava?' Bonnie gesticulates wildly with her hands.

'I need him to invest. And so do you if you want to keep your job. I knew starting a business like this would be hard, but it's sucking every cent I saved.'

'Boss,' Cleo calls across the office, cocking her purple tinged bob to the right. 'We have a bit of a weird one. You've got to take a look at this ...'

HeartSync Registration Form

Congratulations for committing to finding your forever. Please answer the following questions in as much detail as possible, for us to secure your most suitable match.

Name: *Cillian Callaghan*
　　D.O.B: *Old enough to know better ...*
　　Email Address: *divorcedaddy@gmail.com*
　　Phone Number: *0876665238 – don't hold your breath for dick pics*
　　Occupation: *Lawyer*

. . .

1. Describe your ideal partner in as much detail as possible.

Must possess the ability to convince my cheating ex that I've moved on and am in a committed long-term relationship.

2. Describe yourself in as much detail as possible.

Diligent. Dysfunctional. Desperate – given I'm filling in this form

...

Do you want to know my penis size too?

3. Describe your ideal first date.

A blow job and a whiskey – a man can dream right?

4. Describe your ideal holiday.

I own a law firm. I don't have time to holiday.

5. What are you looking for from a life partner?

Ha! There's no such thing.

6. Have you ever been unfaithful?

No. I might be a grumpy workaholic, but I'm not a twat.

7. Provide a brief description of your parents' relationship.

Fucked-up.

8. Do you have any siblings?

Knowing my father, anything's a possibility …

9. How important is marriage to you?

Very important – given I make a serious living from their termination.

10. What are you hoping to achieve from signing up to HeartSync?

A fucking miracle.

Cleo isn't joking. Divorce Daddy has serious issues. But I'm not sure HeartSync is the right company to help him.

Unless …

CILLIAN

One day earlier

Monday 27th November

I don't believe in true love.

I don't believe in soulmates.

And I don't believe in 'until death do us part.'

The only girl who's ever stolen my heart is six years old, three-and-a-half feet tall, has pigtails and a lisp, and calls me daddy.

Being a single father is tough. It makes standing in court tearing strangers' marriages apart feel effortless in comparison. But I wouldn't change it for the world.

Phoebe wasn't planned. Not by me at least, but she's the best thing that ever happened to me. Her mother, Teagan, on the other hand, is a piece of work.

Any woman who leaves their partner and child for a man they met while away on a girl's weekend in Marbella, doesn't deserve to be a parent, let alone to a little girl as awesome as Phoebe.

Teagan blows in and out of our lives like a tornado, leaving me to repair the destruction each time she leaves. Which is, coincidentally, each time she gets a new boyfriend, or the offer of an opportunity to party some-where sunny.

And people ask why I don't date.

Even if I had the time, I don't have the inclination.

Not after Teagan.

Not after my parents.

And not with what I see day in and day out in the courtroom.

I nod at the stoic-looking judge at the front of the high-ceilinged courtroom, straighten my impeccable suit, and congratulate my client on her divorce. The terms are every-thing she asked for, and I managed to secure her more assets than she'd dared to dream of.

And that's exactly why I'm the best divorce lawyer this country has ever seen.

My work here is done.

A quick glance at the chunky Swiss metal on my wrist reveals it's too late to go back to the office. The staff wouldn't thank me for it anyway. They're all terrified of me. Well, except Beth, my PA. We spend way too much time together for me to maintain the marmoreal mask in her presence.

I button my jacket, grab my briefcase and head out into the crisp November evening with two things on my mind: a neat whiskey, and a hug from my baby girl.

My black X5 BMW waits for me in the car park. That unique, luxurious new car scent saturates the air and seeps into my nostrils as I slide behind the leather steering wheel.

It takes forty minutes to get through the rush hour traffic to Sandymount. Finally, I reach the electric gates of the refur-bished Victorian house we call home. Soft light glows from the upstairs corner windows. Phoebe isn't in bed yet. A warmth heats my chest and tingles through my torso.

The gates swing open, and the wheels crunch up the gravel driveway past the wrought iron lanterns lining the path to the teak front door. I park besides the metallic pot plants overflowing with this year's dusty pink and white violas.

I bought this house the week after Teagan announced she was pregnant. In truth, it's probably too big for just Phoebe and me, but I love the space, the seclusion, and the security of it. With a full-sized gym, an outdoor jacuzzi, and an acre of meticulously maintained lawns, it's the only place I can take sanctuary in the city.

The front door swings open as I approach, but instead of Phoebe's smiling toothy face grinning back at me, I'm greeted by Matilda, our amazing housekeeper/nanny. Matilda's like a middle-aged Mary Poppins, and she's the sole reason I feel comfortable leaving my daughter each day while I earn enough money to maintain this lavish lifestyle.

Tonight though, Matilda's usual warm smile is replaced with a tight-lipped grimace. 'She's back.'

I don't need to ask who.

It's etched into every line creasing my housekeeper's forehead.

Teagan.

For fuck's sake.

It took weeks to settle Phoebe after the last time Teagan swanned in, then swiftly out again. Weeks of sobbing. Weeks of night terrors. Weeks of reassuring my baby girl that I'll never walk out on her the way her mother does.

'Where is she?' My voice rumbles like thunder.

Matilda steps back as I bulldoze into the huge rectangular hallway, frantically searching for my daughter.

'Teagan insisted on putting Phoebe to bed.' Matilda nods to the wide centre staircase sweeping up to the second floor. 'Reminded me in no uncertain terms that I'm "just" the housekeeper.'

I charge up the stairs, my blood boiling beneath my skin.

'Phoebe?' It takes every ounce of will power I possess to keep an even tone.

'We're in here.' My ex-girlfriend's excessively upbeat tone rings from Phoebe's bedroom, like her presence here is the most natural occurrence in the world.

Adrenaline propels me through the doorway. Our daughter is nestled into her pink princess themed bed, complete with white twinkling fairy lights. Her blonde hair falls in soft curls across the pillow. Wide silver eyes, almost the exact same shade as my own spark with sheer undulated glee. 'Mammy's home!' she announces, like it's a good thing.

'So I see.' My gaze falls to Teagan who's kneeling at the foot of the bed, wearing a ridiculously revealing black dress, clutching Phoebe's tiny hand like a lifeline.

My ex is a beautiful woman. Stunning in fact. With long blonde hair and a figure to die for, I'm sure she's the epitome of many male fantasies.

Just not mine.

She's my worst nightmare. Or rather, the hurt that she causes our child every time she waltzes in and out of our lives again is.

'I came home,' Teagan whispers wistfully, the same way one might declare they've saved an orphan from a burning building, donated a million euros to Save The Children, or been awarded a badge of honour for carrying a bleeding comrade home from battle.

'So I see.' My leather loafers sink into the plush, pink carpet as I cross the room. Placing a tender kiss on Phoebe's smooth, sallow cheek, I inhale the familiar scent of her bubble-gum scented shampoo into my lungs.

'How's my princess? Did you have a good day?' I choose to ignore the living, breathing, albeit stunning, elephant in the room in favour of a little normality.

'I'm great, Daddy. Matilda made cupcakes after school.

And ...' Phoebe wets her lips and pauses for effect. At only six years old, she's already harnessed her dramatic streak. 'Teacher told me I'm going to play Mary in the nativity play next month.'

'Wow. That's amazing, honey!' Teagan coos from behind me. 'I can't wait!'

I jerk my head to my delusional ex and fire her a warning glare. We both know that she'll be long gone before it comes around. And the sooner the better because the longer she stays, the more hope Phoebe gets that this time it'll be for good.

'You'll be the best Mary that there ever was, princess.' My fingers brush across Phoebe's cheek, smoothing back stray wisps of hair from her forehead. I tuck the duvet tight beneath the mattress. 'Shall I read you a bedtime story?'

Phoebe sucks a low slow breath into the gap where she lost her two front teeth, glancing dubiously between Teagan and me. 'Do you mind if Mammy does it tonight?'

My heart slices open for her. Not just because she's desperate to get whatever limited time with her mother she can, but because the hint of regret welling in the whites of her eyes suggests she feels guilty for picking Teagan over me.

'Of course not, princess. Mammy can do it tonight, and I'll do it tomorrow.' And every night after that, until Teagan breezes in here again.

I'd never stop Teagan seeing Phoebe, but I wish she'd agree to more structured visits. A routine would provide Phoebe the stability every little girl needs.

I brush my lips over Phoebe's forehead. 'I love you, Feebs, sweet dreams.'

'I'll see you downstairs.' I frown at Teagan pointedly as I barrel past her in search of a strong drink. If I didn't need one before, I do now.

. . .

Twenty minutes later Teagan drifts down the staircase like she hasn't got a care in the world, which I suppose, she hasn't. She lives off her ridiculously generous trust fund, flitting from place to place depending on who she's dating. The woman is about as far removed from the real world as Neil fucking Armstrong when he set foot on the moon.

Teagan's heels click across the varnished original wooden floorboards as she waltzes through the hallway like she owns the place. Thank God I didn't cave to her demands and marry her, or she would. I tried to love her; I really did, but we were never compatible.

The truth is when she left it was a relief.

'She's asleep.' My ex hovers in the doorway, gripping the thick architrave in her slim fingers for a second before heading to the crystal decanter and helping herself to my fifteen-year-old Redbreast whiskey.

I place my own glass on the mahogany coffee table in front of me and drop down to perch on the arm of the leather couch.

She turns purposefully, caressing the crystal glass with her thumb. Her jade eyes rake over my fingers as I remove my tie.

I wait with a stiff spine for whatever horseshit excuse she's going to spout for dropping out of Phoebe's life for the last six months. Though, none of it matters. What matters is Phoebe, and minimising the damage Teagan will cause when she disappears again.

'A phone call would have been nice.' I pick up my glass and gulp, eyeing the woman I made a human with over the crystal as the honey-coloured liquid slips down my throat.

Teagan's answering smile is both victorious and flirtatious. 'I knew you missed me.'

The alcohol splutters on my lips. 'Oh, I missed you alright. Like a hole in the fucking head. Your daughter on the other hand, she cried herself to sleep every night for six weeks straight after you upped and left – again.'

Teagan's symmetrical features wrinkle into a wince. She shrugs her bare shoulders, shaking the thin straps of her dress. 'I'm sorry. I should have called. I meant to ... then the longer it went on, the harder it became.'

Jesus, you'd think we were discussing an item at the grocery store that she neglected to pick up, not the neglect of her only child. Fury burns like fire through my veins.

She appears at my side, placing a palm on my bicep. 'I'm sorry, baby.'

'What the fuck, Teagan?' I flinch and shrug her off.

'Come on, Cillian. Don't be like that. I'm here now.' She shimmies against me, brushing her breasts against my chest. 'Let's have a drink. Catch up. Curl up, if you like.' Her tongue darts out over her lower lip. 'You're still working out, I see. You know, you pull off a suit better than any man I've ever met.' Her hand drops to my crotch.

'Yeah – of which there have been many.' I push her hand away and leap to my feet, desperate to put some distance between us.

The woman is delusional if she thinks there could ever be anything between us now. Hell will freeze over first. I wish she'd get it into her head. Phoebe might want a relationship with her. But I don't.

Both scenarios can coexist in harmony if she'd just grow the fuck up and start behaving like a parent.

It's been a long day. I exhale a weary breath. 'What do you want, Teagan?'

The column of her throat bobs as she swallows hard. 'I want you, Cillian.'

I suppose that explains the dress. She does this now and again, tries it on with me. She fooled me once; she'll never fool me again.

Teagan mistakes my silence for surrender. Her pupils trail across my torso as she prowls across the room. 'You never moved on ...' Her fingers trail across her exposed shoulder and she lowers the strap on her already revealing dress. 'You still want me. I know you do. We still have a chance. We could still be a family.'

A bitter laugh hisses from my mouth. 'Oh, I've moved on, sweetheart. You better believe it.'

I haven't but it has absolutely nothing to do with pining over Teagan.

Once bitten, twice shy.

Plus, by the time I've met every one of Phoebe's needs, I haven't got enough energy to entertain any of my own.

But if Teagan thinks I have someone else in my bed, maybe she'll stop this ridiculous farce.

'Liar.' Her irises flash with heat, but all I see is the cold heart of a woman who can leave our child without so much as a backwards glance. 'You and I are meant to be, Cillian. That's why you've never met anyone else. Oh, I'm sure you offer some "out-of-office services" to some of your desperate needy clients, but there's never been anyone serious since me. I still have a few little birdies in your office that tell me everything I need to know. There's never been anyone else. No one meaningful anyway. You still have feelings for me.'

There's many a newfound divorcee searching for someone to celebrate their freedom with, but that's not me. And that Teagan would even think I'd take a client to bed highlights exactly how different our moral compasses are.

'I'm seeing someone.' The lie is out of my mouth before I've had the chance to think it through. It's the quickest way to shut down her bullshit and get her out of my life. 'It's early days, but it's serious.'

Teagan's mouth drops open. 'I ... I ...' She palms her sternum like she's in pain. 'Who is she? What's her name?

Has Phoebe met her yet? Do you love her?' A thousand inse-curities flit across her face.

I don't usually condone lying but in this instance, if it helps to rip the plaster off, it's worth it. If Teagan thinks she has some competition with Phoebe, she might make more of an effort to be a parent to her. Or at least stop dropping in and out of her life on a whim. It's not healthy for any of us.

'Like I said, it's early days. Phoebe hasn't met her yet. But she will when the time is right.'

Teagan takes a step back. A faraway look clouds her expression. 'I want to meet her. In fact. I won't feel right leaving Phoebe again until I do. I want to know what sort of woman is going to be hanging around my daughter.'

Oh fuck.

And that's the only reason I fill in the sign-up form for a dating agency, two hours and three whiskeys later.

Chapter Three

AVA

Tuesday 28th November

I'm hunched over my desk long after Bonnie, Cleo, and Violet head home. I've scanned the entire database for a potential date to take to next week's anniversary party, and Nate's wedding, with no success.

My thoughts return to the weird registration form that came in earlier. Cillian Callaghan's desperation is on par with my own.

Initially, I'd wondered if it was some sort of prank, but he paid the hefty sign-up fee in full, so clearly, he's looking for something.

Or someone.

His brutal honesty on his form combined with those sarcastic one-liners has me pondering exactly what type of man he is, other than a grumpy, cynical son-of-a-bitch, that is.

He's everything this agency shouldn't attract.

Typing his name into Google, I scour Cillian Callaghan divorce lawyer. Article after article floods my screen. It seems Mr Callaghan wasn't exaggerating when he claimed to make his living by tearing marriages apart. His success statistics are scarily high, and from the A-List names mentioned in these articles it looks like he represents some seriously high-profile clients.

His gold and black website is embossed with fancy metallic calligraphy but there's no photo of the man himself, which only serves to intensify my interest in him. Looks like his company covers every aspect of law, from criminal defence to family interests. Why did he choose to specialise in divorce?

I pull up his sign-up form and dial his number before I can overthink it. It's later than strictly professional, but the man is a self-professed workaholic. He's probably still dreaming up ways to destroy people's relationships.

'Hello?' A deep velvety voice snaps with a tinge of irritation.

'Cillian? My name is Ava Jackson, I'm the owner of Heart-Sync, the dating agency you signed up to.' My heart accelerates in my chest. This was a stupid idea. What was I even thinking?

'Oh. That.' He exhales heavily.

'Is this a good time to talk?' I rest an elbow on my desk and try to conjure an image of the man on the other end of the phone.

Is he tall, dark, and handsome?

Short, round, and bald?

His voice suggests the former, but his sign-up form implies the latter.

'It's as good as any, I suppose.' His reluctant drawl suggests he'd rather stick needles in his eyes. 'I'm just having a whiskey.'

'No blow job with that?' It's out of my mouth before I can help it. That's what happens when you're raised by Penny and Frank 'zero-boundaries' Jackson. My parents would be so proud of me.

He pauses for a beat. 'Are you offering? Because it's been a while. I can send a car for you in ten minutes if that's the case.' I swear there's a hint of a smirk in that tone.

'We're not that kind of agency. Careful, or you could get sued for harassment.' I bite my lip; grateful he can't see the blush flashing across my cheeks.

'Given your initial remark, you wouldn't have a leg to stand on.' His voice oozes certainty.

'I might, if I had a decent lawyer.' What am I playing at?

Seriously, am I flirting with the one of the strangest, most surly clients I've ever encountered?

This is what happens when I avoid men for the best part of a year. Though, that voice might be sullen but there's a sublimely sexy edge to it. The man could audition as an audiobook narrator. I'd listen to War and Peace in Russian just to have that rich smooth tone slide into my ear and straight over every notch of my spine.

'I *am* a decent lawyer and I doubt even I could help you.'

'You know what, Mr Hot Shot Lawyer, maybe you *can* help me.' The idea I've been subconsciously toying with spurts like a volcano. 'Just not in a courtroom.'

'And here was me thinking I paid a hefty sign-up fee for you to help me ...' He muses.

'Perhaps we can help each other.' I nip the inside of my cheek, trying to articulate the right words. 'From your registration form, I gather you're not actually looking for a love match, is that correct?'

'There's no such thing.' He says it with such certainty, if I didn't know better, I might even believe him.

'Well, given your chosen profession, I suppose I can understand why you might think that but—'

He cuts me off before I can finish. 'It's a fact, but given *your* chosen profession, I suppose we'll have to agree to disagree.'

Someone's clearly done a number on him. It has to be the cheating ex he's trying to get rid of.

'Mr Callaghan, please hear me out.' I pick up the pen that's lying on my desk and draw tiny hearts on the wad of pink Post-It notes in front of me. My new client might not be a hopeless romantic, but it looks like I still am, despite this year's abstinence. 'Given the way you answered the question-naire, it would be utterly unprofessional and detrimental to even consider matching you with anyone in HeartSync's data-base. We join hearts, not break them. Given you're clearly not looking for love, it's a recipe for disaster.'

'So, you're ringing to issue me a refund?' That voice. It's liquid gold. So rich. So smooth.

'I'm ringing you to offer a different solution. I wasn't joking when I said perhaps, we could help each other.' Espe-cially if you look even a fraction as sexy as you sound.

'Go on.' His voice piques slightly.

'I find myself in a similar situation to you.' I confess, cradling the phone against my shoulder.

A tutting sound follows. 'You have a cheating ex who's hanging round like a bad smell, trying to get into your pants while simultaneously wrecking any bit of routine you put in place for your six-year-old daughter?'

Wow. No wonder the man is a cynic when it comes to relationships.

'Not exactly.' I stare down at the hearts I've drawn on the Post-It notes and am surprised to see I've scrawled the name Cillian in the centre. I tear it off and toss it into the waste-basket tucked beneath my desk. 'It seems to me that you could benefit from a fake-girlfriend. And I find myself in need of a date for several events in December ...' I trail off and wait as my suggestion settles in.

Deep even breaths tickling my ear are the only reassur-ance that he hasn't hung up on me.

This is madness.

I should hang up.

'You own a dating agency, but you need a fake boyfriend?' He snorts. 'I'm not sure if that's tragic, amusing, or if I should demand a refund after all.'

And that right there is precisely my problem. He's right. I'm a lost cause. This is a lost cause.

'It was a stupid suggestion. Inappropriate too.' I blow out a huge lungful of air, deflating both physically and emotionally in unison. 'I'll issue your refund immediately.'

'Don't you dare.' A low growl follows. 'You, Ava Jackson, might be the only woman who can help me.'

'Really?' Surprise surges through my soul replacing the stupidity weighing down on me.

'I think we'd need to meet in person, to see if this could work.' Code for, 'to see if you've got three heads.' I hear a thrumming. Like he's tapping his fingers on a desk. Or his whiskey glass. 'When are you free?'

'I, errrr ...' I glance at my watch. It's not quite nine o'clock.

'If I send a car for you now, will you come?' His question is loaded with intensity. Or maybe that's just in my head.

'If you're looking for that blow job, you can forget it.' I tease, but I'm not entirely joking. This will only ever be business.

I've never even laid eyes on this man, but going by his sign-up form, he's not exactly my usual type. Mind you, my usual type are usually assholes.

'That would imply this is a first date, when in fact, it's a business meeting.'

Good. At least we're on the same page.

He clears his throat. 'But if you want to add a sweetener to the deal, I suppose I could consider it. I wasn't joking when I said it's been a while.' There's that hint of humour again. If I was a betting woman, I'd bet my life his smiles are rarer than black diamonds.

'In your dreams.' Though if his utterly sexy voice is any reflection of the rest of him, it might just star in mine. 'Can you meet me in the city? Forgive me for not feeling entirely comfortable heading to a strange man's house.'

He pauses like he's thinking about it for a beat. 'I'll need to see if my housekeeper can stay late to babysit. I'll call you back in five minutes on this number.'

The call disconnects and I'm left cradling the phone wondering what the hell I've done.

Chapter Four

CILLIAN

I stare at the phone wondering if I've lost my mind. What kind of a woman owns a dating agency but can't even get a date herself? I mean, who is she? Does she have three heads? Is she purple with scales?

How can a woman with the confidence and sass to call me out on my blow job comment possibly need to fake-date anyone? She must have access to thousands of single guys at the tips of her fingertips.

There's something off here.

I just can't work out what.

Matilda pops her head round the living room door, her quilted coat buttoned up to her chin. 'I've made a lasagne for tomorrow. It's on the third shelf in the fridge. Phoebe's packed lunch is on the second shelf next to her breakfast smoothie. I left pancake batter in the fridge door. I'll see you tomorrow, okay?'

It's on the tip of my tongue to ask her to stay but apart from the fact it's not fair, the idea of going to town to meet a woman I might potentially fake-date seems absurd now that said woman's sexy voice isn't purring into my ear.

Ava sounded like a lot of fun, something I don't have enough of in my life. But fun to me has always equalled flighty. And that's something I've had a lifetime supply of.

'Thanks for everything, Matilda.' I stand to wave her off. 'You are a godsend.'

Matilda's cheeks flush at the compliment as she shuffles out to the hallway. 'See you tomorrow.' The front door clicks behind her and an engine roars to life on the driveway outside.

I sit back on the leather recliner, gaze at the honey-coloured liquid in my glass and contemplate ringing my mother. She might pop over for a couple of hours, especially if she thought I was going on a date.

Well, a fake-date.

Date to secure a fake-date?

Whatever.

My parents live ten minutes away, in a ten-thousand-square-foot mansion that makes this place look like a hovel. They are living proof that money does not buy happiness.

Lillian Callaghan oozes glamour. At sixty years of age, my mother could pass for fifty. I have never, and I mean never, seen my mother without a full face of make-up and a killer designer outfit on. Probably for the benefit of my utterly undeserving father. I'm pretty sure it's her way of trying to entice him to keep it in his pants each time he disappears on 'business'.

Her love is unconditional. It knows no bounds. Even when it should.

Phoebe adores her. We're lucky to have her in our lives. But she has some seriously outdated views when it comes to relationships. Which is why she won't even contemplate leaving my father, even though his infidelity is as notorious as his multi-million-euro transport company. I can barely look him in the eye. I have no idea how she suffers him. She lives in denial.

I flip the phone over in my hand and stare at the screen.

Fuck it, what have I got to lose?

She answers on the first ring. 'Cillian? Is everything okay?'

I glance at the clock, it's nine pm. Does she think I should be in bed or something? 'Everything's fine. How are you?' I take another sip and revel in the burn as it slips down my thorax.

'Good. We're at a fundraiser at the golf club. Your father is about to take the stage.' Of course he is, the pretentious prick. William Callaghan, generous sponsor of just about any cause that makes him look honourable, and all-round smarmy asshole.

When I was thirteen, I walked in on him balls-deep in the nanny. All he could say was, 'don't tell your mother about this.'

'Oh, sorry. I won't keep you.' There goes the drink with Ava Jackson in the city. Probably for the best. It was madness anyway.

Maybe I can convince one of my clients to call to the house and pretend to Teagan that we're an item? Charlotte Mulrooney's divorce went through last week and she made it clear she'd like to 'compensate' me for going above and beyond.

No. That's too messy. I could never even pretend be associated romantically with a client. Very unprofessional.

'Are you sure you're okay, son?' Mam asks. The echoing sound of her heels clicking against the flooring suggests she's moving somewhere quieter to continue the conversation.

I exhale a heavy breath. 'Teagan is back.'

'I see.' She gasps.

'I'm just concerned she's going to upset Phoebe. Again.' It

feels good to admit my fears out loud rather than have them race through my brain like a silent but deadly poison.

'How long is she staying for this time?'

'I have no idea. You know what she's like. She flits in and out on a whim.' Teagan always liked my mam. And the feeling was mutual. Maybe Lillian Callaghan could be the one person capable of talking some sense into her? Explain the need for stability for our daughter, though God knows, no one should have to.

I hear my mother swallow thickly. 'Son, I'm going to say something you might not want to hear.'

Tiny hairs prick on my neck. 'What is it?'

'Just think about it, before you jump down my throat, okay?' she urges.

'What?' Suspicion swamps me.

'Did you ever think about giving it another try, you and Teagan?' I can practically hear her wince, waiting for the horror she surely must know she's rousing.

'What? You've got to be joking?' Apart from being the most conniving, unreliable, inconsistent woman I've ever met, Teagan is about as faithful as my father.

'Just hear me out for a second.' My mother pauses for a few seconds while she builds her case. 'Teagan is Phoebe's mother. She's always been a bit flighty, but she was so young when she had Phoebe. Maybe she panicked. She's not a bad person. You know that. Unreliable yes, selfish, absolutely. But I know she still has feelings for you. She wouldn't keep turning up if she didn't. Maybe you could find it in your heart to give her another chance? For Phoebe's sake?'

My molars clamp so hard they could crack. 'I can't believe I'm hearing this.'

'What? Come on. No relationship is perfect. They all take hard work, son. Look at your father and me.'

Case in point. Their marriage is a farce. She turns a blind

eye, so long as he doesn't shit on the doorstep. Whatever he does when he's away is one thing, but my mother is a proud woman. She won't tolerate being made a fool of here in Dublin.

'Teagan is troubled, that's all. She comes from a fantastic family. I know her parents would love to see you back together. To see her settling down. In fact, her parents are here somewhere ...' She trails off.

Of course they are. Our parents move in the same exclusive circles. Circles where marriage is a glorified business transaction between affluent families.

I slump back in my chair, nowhere near as shocked by my mother's suggestion as I should be. She's hinted at it several times before, and I did mention she has some outdated views on relationships.

Lillian Callaghan might be happy to spend her days with a philanderer, but it won't work for me. Not in a million years. In fact, I don't plan on spending my days with anyone apart from Phoebe.

I exhale a weary sigh. I'm not mad at my mother's suggestion. I'm sad. Sad that she tolerates being disrespected by my father. Sad that she thinks I should do the same with Teagan.

'Never gonna happen, Mam. Sorry.' I'd rather be alone forever than tied to someone who makes me miserable.

I reach across the table and pour myself another large measure of whiskey.

Lillian Callaghan hasn't got a bad bone in her body. Sadly, when it comes to her marriage, she doesn't have a backbone either. Oh, how I would love to represent her in their divorce. I'd take my father to the cleaners for her, if only she'd give me the green light.

'Look, son, I know she hurt you, but that's what we do to the people we love sometimes.'

'I can't agree with you, Mam. Look, I just called to say hi.

Enjoy your evening. I'll call over at the weekend with Phoebe, okay? Love you.'

'Love you too.' Her words are weighted with sadness.

I'll think of a way to show Teagan I've moved on alone. Hell, I might not even have to. She'll probably get bored of these dark November nights all on her own. I'm about to call Ava Jackson back and tell her I can't make it when a knock sounds from the front door.

Did the gates not close behind Matilda? They can be temperamental at times.

I drag myself up, drop my drink onto the coffee table and amble out to the hallway.

Teagan stands on the top step in a knee-length forest coloured trench coat belted at the waist. Her long blonde hair is styled across her shoulders and her lips are painted a bright shade of pink.

'Phoebe is in bed,' I tell her, leaning against the door-frame, blocking her entrance.

'I know.' She flashes a row of too-white teeth in my face. 'I came to see you.' She tugs the belt of her coat, and it falls open. She's wearing nothing except a set of decadent ivory lingerie.

'For fuck's sake, Teagan.' I tear my eyes away from her porcelain skin. She might look like an angel, but history has taught me she's the devil in disguise.

'Are you going to let me in, or what?' She pouts.

An idea bursts to the front of my brain and I step back, allowing her entry. This is the perfect opportunity to kill two birds with one stone.

Teagan might be unreliable, but there's no way she'd ever leave Phoebe alone. She's far from the perfect mother but I trust her to guard Phoebe with her life, when she's in the country that is. 'Can you stay for a while?' I ask over my shoulder as she follows me back through to the living area.

Cat-like eyes light and sparkle. 'Absolutely.'

'Great.' I grab my phone and hit Ava Jackson's number. It rings and rings.

Pick the fucking phone up, Ava. Okay, it's been ten minutes instead of five, but she can't have given up on me already, surely?

Eventually she answers. 'That was an unusual five minutes.'

'Oh, you have no idea.' I glance at my ex who's shrugged out of her coat and is now sprawled out in some sort of supposedly seductive pose on my couch. 'Are we still on for that drink? I have a babysitter.'

Teagan's pupils narrow thunderously. She bolts up into a seating position.

'Absolutely. But you're buying. Meet me in Elixir in half an hour.' I'm not sure if it's Ava's sunny voice resounding loudly through the speaker phone that causes Teagan's jaw to drop open, or the mention of a drink in Dublin's new exclusive cocktail bar.

'Can't wait to see you,' I throw in a 'sexy' for good measure.

'Keep it in your pants,' Ava warns me. There's an edge to her teasing tone.

'I can't promise.' Hello? Who is this flirtatious fucker hijacking my voice?

From the horrified look on Teagan's face, I couldn't have planned things better if I tried.

I owe Ava Jackson a drink. Or ten.

Chapter Five

AVA

No expense has been spared on the interior of Dublin's newest, hippest cocktail bar. Crystal chandeliers hang from the ceiling, reflecting light from their multifaceted surfaces, creating dazzling patterns across the brilliant white walls and marble floors.

Carefully curated art, ranging from modern pieces to vintage prints adorn the walls. Strategically placed mirrors enhance the sense of space. Plush, comfortable seats are scattered throughout the huge opulent space, deep-cushioned leather couches, velvet banquettes, and high-backed chairs.

Groups of people dot the room in small clusters, but given it's a Tuesday in November, it's not thronged. I smooth down my black Sandro pencil dress and stride towards the bar, pretending to everyone, including myself, that I'm not completely out of my depth here.

Even if Mr Callaghan isn't the devil in disguise, he's clearly not who Frank and Penny 'zero-boundaries' Jackson will be expecting their youngest daughter to rock up to the island wedding celebration with.

Oh god.

Four days with any man I've just met could be torture, but four days with a man who professes not to believe in life partners and happy ever afters? I'm not sure we could convince anyone we have a future, let alone my overfamiliar, 'let's-talk-about-our-sex-life-over-the-dinner-table' family.

This has disaster written all over it. I swat away the internal worry-worm wiggling in my stomach, pick up a leather-bound drink's menu from the sleek bar counter and thumb through it. Hard liquor is the only way to get through this awkward ... whatever this is.

'What can I get you?' A blond-haired barman asks with a flirtatious wink as I slide into one of the high-backed stools flanking the bar counter.

I swallow hard and glance nervously to the door, then back to the barman, who's waiting patiently, armed with a gleaming chrome cocktail shaker.

Cillian said half an hour. It's only been fifteen minutes. I thought getting here earlier might provide an advantage, but it's giving me too much time to overthink things. To question this stupid idea for the millionth time. To compile a mental list of why this is one of the most ridiculous ideas I've ever had.

'I'll have a classic champagne cocktail, please.' As much as I'd love to try a Harvey Wallbanger or a Rose Berry Bliss, tonight, I'm safer sticking to something I know. I very much doubt Cillian Callaghan will sign up to date me for December if he has to spend the evening holding my hair out of my face while I projectile vomit my nervous drinking binge.

'An exceptional choice.' The barman nods. 'You're clearly a woman of good taste.'

'We'll soon find out.' A ripple of apprehension surges over my spine.

· · ·

At twenty-nine minutes past nine, a gust of air blows in as the front door opens again. I don't need to turn around. It's him. Instinctively, I just know. Every cell in my body sparks to life. Like we're somehow connected already.

Inching my head round, I aim for casual as I seek out the man who entered the room. The one whose sheer presence commands the air around him.

Our eyes meet with a charged intensity.

Cropped dark hair.

Strong square jaw.

Cheekbones that could cut glass.

Silver eyes that glint like liquid metal.

My pulse quickens. Heat floods my veins.

This man can't be Cillian Callaghan.

It can't be.

Because the man who's striding towards me is the very same man I've spent every morning salivating over for the best part of a year. The same man whose sheer proximity sucks the oxygen from my lungs. And he's not a divorce lawyer.

No.

He can't be.

He might look dark and broody, but Mr Suave Suit Guy is a secret superhero. A romantic one too.

He has to be. Because otherwise my siblings were right.

I'm not qualified to matchmake a bitch in heat.

All my decadent early morning fantasies have gone up in a putrid puff of surreal smoke. It's official, I do have the worst taste in men.

I had this man all wrong. He's not good, He's not romantic. He makes money on the back of other people's misery. On their divorces.

A fitted expensive-looking overcoat perfectly encapsulates

familiar broad shoulders. His sullen expression is trained intently on me.

'Ava.' His attention is thrilling and terrifying in equal measure.

'Cillian?' The squeak in my voice is downright embarrassing.

He extends a hand. Several seconds pass while I stare at it in horror before extending my own. My palm slips into his and a jolt of electricity surges straight up my arm, through my core and straight down to my panties.

His gaze falls to our entwined fingers, and he rapidly retracts, twitching like he too felt the burn.

This cannot be happening.

I'm torn between disappointment that the man I had on a pedestal for all these months is the king of divorces, and elation that he's equally as hypnotising up close.

'You're not what I was expecting,' I blurt, picking up my half-empty champagne flute.

He studies my face intently. Those sterling twin pools hold me captive. 'What did you expect?'

'I don't know, maybe a beard, a tail and two red horns?' I take a huge mouthful of my drink, willing the alcohol to take the edge off this bizarre encounter.

Cillian makes a tutting sound. 'You have a very a low opinion of me.' He slips off his coat and hangs it on the back of the stool next to me. He's wearing navy trousers and a white, slim-fitting shirt, with the sleeves rolled up to the elbows. Tanned, powerful forearms steal my attention from his face. The man is like a living breathing god, never mind the devil.

'You make a living from other people's misery.' Finally able to tear my eyes from his masculine body, I search out his with a defiant glare.

'On the contrary, in fact. I make a living from setting

miserable people free.' He signals the barman over and orders a neat whiskey, and another cocktail for me. Good, I'm going to need it.

'Haven't you ever made a mistake in life?' His deep gritty tone's as sombre as his expression. 'Ever thought you knew someone, then discovered they're something or someone completely different behind the mask?'

An image of Josh, the married ankle-tag-wearing douche, slaps me with the reality stick. That's different though, we weren't married. Primarily because he was already married to somebody else ... Shame floods my cheeks.

'If you'd done your homework on me like I did on you, you'd know that I specialise in representing vulnerable women, freeing them from their unfaithful or overbearing husbands.' He arches one thick dark eyebrow and takes a sip of his drink.

My throat thickens. 'You only represent women?'

'Mostly. But primarily, I only represent decent human beings. Criminal lawyers, on the other hand, really are the devil. Or at least they sold their soul to him somewhere along the way.' Thick fingers thrum against the bar counter thoughtfully.

Words fail me. Mr Suave Suit Guy, AKA Cillian Callaghan might not be the hero I'd conjured him up to be, but he's got some redeeming qualities. Even if he is the most solemn man I've ever met.

'Now we've cleared that up, shall we get to business?' His unapologetic perusal of my figure sets goosebumps rippling across my skin.

'Business, yes.' I swallow hard. 'Because we've already established that this isn't a date.' I nod at his whiskey glass.

His lips twitch and for a split second I wonder if Cillian 'can't-crack-a-smile' Callaghan is about to laugh. He doesn't.

But his eyes do linger on my mouth for a beat longer than professional.

'What do you need me to do?' That came out way more suggestively than I intended.

He rubs his thumb across the dark stubble dotting that sculpted jawline thoughtfully. 'I need you to pretend that you're in love with me.'

Shouldn't be too hard, given that up until about ten minutes ago, I thought I was. I mean, the man is exceptionally easy on the eye. Which is the exact reason my heart is beating like a drum in my chest.

'Okay ...' I plaster a smile onto my face and wait for the details.

'Teagan, my ex, is back. And she's got this mad idea that we should get back together. She's convinced that because I haven't had a serious girlfriend since her, that she's in with a chance.'

I drain the remainder of the first cocktail and reach for the second. 'I can do that.'

'Good.' He pins me in another pensive stare. 'What do you need me to do?'

Oh my. What I need him to do, and what I want him to do are two completely different matters. Because even though my original illusions about Mr Suave Suit Guy have been shattered, my delinquent brain is conjuring up a magnitude of smoking hot new ones.

I squeeze my thighs together and will away the want that's curling round my core. 'I need you to come to a company event with me next week and pretend to my family that we're dating. And that it's serious.'

He contemplates it for a second and offers a curt nod.

May as well lay out all my cards on the table. I shoot him my brightest megawatt grin. 'I also need you to come to my brother's wedding with me next month.'

'I'm allergic to weddings.' He scoffs.

'And I'm allergic to ex-girlfriends who are going to want to claw my eyes out when they see me with their baby daddy.' I singsong.

'Fair point.' Those huge shoulders dip in a reluctant shrug.

'I should mention that the wedding is a four-day event on a remote island.' My smile remains firmly in place like a shield as I brace myself for the reaction I already know is coming.

'Talk about self-indulgent. Who thinks I've got four days to give up for a goddamn wedding?' He shakes his head with obvious disgust.

A tiny laugh tinkles out of my lips. 'A Hollywood celebrity, of course. Your research clearly didn't extend to my family members, I see.'

'I only had ten minutes in the taxi. My priority was to make sure you weren't a serial killer with a track record of luring men to fancy bars before seducing and killing them.' He's joking, I think. But he still doesn't crack a smile.

'Look, can you do it or not? I have a lot riding on this.' Like proving to my entire family that I'm not entirely incompetent when it comes to dating, and that Nate's investment in my business is a solid one.

Cillian exhales a heavy breath and rolls his eyes. 'I'll do it. December's usually a quiet month for me. Most couples wait until after Christmas before filing for divorce.'

'How romantic.' I beam, clapping my hands together sarcastically. 'Do we have a deal?'

'Deal. But do you have to be so goddamn smiley all the time? Your teeth are blinding me.' He extends one huge hand again, and against my better judgement, I take it. That invisible circuit short cuts between us again. Sparks ignite and burst into flames beneath my skin. The smile freezes on my face.

This time it's me who rapidly retracts. 'It takes more muscles to frown than it does to smile.'

'Huh.' Cillian's expression is deadpan. 'So, what now?'

'We should probably go on a couple of non-date dates to get to know each other, if we're going to pull this off properly.' It's imperative that I convince my family this is real. Given that the man looks like he's just stepped out of a modelling shoot, it shouldn't be too hard. But I know nothing about him. Other than we'd never cut it as a couple in the real world.

'But we need to lay out a few ground rules.' His eyes bore into mine with a depth that makes me want to dive into them.

'Okay ... shoot.' I drag my gaze back to my drink.

'No touching.'

'I come from a family where PDAs are massively encouraged. And not so public displays of affection are discussed over dinner. Right down to the most minute details.'

'Course you do.' He rolls his eyes. 'I'll hold your hand, maybe. But no kissing. No funny business.'

Does he think I'm going to throw myself at him? Pleeaassse! Well, I might have done before I found out he's the most cynical divorce daddy in Dublin.

'And whatever you do, don't actually fall in love with me, okay?' He drains his whiskey.

Big headed. Much? 'Honey, I don't even like you, so don't worry your handsome head about the other L word.'

'You think I'm handsome, though.' There's a slight smugness to his tone.

'As my mother always says, "there's many a good-looking bastard out there".' I down the rest of my cocktail and stand. 'I'll be in touch to arrange a date.'

'One second.' Thick fingers circle my wrist, bringing it to

his face. He takes a slow deep inhale before rubbing it against his neck in a motion that sets my soul alight.

He's marking his skin with my scent. And it's utterly fucking arousing.

No need to ask who's babysitting tonight. As if the 'can't wait to see you, sexy' didn't give it away on the phone earlier. I've spent ten minutes with the guy, and I already know that line was completely uncharacteristic of him. He must want rid of the ex, badly.

'Want some lipstick on your collar to go with that?' It's a joke but to my surprise his head cocks to the side, giving me access to his neck.

Against my better judgement, I press my lips fleetingly against his flesh. The throbbing of his jugular is in sync with the throbbing in my underwear. Subtle musky notes of his cologne evoke a primal reaction in my core that I haven't felt in forever. His taut skin is soft, it's an effort to tear myself away. Standing back, I admire my handiwork. The rich deep claret outline of my mouth marks his skin like a tattoo. 'You owe me one.'

I spin on my heels and stalk away from my already smug, fake boyfriend before he gets a whiff that my attraction is real.

And it has been for a long time.

Chapter Six

CILLIAN

Wednesday 29th November

'How's Phoebe?' Beth, my long-standing PA, strides into my spacious office and perches on the edge of my sleek grey desk. The heavy door swings shut behind her.

Out of all the people I employ at Callaghan and Co, Beth is my favourite. She brings me coffee, strong and black, just the way I like it and fends off my accountant's inappropriate advances. She even collects my daughter from school when Matilda is unavailable.

'She's doing well.' I rest back on my leather chair, thrumming the desk with my fingers. 'She was, anyway.'

It's a rare day where I'm not in court, but like I said to Ava last night, this close to Christmas, most people suck it up for a few more weeks. January is always my busiest month.

'Was?' A small frown line indents the space between Beth's eyebrows.

'Teagan.' Her name is an explanation on its own.

'Oh.' Beth sucks in a breath. 'Is she staying at yours?'

'God, no! Thankfully, I had the insight to change the locks when she ran off the first time, though she still has a fob to get in the gate.' Which is why she was able to appear half naked on my doorstep last night. My temple twinges at the memory.

'She'll get bored, boss. She'll be out of your life again before you know it.' Beth's been around long enough to know the drill. She would have been the perfect ruse to get Teagan off my back, if she wasn't already happily married to another woman.

'Which is great for me, but not for Phoebe.' A photo of my daughter in a gold frame stares back at me from my desk. My heart breaks for her a little bit more.

'Will Teagan stay for Christmas, do you think?' Beth flicks imaginary lint from her tailored suit pants.

'Not if I can help it. I'd love her to play a steady role in Phoebe's life, but I don't think she's capable.'

'Be careful.' Beth warns me. 'You know I like Teagan. It's impossible not to like her. But she's troubled.'

'Don't worry, I have a plan.' Ava Jackson's stunning face pushes itself to the forefront of my mind.

Ava was not what I was expecting, despite having stalked her Instagram in the taxi last night. Technicoloured, heavily filtered pictures did nothing to capture her natural beauty. The woman is an absolute knockout. If she hasn't got a date for her brother's wedding, and whatever work function next week, it's not because she *can't* get one. It's because she doesn't *want* one.

'Should I be worried?' Beth's eyes widen in mock horror.

'Drastic causes require drastic measures.' My lips lift into a rare tight smile.

A knock sounds on the door and it inches open. My head snaps up to see Elena, our receptionist hovering in the doorway, wearing an apologetic smile. She knows not to disturb me unless it's urgent.

'Mr Callaghan, there's someone in reception demanding to see you.' She wrings her fingers nervously.

Beth and I lock eyes. I glance at the paperwork on my desk, photographic evidence of a well-respected judge entering a Thai massage parlour, wearing a seedy smile and unbuttoned suit pants. Has he come to try and buy his way out of his predicament? If so, he's in for a big disappointment. This is exactly what his long-suffering wife, Dolores, needs to be free of him for good.

'I'm not expecting anyone.' The words sound harsher than I intended. I shouldn't be so clipped. It's not Elena's fault there's someone downstairs demanding to see me.

But 'clipped' keeps people out.

'Clipped' says 'don't get familiar'.

'Clipped' doesn't let anyone in close enough to get hurt. Or made a fool of.

Beth stands, flanking my side ready for a battle. 'There's nothing in Mr Callaghan's diary.'

'She says it's personal.' Elena squirms, looking anywhere but at me.

Oh fuck. If Teagan's out there now causing a scene, I will escort her out of this five story Georgian building myself. Beth and I exchange a knowing look.

'Who is it?' I adjust my collar and straighten my spine, readying myself for confrontation.

'Dark haired. Huge hazel eyes. Impeccable dress sense, and a figure most women would kill for,' Elena blurts. 'She says she's your girlfriend.'

My head rolls back against the chair. 'For fuck's sake.'

It can only be Ava.

She said she'd be in touch, not that she'd rock up to my office and set every tongue within a mile radius talking.

'You kept that quiet, boss.' Beth is the only one of my staff brave enough to tease me. Another reason I have so much respect for her.

'Not as quiet as I'd have liked apparently.' I groan. 'Send her up, Elena.'

Three minutes later, Ava Jackson struts into my office with a smile the size of Africa. Gold-flecked eyes glint with mischief, and her cheeks glow rosy from the cold. She's wearing a camel-coloured coat that caresses her curves. The hemline stops gracefully just above her knees revealing toned calves propped up by six inch patent stilettos.

Is she wearing tights or stockings under there?

What? I'm only human. Just because I choose to abstain from dating, that doesn't mean I can't appreciate a good-looking woman when I see one.

'Hello, sexy.' She leans across my desk and plants a kiss on my cheek, much to the amusement of Beth, who's 'filing paperwork' in the corner. Any excuse to watch the show.

'You could have called. Or emailed. Or text.' Anything but show up here looking so damn delicious. Mind you, she'd have to look good enough to eat to persuade anyone that knows me that she's my girlfriend. The world and his wife know I don't date. I've made sure of it. I've had to brush off more than one unwanted advance from clients. Neighbours. Mothers at the school gate. Married ones too.

'Where's the fun in that?' Ava beams. 'Did that lipstick come off your collar last night?' She runs her finger over the same spot she pressed her lips against only hours earlier. My dick twitches in my pants at the memory of her breasts brushing against my chest. Her feminine scent. The sensuality of her fleeting kiss.

Oh god. It's been too long since I got laid.

Ava Jackson is everything I avoid in a woman: openly affectionate and romantically delusional. But there's no denying she is smoking hot, and apparently committed to the deal we made.

'It stayed long enough to make a difference.' Teagan was

livid. So much so, that she stormed out the second I got home. I'm under no illusion that's the end of it though. She's one of the most competitive people I know, and this new competition will drive her over the edge.

Ava's smile widens, revealing naturally white teeth fit for a Colgate ad. 'Good. I was hoping today, you might return the favour.'

Beth clears her throat from the corner of the room. 'Hi. I'm Beth, Cillian's long-suffering PA.'

'I'm Ava.' She's sporting a full-on grin now. 'Lovely to meet you.'

Surely the woman's face has to hurt from smiling all the damn time? I'm exhausted even thinking about it.

'Ditto.' Both curiosity and amusement flash across Beth's features.

Ava turns her attention back to me. 'I thought I'd drop by and see if my man is free to take me for lunch.'

'I'm not.'

'He is, of course,' Beth gushes.

I give Beth the same look I've given her countless times over the years. The one that says, 'extract me from this situation, immediately.' But today of all days, the conspiring witch chooses to ignore it.

'There's nothing in the diary at all. Take the entire afternoon if you like. I've got everything under control here.' Beth's enthusiasm matches Ava's as she practically shoves my coat at me.

'Wonderful.' Ava rubs her hands together gleefully.

I pinch the bridge of my nose and exhale. 'Fine. Lunch. But that's it.'

The heat of every set of eyes in the building scorches my back as I escort Ava through the building. Thankfully, she adheres to the rules and doesn't touch me. I had an awful premonition she might try and take my hand and ruin my badass-boss reputation forever. Though if Teagan was serious about her 'little birdies', Ava's probably just done me a huge favour. Again.

Outside, the afternoon is fresh. Weak winter sunlight peeps from behind the clouds. Grafton Street is hopping with tourists as usual. Shoppers bustle about the busy street admiring the lavish window displays.

I crane my neck at Ava who's gone suspiciously quiet. 'Was that necessary?'

'Absolutely.' She smirks. 'I told you, you owe me.'

'I didn't expect you to cash in on it less than twenty-four hours later.' I steer her towards one of the quieter side streets. 'Are you hungry?'

'Yes. Starving!' she exclaims. 'Do you know how much of an appetite you can work up matchmaking the singletons of this country?'

'Do you know how much of an appetite you can work up building a case against unfaithful spouses?' I counteract, stopping outside a small but exclusive Italian restaurant called La Dolce Vita. It's almost impossible to get a table here but the owner, Maria Romano, is a previous client and she always finds me a table.

Ava hesitates in the doorway. 'Do you have a reservation?'

'I don't need one.' I open the door and usher her in.

'Confident, aren't you? I suppose your gentlemanly manners compensate for your arrogance,' Ava teases.

'Don't be fooled. I'm no gentleman.' Primarily because my eyes can't stay away from her ass.

Maria is working the floor. Her head whips round as we enter, and a gigantic smile lights her face as she rushes to greet us.

'How is my favourite lawyer?' She presses a kiss to each of my cheeks, examining me from head to toe in a maternal fashion before turning her attention to Ava. 'And who do we have here?'

'This is Ava, my—' I'm about to say associate when Ava butts in with 'girlfriend.'

'My oh my.' Maria's chocolate brown eyes glitter. 'Let me get you the most romantic table in the house. I knew you'd meet someone eventually. A man like you is too handsome to be alone forever.'

Heat creeps across my neck. Mortifying. Why did I think this was a good idea? Now every time I want to come for a decent meal, I'll be plagued with questions about what went wrong. Clearly, I didn't think this through at all. 'Anywhere is fine. Don't go to any trouble.'

'Nonsense. For the man who set me free, I will do anything.' Maria motions to a passing waitress and asks her to set up a table in the window overlooking the lights on the street outside.

We're handed menus and given a complimentary glass of champagne. 'Set her free?' Ava whispers as we take our seats.

'Her husband had some unsavoury connections. Not many were willing to take him on.' It was one of my most challenging cases, and one I wouldn't have risked if Phoebe had been born.

Ava raises her eyebrows while she digests this nugget of information. The air falls silent between us but there's no denying the chemistry. It swirls between us fogging the air. Why does she have to be so damn alluring? It's distracting.

I scan the menu pointlessly. I already know what I'm going to order. The same thing I order every time I eat here. The ravioli is to die for. If I wasn't going back to work, I'd wash it down with a glass of red.

'Italian's my favourite.' We both say at the exact same time, though her excited tone is decidedly more enthusiastic than mine.

'At least we have something in common.'

'So, what exactly do I owe you?' I ask, after the waitress takes our order.

'Lunch.' Those hazel-hued eyes sparkle with mischief.

'Does this lunch count?' I motion to the chequered table-cloth on the table between us.

Her plump lips roll into yet another grin. 'With my parents.'

Fuck. My. Life.

Chapter Seven

AVA

My brother has a big mouth. I mean, that's not news per se. Which is why I woke up to five missed calls from my mother, Penny 'zero-boundaries' Jackson, demanding to know every single detail about my new boyfriend, including his penis size.

I really should have included those questions on the HeartSync sign-up form after all, because that's the only way I'll ever find out the truth about Cillian's.

I imagine it's big. It has to be. A man with his confidence couldn't be walking around with anything less than eight, maybe nine inches in his pants, right?

'With your parents?' Cillian repeats, dragging my mind out of the gutter. His jaw tightens and a pulse ticks in his temple. He needs to lighten up.

I read an article once about men with stressful jobs that caused heart conditions. Cillian looks like he's liable to keel over at any second. And if he did, I'd be obliged to perform mouth to mouth. Which would mean I finally get to place my lips on Mr Suave Suit Guy, but for all the wrong reasons. He might be a cold-hearted grump, but he is the hottest cold-hearted grump I've ever come across.

'Seriously, Cillian. It's only lunch.' I'm lying. It's not only lunch. It's the Spanish Inquisition. But given he's used to being interrogated in the courtroom, and apparently liberating mafia-connected wives, Frank and Penny's questions should be a walk in the park. No point taking him to Nate's wedding if he can't survive a simple family dinner.

'When?' He lifts his glass of water to his lips. Even the rippling tendons in his neck are masculine. Which is probably why I willingly pressed a kiss there last night. And subsequently spent hours overthinking the level of heat radiating from his body. Remembering the expensive enticing smell of his cologne. The 'I could fuck you into next week' vibe that oozes from his every pore.

It's not my fault.

I've been fantasising about this man for the best part of a year. Before I knew he was a moody, pessimistic workaholic, of course.

'Sunday. Jackson family roasts are a tradition. Come on, we both know you don't already have a hot date.'

'That's where you're wrong.' He rakes his fingers through his cropped dark hair. 'I'll have to check my mother will take Phoebe for a couple of hours.'

My scalp prickles. How would those fingers feel raking through mine?

'Phoebe?'

'My daughter.' His voice hitches with pride at the mere mention of her name. Tingling sensations spark in my ovaries.

What is it about single dads that's so freaking hot? Seriously, it's my favourite romance trope. Throw in a bit of an age gap and it's a one click wonder for me. I'd put Cillian at about eight years older than me. Old enough to have experience anyway.

I cross my legs under the table and press my thighs together. 'How old is she again?'

'Six going on sixteen.' Cillian's entire face transforms. A dimple indents his left cheek as his lips curl into an actual smile.

My underwear is on fire.

He was attractive when he was sullen, but when he's smiling, he's devastating.

'Want to see a picture?' He whips his phone out of his pocket before I have the chance to even reply.

The most beautiful little girl stares back at me from his mobile. She's wearing a pink polka dot dress and matching headband. She has her father's molten silver eyes, but her hair is blonde. She must take that from her mother. A gappy grin shows the tooth fairy is no stranger to their house. 'She's stunning.'

'Thank you.' He slides the phone back into his pocket and resumes his poker face. It's too late though, I've seen the man beneath the mask. Cillian Callaghan isn't the devil in disguise. He's a fucking teddy bear. For one lady at least.

Would he ever find room in his life for another?

For fuck's sake, Ava.

The man doesn't believe in hearts and flowers. He's allergic to romance. And he doesn't believe in relationships.

Get a grip.

This is an arrangement, not a real date.

Though that doesn't mean I can't enjoy it. Underneath that hard shell, there's a heart beating somewhere in that broad chest. Dating for December could turn out to be fun if he'd only lighten up a little.

'Phoebe wasn't planned.' He admits, taking a sip from his drink. 'Not by me, at least.'

'Oh.' Realisation sinks in. Did his ex trap him? Is that why he's such a cynic about love and relationships? Or does that stem from his career choices?

'Teagan does what she wants when she wants. Which is

why I need your help. She needs to know I've moved on or she'll never give up.' His gaze shifts to meet mine. 'You have no idea what the woman is capable of. She took a job in my office, way below her paygrade just so she could have access to my calendar. She waited a full year before making her move. She's ten years younger than me. Beautiful. Bubbly. I was foolishly flattered.' He shakes his head. 'My mother made no secret that she'd like to see us together. Our parents have been friends for years.

'I warned Teagan from that first night it would only ever be a bit of fun between us. I warned her not to fall in love with me. Marriage has never been part of my life plan. But Teagan wanted to be the one who changed me. It became an obsession for her. One night she caught me drunk enough to sleep with her without protection. Nine months later we had a daughter.' He shrugs casually, but there's nothing casual about his confession.

No wonder the man has trust issues.

He stares into space, seeing something faraway. 'She was determined to be the one to tie me down. And in some ways, she did. Having a daughter is a bigger commitment than marriage. I wouldn't be without Phoebe for all the money in the world. But just because I'm tied to Phoebe, I refuse to be tied to Teagan – romantically at least. I tried. I really did. But when she cheated on me and left, all I felt was relief.'

'I'm sorry she did that to you.' I reach across the table and touch his hand. He jolts back as if feeling the same million vaults of electricity coursing through his skin that coursed through mine.

'It sounds ridiculous when I say it out loud.' He swallows hard, thrumming those thick fingers on the table again. 'But it was a violation. She watched me from afar, stalked me like a preying lioness and made her move.'

A sliver of guilt crusades through my core.

I've been watching Cillian from afar for the best part of a year and fantasising about him.

But then again, that's all they ever were, fantasies. I'm not scheming to have his children. Even if my ovaries have started ticking like a deadly time bomb since Nate and Holly had Harriet.

It's on the tip of my tongue to confess. To admit I've seen him around. But what would that achieve? He'd run a mile.

Instead, I bite my lip and put myself in his shoes. 'It doesn't sound ridiculous. If you were a woman and a man forced you to become a parent, it would be a serious crime.'

His face softens slightly. 'Now you know why it's imperative I get rid of Teagan from our lives. She's dangerous.'

'I'll do whatever it takes to help,' I promise.

The enticing scent of pepperoni wafts beneath my nose as the waitress places our plates on the table. It's the perfect way to draw a seamless line under a conversation that was disturbing on several levels.

My thin crust pizza is Instagram-worthy. And so is my super sexy fake-boyfriend.

'Can I get you anything else?' the waitress asks with a smile.

'Would you mind taking a picture of us?' I hand her my phone as Cillian rolls his eyes.

'Sure, no problem.' She stands backs and snaps several different angles while I tilt my head and pose. Cillian's jaws clench so tightly together; he looks like he's in pain.

'Thank you so much.' I slip her a twenty-euro tip, returning my attention to my non-date. 'Where were we?'

'You were publicly embarrassing me. Again.' He picks up his fork with his right hand and stabs his ravioli aggressively. 'As if you didn't do enough damage in my office already.'

'Damage? That was a PR stunt. You can bet your life your

ex will have heard about it by tomorrow.' I tear off a slice of pizza and pick it up with my hands.

'Sorry for getting so serious. I just want you to understand what I'm up against. I'm not trying to scare away the mother of my child for no good reason.'

'I would never judge.' I feel obliged to lighten the mood. 'I'm going to ask you some questions and you're going to answer them, okay? We need to at least appear comfortable with each other if we're going to convince my family we're an item.'

'Fine.' His lips part and he shoves a fork full of food in. It's a battle not to stare.

I start with an easy one to get him warmed up. 'What's your nickname?'

'Nickname?' He repeats like I've asked him to translate the Koran for me.

'Yeah. What do your friends call you?'

His eyes narrow. 'I don't have many friends. I have colleagues. I like to keep my circle tight.'

My mouth falls open. 'Seriously? Isn't that lonely?'

A brief flicker of something flashes through his eyes and I realise I've hit the nail on the head. Cillian Callaghan is lonely. A pang of sympathy twinges in my chest. This poor man, I can't even comprehend his life. What he's been through. What he's still going through.

'It's safer. Besides, between work and Phoebe, I don't have time. Beth's kind of a friend, my PA. She helps with Phoebe sometimes. Beth's nicknames for me range from, "The Marriage Melter" and "The Divorce Deliverer", to "you abso- lute arsehole."' He flashes a small smile, but it doesn't reach his eyes.

'From what I can see, she has the measure of you.' I shoot him a wink to show I'm only playing.

'There's also Alex Benedict. He's been my friend forever

but truthfully, he's more of a pain in my ass. He lives to goad me at every opportunity. Our families have been friends forever.' He closes his eyes for a long beat and rolls his lips. 'He works for me too. Fuck, I'm sensing a theme here.'

'They don't count as friends if you have to pay them.' I tease. 'Okay. Next question. What's your weirdest habit?' I take another bite of my melt-in-the-mouth pizza and wait for his response.

His left fingers thrum against the tabletop, the same way they did against the bar counter last night. 'I don't have any weird habits.'

'Is that right?' I deliberately tap my own fingers against the chequered tablecloth and gaze pointedly at his.

He snatches his hand away and grabs his fork again. 'What's your weirdest habit?'

'Easy.' I shoot him a lazy smile. 'I love sniffing books. I can't help myself. The pages call to me. They say a picture tells a thousand words, but I disagree. A picture can be falsified. Filtered. Edited. The smell of a book tells so much more. It's age. Where it's been stored. The smell of an old book is my absolute favourite. Like a first edition Bronte. All that history between the pages.'

Cillian rolls his eyes once again. 'Why am I not surprised you read romance novels?'

'I don't read them. I devour them.' I shrug. 'I also love romcoms. I mean, I hate the third act break up, but you know you've got to suffer it to get the grand gesture.'

'Suffer is the only word for it.' Cillian facepalms. 'Like that prat Richard Gere rocking up outside Julia Roberts' place in a white limo clutching some store-bought roses like a lifeline.'

'Ohh!' I lean forward in my chair. 'I love a man who's educated in romance!'

'Huh! More like been tortured with it. Blame my mother.

She doesn't get the romance she requires from my father, so she gets her kicks bingeing cheesy romcoms instead.'

'*Pretty Woman* wasn't cheesy. It was taboo for its time.'

'Whatever. You'd never in a million years catch me rocking up in a white sports car, brandishing a bad bouquet of flowers and blasting classical music.'

'Ah what?' I push his arm playfully. 'A girl can dream, I suppose.'

'There's being a dreamer, and then there's being delusional.' It's Cillian who asks the next question. 'Where did we meet?'

'Duh, you signed up to my dating agency. I read your form and immediately knew you were "The One." It'll be great for business.' I do a little shimmy with my shoulders.

'Yeah, great until we break up,' he says drily.

'According to you, everyone breaks up in January anyway. Hopefully, we'll get lost in the statistics.' I readjust my legs beneath the table and the top of my foot brushes his knee. He jolts again, while I pretend there aren't a million butterflies soaring through my stomach.

He arches a single dark eyebrow. 'Nothing about our "relationship" is going to get lost as a statistic after you waltzed into my office earlier. Everyone knows I don't date.'

'You do now.' I flutter my eyelashes playfully. 'Who knows, maybe I'll open the floodgates for you.'

'Maybe I'll open yours.' Big black pupils dart across my lips.

'As long as you don't forget the rules. No touching. No kissing, and definitely don't fall in love with me.' I quote him his own words from last night, teasingly.

'You're safe.' Cillian 'can't-crack-a-smile' Callaghan's luscious lips twitch. 'From the latter, at least.'

Saliva pools in my mouth. 'Be careful, or I might think you're flirting with me for real.'

Those molten metal eyes flicker and smoulder. 'I'm practicing for this wedding you're dragging me to. When I commit to something, I like to do it to the best of my ability.'

Great.

Now I'm left wondering what else he does to the best of his ability.

Chapter Eight

CILLIAN

Thursday 30th November

I make it my business to finish early on Thursdays when possible. Phoebe has ballet class. She loves it when I watch but it means fending off the desperate housewives of Dublin. Even my meanest scowl isn't enough to deter them from sliding into the seat next to mine, brushing against me 'accidentally', and leaving their lingering hands for five seconds too long on my thigh.

It's common knowledge I don't date but that doesn't stop some women trying it on.

Majella, a tall blonde former Miss Ireland, slips into the seat next to me this evening. 'Darling, it's so good to see you.' She paws my arm and I flinch. Apart from the fact she's more plastic than Barbie, she's married to a local politician, Stanley Howard. He's the youngest, slickest MP around. Rumour has it that Majella and he have an open marriage, but that's one party I do not want to be part of.

I manage a grunt in response.

'We must get the girls together for a playdate. Cecilia would love it if Phoebe could come to our house. You should come too.' Her fingers brush over my leg. 'How about this

Sunday? Stanley's in the States on business. I could cook if you like?'

I swat her hand away. 'I don't think so.'

She straightens herself and fluffs her coiffed hair. 'You know it really is time you got over Teagan. A woman like her is no good for a man like you.'

'It's none of your business.' I grit out, keeping my eyes trained intently on my daughter.

'I know but you could have it all.' Majella purrs, leaning into my shoulder.

'Who says I don't already have it all?' Where's Ava when I want her to waltz in and cause a stir?

At that second my phone buzzes in my pocket.

The name Ava Jackson flashes across the screen. The woman is a telepath. My lips curl upwards as Majella cranes her neck to squint at my phone.

I clear my throat and adopt the most flirtatious tone I can muster. It's not as difficult as one might imagine, given the woman on the other end of the phone is sex on legs. But after our fake-date yesterday, I realise she's so much more than just the way she looks. She's quick and witty, and from the way her eyes filled when I showed her Phoebe's picture and explained the situation with Teagan, she's full of compassion too.

She's everything I need in a pretend girlfriend, and everything I don't need in a real one – deliriously optimistic, emotionally intelligent, and an advocate for everything I don't believe in.

Especially 'happy ever afters'.

'Hello gorgeous.' I cradle the phone to my ear. Majella stiffens beside me. 'I missed you today.'

'You did, did you?' Ava's voice is filled with glee. 'I'm assuming you have company.'

'Something like that.' I chance a sideways glance at

Majella who's staring in wonder. 'Hoped you'd turn up at the office in those stilettos again.' It's not a complete lie. I found myself glancing at my office door more times than is normal, wondering if she'd waltz in unannounced for a second day in a row.

'I never had you down as having a foot fetish.' Her laugh tinkles into my ear and I find myself smiling for real this time.

'What did you have me down as then?'

'An uptight workaholic in need of a good laugh and a good shag. Not necessarily in that order.' She chuckles.

'Are you offering?' The flirtation is supposed to be for Majella's benefit, but I'd be lying if I said I wasn't enjoying it.

'I wouldn't dream of it, seeing as it goes staunchly against your rules. I'll cut to the chase. I bought tickets to a wine tasting experience at The Conrad Hotel tomorrow night, but my sister cancelled on me. She has a date. I thought it might be a good opportunity to get to know each other. Do you want to come? Seeing as we are you know ... dating.' She emphasises the word 'dating' heavily.

'Do I want to come?' I repeat every word in a low seductive voice. Majella bristles beside me, crossing her legs.

'It'll be fun. You could do with some fun in your life, you know.' Amazing how Ava has the measure of me after one date.

Phoebe's going to Sarah Snowden's house for a sleepover. If I stay at home, I risk Teagan turning up in her lingerie again.

'Count me in. What time?'

Majella finally stands and stalks away. This fake-dating deal is turning out to be even more helpful than I thought.

'Eight pm. I'll meet you there.'

· · ·

Friday 1ˢᵗ December

The following night, I find myself in the basement of one of Dublin's most prestigious hotels. An open fire crackles and roars in the wrought iron fireplace nestled into an exposed stone wall. The room is set with small tables adorned with pristine white tablecloths and a variety of wine glasses.

There are about fifteen people tasting wine, but only one I can't take my eyes off. Ava looks stunning tonight in a black lace dress and those damn stilettos again. Maybe I do have a foot fetish after all. Her dark glossy hair's blow-dried into curls that fall down her back and she's wearing that rich wine-coloured lipstick again. The one I stared at on my neck long after Teagan left the other night.

At the front of the room, an experienced sommelier is explaining the characteristics of the third wine of the evening, describing its origin, grape variety and tasting notes. I'm only half listening, my mind occupied with the woman sitting a foot away from me.

The more I sip, the more I wonder what it would be like to taste Ava. This is technically our second date and if it was a real date, I would have kissed her the second I laid eyes on her. She might be infuriatingly cheerful, but she's also the most beautiful woman I've ever met. Those full, luscious lips. The way her tongue keeps darting over her perfect Cupid's bow. I know what else I'd like it to dart over.

Get a grip, Cillian. The woman is doing you a favour. And you're supposed to be doing her one. Not imagining her on her knees for you.

'What are you thinking?' She tilts towards me, offering a stellar view of her killer cleavage.

It's been way too long since I've been with a woman, because all I can think about is bending you over the table, lifting that dress up, and leaving those shoes on.

I swirl the wine in the glass, watching as it trickles back

down to the base. 'I think I prefer the first one. What are you thinking?'

She holds her glass under her nose, takes a small sniff, then downs the contents in one mouthful. 'I'm thinking you'll be able to tell Frank and Penny on Sunday that their daughter swallows.' Neat dark eyebrows wiggle suggestively.

I almost spit my drink out all over my shirt. What a visual. Sliding further under the table, I will my delinquent dick to stay the fuck down.

Ava is beautiful on the outside, but her playful personality is every bit as alluring too. Even if it's the polar opposite of mine. 'Yeah, because I'm sure that's exactly what your parents are going to ask over Sunday lunch.'

'Oh, Cillian. You have no idea what you're letting yourself in for.' Her bright eyes glitter. 'My mother is a retired midwife. She'll tell you herself, she's seen it all. And both my parents believe in talking about everything over Sunday lunch. And I mean *everything*. Don't say I didn't warn you.' The glasses are cleared away and we're handed the next wine to sample.

They can't be that bad. They raised her.

I scoot my chair closer to Ava. The desire to talk to her is way stronger than the desire to discover the origin of the grape.

I keep my voice low, grateful we're at the table furthest away from the sommelier. 'Speaking of Sunday lunch, we should probably prepare for it.' I've come up against some mean motherfuckers in court, but the prospect of facing the parents of any woman I'm 'dating' sets an apprehensive shudder over my spine.

'Honey, there is no preparing for Sunday lunch with my family.' Ava presses her palm to her chest; a buoyant bout of laughter escapes her expressive mouth. Several eyes glare from the table in front of us. 'But if it makes you feel better, we can ask each other more questions to get to know each other better.'

I want to know more about her. But not because we're fake-dating. Because she's intriguing. Funny. And sexy as hell.

It's a good job I don't really date. Because if I did, I'd date her properly. Spending time with her is effortless. Her warm honeyed laugh is infectious. Her ease in her own skin is ridiculously attractive. I don't doubt the sex would be amazing.

But then it would end in disaster. A woman like Ava would never settle for something casual. She'd want the whole bells and whistles. A big white dress. A church overflowing with family and friends. A promise of forever. And that's something I'll never be able to give anyone.

Which is precisely why I need a fake girlfriend and not a real one.

'I'll start.' I offer. 'What's your favourite food?'

'Pizza. Couldn't you tell by the way I demolished my lunch on Wednesday?' She crosses her legs, and my eyes are drawn to her shapely thighs and those sexy heels again.

'I noticed you didn't offer me a slice.'

'We're only fake-dating,' she whispers in my ear. 'If you were my real boyfriend, I'd have given you a slice.'

My lips brush across her ear. I'm playing with fire but between the drink, and the desire crusading through my cock, I can't stop. I haven't had this much fun in years. 'Not quite the benefits I was expecting a real boyfriend to get.'

Goosebumps ripple across her arms and she gazes up at me from black lash-framed eyes. Our pupils lock and smoulder. The air crackles and time stops. The rest of the world disappears.

Fuck.

This attraction between us, it's mutual.

And if we're going to be 'dating' for December and spending this much time together, I'm going to need a will of steel not to act on it. Regardless of the consequences.

Chapter Nine

AVA

Cillian might have a cold heart when it comes to love, but the rest of him is blisteringly hot. The man radiates heat, promise, and what Bonnie calls Big Dick Energy. It's just a shame he isn't willing to use it on me. A single man that exceptional looking is a cruel waste.

Though just because he doesn't believe in love and commitment, that doesn't mean he believes in celibacy, does it?

Does he have a fuck buddy? Someone who takes care of his needs?

Or does he take care of them himself?'

I'm nothing if not Penny Jackson's daughter. I snap my eyes away, breaking our sizzling stare. 'My turn to ask the question.'

Those silver eyes dart over my lips again. 'Go on.'

'When did you last have sex?'

His face remains in its usual deadpan expression, but his voice is tinged with amusement. 'Is that something your parents are going to want to know?'

'I wouldn't rule it out.' I smirk, handing over my dirty glass to one of the passing servers and accepting the next one.

He inches towards me, until there's only millimetres between us. 'I'll answer the question, if you do.'

Disgust curls around my core at the thought of Josh, the married ex-convict, but I nod. I may as well confess because it'll take all of three seconds for one of my family members to out me about Josh and his ankle tag.

'A year ago.'

Mr Deadpan sucks in a sharp breath demonstrating a rare flash of emotion – surprise. 'That's almost as long as me.' He exhales a low whistle and cocks his head to the side. 'It's been eighteen months.'

Who did he sleep with, eighteen months ago? And why is there an irrational wave of jealousy rolling through my stomach right now?

Cillian continues with the questions, thankfully oblivious to my internal green-eyed monster. 'Why don't you date? A woman with your looks could have her pick.'

A woman with my looks? My stomach flips and the green-eyed monster is placated, for now at least.

I swallow hard, suddenly serious for once. 'Is that your question? Why don't I date?'

He nods before taking a sip of his wine. We're way past even pretending to care about the grape variety. Or the tasting notes, but we're going to need more of it to continue with this line of questions.

'I had a bad experience.' I suck in a mouthful of air and exhale it slowly. 'The last guy I dated, Josh, lied to me. He'd just been released from prison – nothing major,' I add before he thinks I'm completely irresponsible. 'He was one of those environmentalists protesting about dairy farms. Stupidly, I thought that made him one of the good guys. Showed that he cared about the world.'

Cillian's lips twitch and I can't tell if he's amused or angry.

'My family think it's hilarious that I run a matchmaking service, yet I can't find a match for myself. They tease me about Josh relentlessly. They wouldn't joke if they knew how bad it really was.' Water threatens at the back of my eyes, and I blink it away.

Blurting out my deepest darkest secrets to Cillian was not part of the plan. It's only going to reinforce his delusional views on love.

I blame the wine.

Though he did open up to me at lunch the other day about his ex.

'What happened?' Cillian gazes at me with that intensity again. I'd almost swear he cares.

I shrug, like it's nothing, when obviously it's not. Not when it put me off dating for a whole year. 'He was married. When I found out, the shame of what I'd done was almost too much to bear. I couldn't even tell my family.'

'It's not on you.' Cillian's face screws into a ball of disgust. 'I'm sorry he did that to you.' His fingers skim over the back of my hand in a fleeting gesture that scalds my skin. 'Not all men are assholes.'

'Yeah, some men refuse to entertain the idea of marriage completely.' I offer him a wry smile. 'While others are grumpy workaholics.'

'And others, are struggling full-time parents, without the time or inclination for much else.' He raises his glass to his lips.

'Do you really not believe in true love? Soulmates? The concept of marriage or monogamy?'

'I believe in the principle of monogamy. I've just never experienced it myself.' He stares pensively ahead. 'And I don't know anyone who has.'

Wow.

'You're in for a treat on Sunday. That's all I can say.' The sommelier shoots us a filthy look from the front of the room. 'Want to get out of here, before we get kicked out for talking?'

'Probably for the best.' Cillian stands and pushes his chair back.

We slip out the basement and take the dimly lit stairs to the main hotel bar. Where Elixir was trendy, this bar omits another level of class. The walls are decorated with a silver jacquard paper. The couches lining the edge of the room are low, lustrous, and lilac in colour. The room is light and bright, and overflowing with foliage and potted plants. Climbing vines cascade from ceiling corners, softening the sharp edges of the room.

It's the first Friday in December so no wonder the place is packed. I nudge my way through to the bar with Cillian right on my heels. As we make our way through the crowd, a tall, fair-haired guy stops right in front of me, blocking my path. 'Oh my God, is your name Google?'

'Sorry?' I stammer, as he towers over me.

'Is your name Google?' He winks lasciviously, 'Because you, honey, are everything I've been searching for.'

I burst out laughing at his unabashed cheesiness. 'And you, *honey*, are the reason I ensure my computer's safeguarded by antivirus.'

Cillian steps forward and glares at the guy before placing the palm of his hand on the base of my spine, marking me as his. 'She's with me.'

A tingling sensation shoots from my head, all the way to the tips of my toes. My core coils with pent-up need.

'Sorry, man.' The guy steps aside and raises his hands in a peace gesture.

Cillian's palm remains on my back until we reach the bar.

His thumb caressing the base of my spine. It's all I can do not to throw myself at him.

'What would you like to drink?' His lips brush my ear as he leans in to be heard.

You.

'Sex On The Beach.' Flies out my mouth before I can stop myself.

'So predictable.' He shakes his head, a small smirk playing on his lips. 'You could at least have gone for a Flaming Orgasm.'

'You know one of my favourite tropes in a romance novel is "Why Choose".' Whoops. The wine has definitely loosened my lips.

'I knew you were going to be trouble when you walked in.' He cocks his head to the side and smirks, the grouchy mask beginning to slide.

I never had him down for a Swiftie but I suppose he does have a six-year-old daughter. 'So shame on me now.'

His deep rumbling laugh flips my stomach. 'Busted.'

He's educated in romcoms, knows Taylor Swift lyrics, and fills a suit ridiculously well.

He's like an early Christmas present I never knew I asked for.

As long I forget the part where he doesn't believe in romance, love, or marriage, of course. I'm not stupid enough to do a Teagan on it. I'd never try and trick or trap him, but if he offered me the 'bit of fun' he offered her, I sure as hell wouldn't turn it down.

Two Sex on The Beach and Three Flaming Orgasms later, and I'm bent over the hotel's disabled toilets with Cillian holding my hair out of my face. He strokes my hair with a tenderness I never imagined he was capable of.

'I'm so sorry,' I mumble, the second I finish retching my guts up.

He grabs a thick wad of tissue and dabs my mouth dry. If I wasn't so touched by his unexpected kindness, it might occur to me to be mortified. 'You don't need to apologise to me, I'm not your father.'

'But can I call you daddy?' I hiccup.

Clearly not all the alcohol is in the toilet.

'If you did, I'd have no choice but to take you home with me and smack your backside for getting yourself in this predicament.' His Adam's apple dips in his throat, and I swear his eyes strip me naked with one perusing sweep.

'Would that be such a bad thing?' Oh god. I'm drunk. And desperate, obviously.

He has no idea how many times I'd imagined being in his bed, or having him in mine, long before I even heard his velvet voice purring into my ear or felt the heat of his palm on my back. Or read his cynical sign-up form. And after what he told me on Wednesday, he would be horrified if he had the slightest inkling. Which is why he can never ever find out.

'I'm sure it would be a fantastic thing.' His gaze rakes over my cleavage. 'But it's not going to happen, princess.'

I pout like a four-year-old. 'Why not?'

The attraction is undeniably mutual.

The smouldering glances.

The way he stroked my spine.

The way he acted like a caveman to Google man.

'Firstly, I don't sleep with intoxicated women.' His finger coasts across my bare arm. 'And secondly, it would complicate our arrangement.'

At least he didn't say it was because I'm a holy show that can't hold her drink.

'Come on, let's get you home to bed.'

If only.

. . .

I wake up naked, face down on my quilted cream pillow. A thousand memories of the night before taunting me as I force open my eyes.

The cocktails.

Being sick.

The 'daddy' comment.

Thank God Cillian had more sense than me. I will never mock his serious, sullen ways ever again. Well, for a while at least.

I spy a glass of water and headache tablets on the bedside locker next to me and manage to drag my head high enough to swallow two before passing out again.

The next time I wake, it's decidedly brighter and the pounding in my ears is not coming from inside my head. It's coming from my front door.

I live in the penthouse apartment of a stunning block in Ballsbridge; a twenty-first birthday gift from my movie-star brother. He's not all bad, even if he did rat me out to my parents for having a new man.

If it's Frank and Penny dropping in for a surprise visit hoping to catch my 'boyfriend' here, they're going to be sorely disappointed. Almost as disappointed as me. Because as mortified as I am about coming onto Cillian Callaghan last night, I don't need to be drunk to admit I'm attracted to him. Panty-meltingly attracted to him.

My family are right. I literally have the worst taste in men. Because as attractive as he is, Cillian is a commitment-phobe with more baggage than an airplane on a long-haul flight to Australia.

I drag my fingers through my tousled curls, pull on a black silky robe from the back of my bedroom door, and pad through the sunny hallway to the front door. The banging continues. Giles, the building's doorman/porter wouldn't let just anyone in. It must be someone I know. Or a takeaway delivery. And I didn't order takeaway, not yet anyway.

'I'm coming,' I yell.

When I yank it open, it's not my parents' eager eyes staring back at me. It's Cillian's silver ones. And in his hands is a pizza box from La Dolce Vita.

My stomach flips, but it has more to do with the man himself, and his thoughtful gesture than the pizza.

In a pair of dark navy jeans and a blue sports jacket, he looks almost as enticing as the pizza. I glance down at my robe and bare feet. Not exactly catwalk ready, but if we're going to go to Nate's wedding as a fake couple, he may as well get used to it.

'I know it's early days, and this is probably going to come across as forward, but I think I might actually love you.' I hold open the door and beckon him in.

'If you could look that convincing when you meet Teagan, then I could probably look like I love you too.'

Chapter Ten

CILLIAN

Saturday 2nd December

I follow Ava into her spacious living area, wondering for the millionth time, what the actual fuck I'm doing here. I could pretend I'm checking on her after last night, but the truth is, I can't stop thinking about her.

The second I woke I checked my phone for texts, of which there were none.

With Phoebe at her friend's house until this afternoon, I had too much time on my hands to think. Specifically, about the curve of Ava's lips, the swell of her womanly hips, and the way her breasts heaved when she asked if it would be such a bad thing if I brought her home to my bed.

Ava drops onto a plush, L-shaped sofa that wraps around a low glass coffee table. She drops the pizza box onto the couch beside her and motions for me to sit down.

'Are you going to eat that on the couch?' It wouldn't happen in my house. Life is messy enough without adding physical food spillages to the mix.

'Yep.' She tilts her chin out defiantly and grins. Even hungover, and without a scrap of make-up she's every bit as stunning as she was last night. And every bit as cheerful.

'What if you make a mess?' I sound like someone's father. Oh wait – I am someone's father.

'My house, my rules.'

I shrug off my jacket, draping it across the back of the couch before I sit down. 'This is a beautiful place you've got.'

A huge balcony with sliding doors offers panoramic views of Herbert Park and the trendy little boutiques of Ballsbridge. The entire penthouse is decorated in warm neutral tones and exudes sophistication and elegance.

It's not what I expected. For a start, it must have cost a bomb, and if she's looking for investors for her business, I can't imagine she's rolling in cash.

I should have pried last night. If she was drunk enough to ask me to stay, and call me daddy, then I'm pretty sure she would have told me anything.

'Thanks.' She opens the pizza box and dramatically inhales its steamy aroma. 'It was a gift.'

'A gift?' I feel my eyes widen. 'Who did you have to shag for this?'

'Why? Do you want their number?' Ava exhales a loud belly laugh. 'What makes you think I had to shag somebody? Why are you always so cynical?'

'I can't help it. In my line of work, everything comes down to sex and assets. That's what couples fight over. That's usually why they file for divorce. Now and again, it's amicable, but if they're hiring me, it's usually incredibly ugly.'

'Why did you become a divorce lawyer?' Ava takes a bite of pepperoni pizza before sliding closer and offering me the box. Her unique feminine scent clouds the air around my nostrils and my irresponsible dick jerks to life.

'I thought you only shared your pizza with a real boyfriend?' It's the perfect deflection, and hopefully distraction, from the hard-on pushing against my pants.

'Good point.' She snatches back the box before I can take

a slice. 'Though, I'm happy to share a takeaway if there's enough. I'm just not happy with random strangers shoving their fork into my food when I go out for dinner. Comprendo?'

'That makes perfect sense. Then they're shoving their fork into their mouth, then shoving it back into your dinner. You've no idea where anyone's mouths have been.'

'Exactly.' Ava's eyes flicker with amusement. 'Apart from we all know where yours has been for the past eighteen months – nowhere.'

I exhale a heavy sigh. 'I see you didn't lose your memory down the toilet with the cocktails last night.'

She presses the heel of her palm over her sockets. 'I nearly wish I had. I'm so sorry.' She peeps up, her thick black lashes dancing across her cheeks.

'Sorry for spewing your guts up? Or sorry for coming on to me?'

Why am I bringing this up now?

Because it's all I've been thinking about, along with, well... the curve of her lips, the swell of her womanly hips, and the way her breasts heaved when she suggested it.

I'm playing with fire. Testing the water to see if it's warm enough to dive into now the alcohol's worn off. I should know better.

Ava pauses chewing her pizza and swallows hard. A pink tinge flushes her cheeks. 'Both.'

Chemistry clouds the air between us, thick and heavy and full of a promise of something that I can't deliver. Oh, I don't doubt I could satisfy her, physically at least. That's the easy part. It's all the stuff that comes after that I can't handle.

Entwining my existence with someone else's.

Risking letting another woman into mine and Phoebe's lives for her to disappear on us again.

Nothing lasts in the end.

So why chance it?

'Don't be. On either account.' I adjust my trousers and try to avert my gaze from where her robe is gaping open, exposing inch after inch of satiny skin. 'But it can't happen again.'

'I know.' She squeezes her eyelids shut like she's forcing away the memory. 'I'm sorry.'

I nod, unable to speak, because if I do, I'll say something I regret. Like the reason it can't happen again is because I don't trust myself not to bring her home, take care of her, let her call me daddy, or whatever the fuck she wants, once she's in my bed.

I haven't been this attracted to a woman since ... well, ever. And if our views on relationships weren't so different, perhaps we could have a bit of fun with this fake-dating thing, but they are, so we can't. And apart from the fact I don't believe in love, laughter and happy ever after, I have a daughter to care for and a business to run. I don't have time for a relationship. I'll never be able to give Ava what she wants out of life.

So as much as I want to rip open that robe and devour her body with my tongue, I can't. It wouldn't be fair on either of us.

'What are you thinking?' Ava interrupts my silent pep talk.

'Nothing. Everything. Never mind.' The topic of who gifted her this penthouse suite suddenly feels far safer than asking if she'd consider casual sex without the Happy Ever After she seeks for her clients. 'So, who gifted you this place? An elderly relative? An old lady you met at a car boot sale? There's a story here somewhere. I should probably hear it before we go to your parents' house tomorrow.'

She sits straighter and tightens her robe, to the displeasure of my cock, but the safeguarding of my sanity. 'My big brother, Nate.' She pronounces his name with a tone that implies I should know him.

'Nate?' I rack my brain, but nothing comes up.

'Nate Jackson.' She annunciates every syllable slowly.

My eyebrows shoot skywards. 'Nate Jackson the movie star?'

'The very one.' Ava says with an apologetic smile. 'Forgive me for not telling you right away. Once men find out I'm related to a world-famous action star, I tend to just fade into the background. The entire relationship then turns into "when can I meet your brother?" and they fall in love with him, instead of me.'

'No fear of that here.' Not when all I can think about is running my tongue over the perfect dip of her Cupid's bow.

'Yeah, yeah,' she rolls her eyes. 'We all know you don't believe in love of any kind.'

My gaze cruises across her flawless features, her satiny skin, and huge hazel eyes. 'I do believe in love. How can I not, when I love my daughter more than life itself? I just don't believe in a romantic love that lasts.'

'Wait until you meet my parents tomorrow. Then we'll have this conversation again.'

'Can't wait.' Sarcasm punctuates each word as I stand and grab my jacket from the couch.

'Are you going already?' Ava sounds disappointed.

'I have to collect Phoebe from her friend's house. We're having a movie night tonight.' I'm just praying Teagan doesn't crash it.

'Oh, can I come?' Ava darts forward in her seat beaming like a child. 'I could bring the popcorn.'

An image of Ava, Phoebe and I snuggled on my couch under a fleecy blanket sends a strange sensation swirling in my chest. I dismiss the idea immediately. 'Not appropriate.'

Her face falls. 'Sorry. Of course.'

'I've never introduced Phoebe to any female friend, other than Beth. I wouldn't want to confuse her.' It's only the truth. Phoebe knows Teagan has boyfriends. As young as she is, she seems to instinctively understand that they're the reason Teagan isn't at home with us. I can't have her worrying that I'm going to disappear on her too.

'Absolutely. I totally get that. I'm sorry if I overstepped.' Ava stands to see me out, her long toned thigh slipping out from between the folds of that black silky material. Every cell in my body begs me not to leave, screams at me to touch her smooth silky skin. The air is thick with tension. We're one spark from a fire neither of us will be able to put out.

'It's fine. Everything is fine.' Am I trying to convince her? Or myself?

She turns slowly, sashaying towards the front door with graceful, fluid movements. I follow her, her scent teasing my nostrils.

I linger, leaning on the doorframe. 'I'll see you tomorrow. Want me to pick you up?'

Ava nods, her gold-flecked eyes darting up to meet mine. 'It would look better if we arrived together.'

'Okay. What time shall I collect you?' Her face is inches away. It would be so easy to press my lips to hers. To explore her mouth. To taste her. To devour her. Which is exactly why I need to leave right now.

I'm not due to collect Phoebe for another two hours but given the way my penis is a trigger-happy loaded pistol, it's safer for both of us if I go.

My imagination is running riot with all the ways I'd like to take her. And every single one of them obliterates the safe little world I've created for myself. If being with Ava is even half as good as I imagined, my world as I know it would be gone forever.

'Two p.m. Bring your thickest skin. And earmuffs. You're

going to need them.' She leans up on her tip toes and drops a chaste kiss on my cheek. 'Thanks for the pizza. And for last night. You know, I think you could be a lot of fun. If you'd let yourself.'

So do I. Which is half my problem.

Chapter Eleven

AVA

Sunday 3rd December

Nerves spin in my stomach like a Ferris wheel, though it's not like I'm taking a real boyfriend to meet my parents.

For the sake of my brother's wedding, I want them to like Cillian.

But what I really want, is for *him* to like them.

For him to grasp that some relationships do last.

To understand that not everyone is destined for divorce, or a life of misery.

Why?

That's a question I'm not ready to answer. Not even to myself. I only met the guy six days ago. So why am I replaying every minute we've spent together over and over in my mind? It's not healthy. It's supposed to be fake, that's the agreement.

I glance at my reflection in the mirror, smoothing down the coffee-coloured jumper dress I agonised for way too long over. The woollen material clings to my curves without revealing any skin. It's sexy yet understated. Exactly what I need for today.

My phone vibrates with an incoming message.

It's Cillian.

Outside.

I grab my coat, take a few deep breaths, and ride the lift down to the ground floor.

A BMW X5 is double-parked outside the revolving glass doors. I nod to Giles, the white-haired porter, and he shoots me a knowing wink. 'Hot date, Miss Jackson?'

'Something like that.' Poor Giles. He's seen it all since he started here four years ago. There's been many a night I've come home tipsy and shared my curry chips and my woes with him. He's like the grandfather I never had.

'About time you got back out there.' He lifts a weathered hand and gives me an encouraging thumbs up.

'You said it, Giles.' I stalk across the marble floor with a confidence I don't necessarily feel.

Cillian hops out and struts around to the passenger side to greet me.

Oh. My. God. However hot Mr Suave Suit Guy is, Casual Cillian is equally as devastating. The grey round-neck jumper clinging to his broad shoulders makes me want to slide across the muscular planes of his chest and wrap my legs around his waist. His now familiar scent surrounds my senses, luring me in.

'Afternoon.' His lips lift into an almost-smile as he opens the door for me. I'd nearly swear he's happy to see me. Well, as happy as an eternal grump can be.

'And you claim not to be a gentleman.'

He arches an eyebrow. 'Don't be fooled by basic manners.'

Do those same manners apply in the bedroom?

The more time I spend with him, the more I'd love to find out. My mind is in the gutter.

I hop into the vehicle, and he closes the door behind me. The brand-new car smell has nothing on Cillian's cologne.

'Are you ready?' I ask, the second he slides back into the

driver's seat.

'As I'll ever be.'

Cillian pulls into the driveway of my childhood home and the front door flies open so fast, the decorative festive mistletoe wreath hurtles to the ground.

Once again, my date – I mean fake date – opens the door for me, unwittingly securing my parents' seal of approval before he's even had the chance to say, 'pleased to meet you'.

My mother's bob is perfectly styled as usual. It doesn't budge as she hops from foot to foot in excitement. 'Ava! It's so good to see you!'

Really? Is that why her gaze is focused intently on the man beside me? The one whose ever-rigid lips are stretched into what I think is supposed to be a smile but looks more like he's holding back a ferocious fart.

My dad appears in the doorway behind her, snaking an arm around my mother's waist. 'Frank, fix the wreath, please!' She squeezes his hand with the same affection I've watched pass between them for my entire life. And Cillian tells me there's no such thing as true love. He's about to get a first-row seat to the biggest love story I've ever witnessed.

'You must be Cillian.' Mam gushes as we reach the front door. 'It's great to meet you! Welcome to the madness.'

Cillian extends a hand for a formal shake at the same time as my mother lunges at him and yanks him into a typical Penny Jackson overfamiliar embrace. His shoulders stiffen and it's a battle to suppress the laughter bubbling in my chest. If he thinks that gesture's inappropriate, wait until they get started on the wine.

'Hi Dad.' I spring a kiss on his cheek before stepping into the hallway.

'I'm Frank.' My dad shakes Cillian's hand enthusiastically,

but there's a hint of something stern in his gaze. An unspoken warning not to hurt his youngest daughter. No fear there. Can't get hurt from a relationship that's not real. Can you?

'Great to meet you.' Cillian's voice is deep and rich and surprisingly genuine.

Mam links her arm through Cillian's and guides him through to the living room. Dad and I exchange a knowing look.

In true Jackson style, mam and dad have put the Christmas tree up already. They do it every year on the first of December and crack open the sherry.

'Do you like the tree?' Mam's still clinging onto the curve of Cillian's taut bicep. A ripple of envy surges through my stomach. A longing to touch him blooms like an unfurling flower. I push it down and try to remember why we're here.

My business. I need Nate to invest.

'It's beautiful, Mrs Jackson.' Cillian reaches out to examine one of the personalised baubles, another Jackson tradition. Each year we get a new family photo made into a bauble. This year's photo is special. Nate's fiancée Holly is in it, and so is their new baby daughter, Harriet.

'Oh please. Call me Penny.' Mam swats Cillian's forearm playfully, then turns to me. 'Oh honey, I can see why you're so keen on him.'

Thanks Mam.

'He's quite the catch. I bet he's an animal in the bedroom.' A girlish giggle peels from her lips.

Cillian splutters into his hand, coughing through his recovery.

I snigger. 'Mam, this could be your future son-in-law!'

'Precisely!' She throws her hands up into the air. 'It's essential he knows what he's doing down under. Imagine being married to a man who had no idea what to do with it! Thankfully, your father ...'

'Okay, Mam. That's enough.' I hold a hand up to silence her. 'I don't think Cillian's quite ready for those details yet. Not without copious amounts of alcohol, anyway.'

'Who's for a glass of wine?' Dad rubs his hands together, a mischievous glint in his eyes.

'Yes please.' Given the tone pre-dinner, I've got a feeling I'm going to need it. Though not as much as Cillian. As his jaw winds tighter and tighter, I begin to relax. My parents like him. They wouldn't tease him if they didn't.

'Did you not have enough on Friday?' Cillian's sharp eyes flick to mine.

'Trust me. Take a glass of wine. You'll need it when these two really get going.' I nudge my dad and he guffaws.

'Let's go through to the kitchen.' Mam finally releases Cillian's arm, and his shoulders sag in relief.

'So, Cillian. Tell us about yourself. What do you do?' Dad asks as he uncorks a bottle of Malbec. The scent of rosemary and garlic permeates the air in the brand-new kitchen dad installed earlier this year.

'I'm a lawyer.' Cillian gratefully accepts the glass that's handed to him. Wise decision. He won't be driving for ages.

'Oh, that's impressive.' My mother squeals. 'What kind of law?'

'I'm a divorce specialist.' Cillian's tone is clipped, defensive almost.

'Oh.' Mam and Dad lock eyes across the room discreetly telepathing their surprise.

Mam glances to me and shrugs. 'They do say opposites attract.'

'Cillian has a daughter. She's called Phoebe.' I watch on as he squirms, but he needn't worry. There will be no judgement from Frank or Penny Jackson. They love kids. They wouldn't care if Phoebe was conceived on a threesome in Vegas with an Elvis impersonator and a stripper - as long as she's loved. 'I haven't met her yet, it's still early days, but hopefully in the new year.'

'How wonderful. That's something to look forward to.' My mother's eyes light with excitement. 'How old is she?'

'Six going on sixteen.' Cillian treats us to one of his rare genuine smiles. My breath catches in my throat. That smile could light up the city.

'Is her mother around?' My mother asks, stirring a steaming pot of gravy on the stove.

Cillian flinches, as if he's remembering exactly why he's here. 'I have full care of Phoebe. Her mother is ... unreliable.'

'Wow. That's remarkable. It can't be easy, juggling a big job and a daughter.' My dad tilts his head, taking Cillian in again.

'It doesn't leave time for much else.' Cillian rests against the kitchen countertop. He's braver than me. I know what those two animals get up to in here.

'So how did you two lovebirds meet?' Mam's eyes dart between us. I cross the room to stand next to Cillian in a faux show of togetherness.

'Cillian filled in my sign-up form at HeartSync.' I touch his forearm in what's supposed to be a casual gesture, but fire that ignites in my underwear is anything but casual. It's explosive.

'Oh, how wonderful.' Mam abandons the gravy and clasps her hands together. 'That's so romantic.'

'Oh, Cillian is the most romantic man I've ever met.' I can't help myself. All nerves have evaporated. Being in my childhood home provides a security I haven't felt since I met Cillian. It's time to have some fun. 'When I saw how he answered the "describe your perfect first date" on the questionnaire, I just knew he was special.'

Cillian bristles next to me, his eyes narrowing into a glare.

'Oh, what did he write?' Mam gushes.

'Cillian, you tell them. I just can't get the words out.' I nudge him with my elbow.

'I thought those questionnaires were confidential?' If looks could kill, I'd be writhing around on the lino floor in agony, exhaling my last breath.

'Oh, in case you didn't notice, you don't need to be shy in this house, pumpkin.' I shoot him a sickly-sweet smile before taking a huge mouthful of wine.

'Still, I'd rather not elaborate. Not until we've brought that special date to life.' His chin tilts defiantly, a sarcastic smirk stretching his plump inviting lips.

'Well, I'm pretty sure that fantasy could have become a reality on Friday night.' What am I playing at? My parents' over-sharing openness must be contagious.

Frank and Penny watch on with glee. All they're missing is a bucket of popcorn.

Cillian's eyes darken. 'I wanted to wait until you were sober, so we could both enjoy the experience.' Touché. An image of myself on my knees behind Cillian's desk springs to mind and it's my turn to squirm.

'Really?' I clink my wine glass against his. 'Should I switch to water?'

His tongue darts out to wet his lower lip and he pauses for a beat. Is he conjuring the same image as me? Wondering if this fake thing between us could have a few perks? 'Another day.'

'I'll hold you to that.' I pat his arm again, for no other reason than I can't help myself. Heat pulses between us and the air sizzles.

'More like *I'll* hold you to that.'

'Oh, Frank. Check out the chemistry!' My mother shrieks. 'This place is about to blow.'

She has no idea how close to the truth she is.

Chapter Twelve

CILLIAN

Ava's mother is a wonderful cook. Roast lamb with all the trimmings is my death row meal. Still, I'm not convinced it's worth the mortification Ava is subjecting me to.

I take another forkful of melt-in-the-mouth meat, savouring the succulent flavour.

'I take it you're going to the HeartSync anniversary party next week?' Penny asks from her position to my right.

'Of course.' It was one of the stipulations of our agreement. Blow jobs, however, were not. But with Ava teasing me like she did, all I can think about is her sensuous mouth wrapped around me. If her parents had any idea I'm sporting a full erection beneath their dinner table, they'd be horrified.

Scratch that, they'd probably be delighted. I've never met another couple like them.

'I've emailed Beth the details. She has it scheduled in your diary.' I bet she has. Beth has been insufferable since Ava turned up at the office on Wednesday. Even though I explained our relationship isn't real, Beth's got this daft notion that we're going to blossom into the next 'big thing.'

'Where is it again?' I drop my hand beneath the table and

skim over Ava's thigh. I could say it's to support the farce we're putting on, but the truth is, it's because I want to touch her.

Did she mean what she said earlier? *She'll hold me to it.*

And if she did, is that a line we should cross?

This is supposed to be a business agreement. We want different things out of life. Well – that's not strictly true – I should say, we believe life will offer us different things.

Would I like to find a partner? Someone to share my day with, to share the rest of my life with, to take to bed every night until death do us part?

Yes. I would. Absolutely.

Do I believe that could ever be a reality?

No. I don't. Absolutely not. Which is why I've never hoped for it, let alone looked for it.

Ava freezes for a second, registering my palm on her leg. Goosebumps raise beneath her sheer silky tights. Or are they stockings?

'It's in The Shelbourne.' Her voice cracks and she swallows hard.

Good. If she wants to play games with me, she needs to know I'm the ultimate opponent. I don't lose. Ever. I have a heap of freshly stamped divorce decrees to support that statement.

I've only had one glass of wine, but it's enough to lower my inhibitions. Let's see how far she's willing to take this game. 'I love The Shelbourne. Shall we book a suite there to save either of us trying to get taxis home?'

'Oh, that sounds like fun.' Penny nods her approval. 'I knew I liked you, Cillian.'

I inch up higher over Ava's inner thigh in a circular motion. Let's see how she handles a little pressure.

'Careful, or I will start calling you daddy.' Ava whispers into my ear.

Oh, she's good. Is it possible I've met my match?

'It's a big occasion, a year in business. It's essential we mark it.' I tear my fingers from Ava's thigh before I snap completely. The urge to find out exactly what's she got underneath that dress is consuming me.

Note to self – do not touch my fake girlfriend. Because if I start, I don't think I'll ever be able to stop.

Ava smirks, like she knows she won this round of whatever fucked-up game we're playing. But winning a round, and winning the entire game, are two entirely different matters. It's a long month and we're only getting started.

Frank places his cutlery together on his plate and squeezes his wife's hand over the table. 'That was delicious, Pen. Thanks.'

Ava wasn't exaggerating. The love between them is obvious. A tiny hint of yearning tugs at my tummy.

'You're so welcome.' Penny returns his squeeze before picking up her fork again and turning her attention to me. 'So, Ava tells us you're coming to Nate's wedding?'

'Yes.' Although I have no idea who's going to mind Phoebe for four days.

Like a mind reader, Ava's head flicks round to mine. 'Who will mind Phoebe?'

'My mother, hopefully.'

'Phoebe's welcome to come.' Frank offers.

'Nate and Holly wouldn't mind.' Penny backs him up. 'The place will be filled with kids.'

I pause for a beat, trying to articulate the right words but Ava beats me to it.

'Thanks, Mam, Dad.' She eyes her parents steadily over the table. 'It's just that we're so new, and Phoebe has had such instability from her mother, we don't want her to know about our relationship until we're a sure thing.'

She has it in one. I could kiss her. Except I can't. And not just because I made the stupid rule, but because if I do, I might never recover.

'Oh, you two are so cute!' Penny grins across the table. 'You guys are already a sure thing. Trust me. I'm never wrong.'

Ava shifts in her chair, guiltily. Are we the worst people ever for faking this relationship? I rub a thumb across the stubble dotting my chin.

No. It's essential. Ava needs a date for her brothers' wedding to secure his investment.

And I need Teagan out of my life.

'She's right.' Frank gazes at his wife with a wistful admiration. 'You guys are perfect for each other. Even if you don't know it yet.' His eyes twinkle with mischievousness.

We could be perfect for each other. For a while.

But then what?

It's a chance I can't take. Which is why I should keep my wandering hands to myself.

After dinner, Ava and I clean up. Each time our hands brush over the dishwasher, my stomach twists like a corkscrew. I want her. I wanted her from the second I saw her, but now I know how smart her mouth is, I can't stop thinking about all the things she could do with it. And how I'd love to see it drop open as she surrenders herself to me. As she writhes and wriggles beneath me.

I've replayed Friday night in my head a million times, wishing I'd brought her to bed with me. But she was drunk. It wouldn't have been right. Plus, I don't want to complicate our agreement.

But if she keeps going with that dirty mouth, there's only so much a man can take.

'Are you sure you can't stay a bit longer?' Penny puckers from where she's sipping her third glass of wine at the table.

'You could stay for another drink, get a cab home later. Natalie, Ava's sister, will be over after her shift at the hospital. She's a nurse, you know. She'd love to meet you.'

'I wish I could.' And surprisingly, it's the truth. Frank and Penny Jackson are easy company. It's not hard to see where Ava gets her bubbly warmth from. With a family like hers, no wonder she's optimistic about relationships. 'But it's getting late. I have to collect Phoebe from my mother's house.'

'Well, we'll look forward to seeing you at The Shelbourne then.' Penny stands and motions for her husband to do the same. They walk us through the hallway and open the front door. A gust of icy wind whistles through the wreath which Frank hung back in position on the door.

I step out onto the top step and offer Ava my hand for balance. Her petite palm sinks into mine like it was made for it. Fireworks burst beneath my skin.

'Wait!' Penny exclaims. 'You guys are under the mistletoe. You have to kiss.'

I glance at the wreath. Technically, I'm next to it, but Ava is definitely beneath it. Oh god, what I wouldn't do to have her beneath me. I can't kiss her. Because if I do, I might never stop.

'Mam! Don't be daft.' Ava swats the air in front of her face. The moonlight illuminates her cheekbones and high-lights the blush creeping over her skin.

'Traditions are traditions.' Frank insists, dropping an arm around Penny's shoulders. 'We didn't raise any prudes in this house.'

'Oh, come on!' Penny nudges Ava towards me. 'It's only a kiss.'

It's not only a kiss though, that's the problem. It's lighting a match beneath a straw house that's covered in petrol. This attraction between us, it's carnal. Someone's liable to get burned.

The air shifts and thickens between us. Ava hooks me with those huge hazel eyes. Her throat flexes and my heartbeat goes haywire. Lust and logic rage inside my chest.

Desire blazes in her dilating pupils, inviting me in. She inches up onto her tip toes at the same time I stoop downwards, and our mouths collide with a ferocity that neither of us could have predicted. Her soft lips part, allowing my greedy tongue the access it's been longing for from the second we met. She tastes like Malbec and magic. Which is no surprise because she must be some sort of sorceress to invoke this reaction in me.

I don't do this kind of thing.

Ever.

Until now.

Until her.

Her body moulds against mine, her hands curl around my neck, fingers raking through the back of my hair. I grab her waist, palming the swell of her hips as our mouths continue to move and meld like they were made for each other.

My pulse roars in my ears. Blood pumps furiously below. Fuck. She tastes like more. One kiss is never going to be enough.

'Easy.' Frank's teasing tone breaks the spell.

I tear my lips from Ava's and jump backwards, shoving my hands in my pockets. Like that might keep them from reaching out and touching what isn't mine.

Ava blinks hard. She looks as dazed as I feel.

'I told you they had chemistry!' Penny squeals.

I stalk towards the X5 and open the passenger door for Ava.

'Thanks again.' I manage to grit out.

Ava has this faraway look in her eyes as I reverse out the driveway. I raise a hand to wave at Frank and Penny. They're standing with their arms wrapped around each other like they're on honeymoon.

'Your parents are unreal.' They're like none I've ever met before. There's no denying the spark that's still so obviously blazing between them. But it has absolutely nothing on the inferno ravaging my insides right now.

Chapter Thirteen

AVA

The drive back to my apartment is silent, apart from the thunderous humming of my heart. I have imagined kissing Mr Suave Suit Guy a hundred times over the past few months, but never in my wildest fantasies did it live up to kissing Cillian Callaghan. His mouth was the perfect combination of soft and firm. And my god did he know what to do with it.

My lips are ruined. And so is my underwear.

He pulls up outside my apartment, leaving the engine still running. The streetlights cast a dim glow through the car.

'Are you okay?' he asks, thrumming his fingers on the steering wheel, looking anywhere but at me.

'I think so.' I swallow the saliva flooding my mouth. 'Are you?'

He exhales a heavy breath and angles his head towards mine. His silver eyes spin with a million emotions. 'I shouldn't have lost control like that. I'm sorry.'

'Don't apologise. It's every other man that came before you who should be sorry. I've never been kissed like it.' My hand instinctively reaches out to pat his thigh, the heat that burns between us melts all rationale. 'Do you want to come up?'

Darkening eyes pin me with a smouldering stare. 'Do I want to come up?' His voice is incredulous.

He readjusts the crotch of his trousers, drawing my attention to the wigwam tenting his pants. 'Ava, I've been "up" all afternoon. I want nothing more than to drag you up to your bedroom and ravage every inch of your skin until you're screaming my name and begging me to let you come.'

His words steal the breath from my chest. Longing rips through my limbs. 'What are you waiting for then?' It's barely more than a whisper.

His eyes darken. 'What I want, and what I can have are two very different things.' He drags his eyes away from mine. 'I have to collect my daughter.'

Of course. In the heat of the moment, I forgot he has more responsibilities than I can even imagine.

Which is why, the second I get the chance, I'm going to ensure he gets to forget about them, for a while at least.

We might not be a HeartSync love match, but after that kiss I've decided there's no real reason I can't have a bit of fun with Mr Right Now, while I'm waiting for Mr Right.

Maybe what I really need to get back out there again is enough fun to remind me what I've been missing. Though truthfully, whatever chemistry is sparking between Cillian and me is something I've been missing my whole life.

I hop out of his BMW, a plan already formulating in my mind. 'See you Wednesday.'

Those metallic eyes linger on my lips for a beat before he nods.

'How did it go?' Giles motions to Cillian's taillights disappearing into the distance.

'Good. Too good.' I head to the lift. Giles doesn't need to know I have another hot date right now. With my vibrator.

· · ·

Monday 4th December

I'm at my desk early, hoping work will distract me from the memory of Cillian's lips on mine. From obsessing over the bulge in his trousers. And my newfound plan to seduce him.

Sure, we have an agreement, and business is business.

But there's no reason we can't combine it with a little pleasure.

I might even throw in that sweetener he was looking for.

Bonnie approaches, clutching two caramel lattes from the neighbouring Starbucks. The scent of coffee permeates the air.

'Has he passed yet?' Bonnie points towards the window, handing me one of the lattes.

'Who?' I'm buying time. I've yet to confess to my best friend/PA exactly what I've been up to for the past six days, primarily because I know she'll worry about me.

'Duh, Mr Suave Suit Guy. The one and only man you've allowed yourself to drool over since Josh the Dairy Destroyer broke your heart.' Bonnie perches on the desk next to me and scans the commuters outside the window.

'Yeah, about him ...' I spin round to face her and take a large gulp of coffee. 'We're fake-dating.'

She splutters, whacking her chest with her fist. 'What? Since when?'

'Since last week. It was him who filled in that sign-up form. I thought we could be of assistance to each other ... He's looking for someone to scare off his ex. I need a date for Wednesday night. Not to mention Nate's wedding.'

'You are fucking joking me? He's the cynic with the blow job and whiskey hang up?' Trust Bonnie to remember that part of the form. Though I'd be lying if I said I haven't obsessed about that line myself a million times.

'The very one. I nearly died when he walked into Elixir the other night. What are the chances?' I take another sip of coffee and rock back on my chair.

Bonnie's face is a picture of shock and horror. 'You must have been so disappointed! I know you'd built Mr Suave Suit Guy to be something special in your head. Then you get landed with the "divorce daddy" instead.'

I inhale a lungful of air. 'On the contrary in fact. He might not be what I envisioned, but he's so much more, in a different way.'

'Spill.' Bonnie crouches forward so Cleo and Violet can't hear us across the room.

When I reach the part where my parents forced us to kiss, Bonnie actually squeals.

It's cathartic getting it off my chest. And like the school-girl with the silly crush, I love talking about Cillian Callaghan. Hearing his name on my lips feels stupidly good.

'He's never going to be The One. He doesn't believe in love and relationships, but given the chemistry between us, I'm willing to overlook that for a little short-term festive fun.'

'Oh, Ava. I don't know.' A single worry line creases Bonnie's otherwise smooth forehead. 'I'm all for casual sex. You know I am.'

Bonnie might work at HeartSync, but she's a hardcore Tinder dater, and utterly unashamed about that fact. She always claims when she's ready to settle down, she'll try HeartSync, but for now, she's happy with good old fashioned hip syncing.

'It's different for you, Ava. Ever since we were kids you've dreamed of hearts and flowers. The big white dress. The fairy-tale wedding. And you've been obsessed with this guy from afar for the best part of a year. I'm worried you're going to get hurt.'

'I was obsessed with the fantasy of what I thought he was.

And his impeccable ass, it's true. But I don't even associate Cillian with that guy anymore. Cillian is Cillian. I'm obsessed with him in a different way. I know we are utterly incompatible in the real world. The man is a disparaging damaged divorce lawyer, and I'm a hopeful romantic, but he's also sexy as fuck, in that broody "I'd break you in bed" kind of way. There's no way I'm mistaking him for husband material. But would there be any harm in a fling with my fake boyfriend? I feel like I need help getting back in the saddle. You know I haven't been with anyone since Josh. He really knocked the wind from my sails. I had no idea who he was, and I trusted him with my heart and my body and look where that got me. At least with Cillian, I know where I stand. Surely, it will only help both of our causes.'

'As long as you don't do something crazy like fall in love with him.' Bonnie drains her coffee and fires me a knowing look.

'We're going to be spending the month together anyway. It has to have some perks.' I cross my legs and press my thighs together.

'When are you seeing him again?' Bonnie throws her empty cup across the room and fist-pumps the air as it sails straight into the recycling bin.

'Wednesday. He's coming to HeartSync's anniversary party. Are we all set for that by the way?' It's one thing being distracted at home, but I can't afford to take my eye off the ball at work. Not when I want to entice Nate into investing. With his help, HeartSync could open offices across the country, Europe, who knows, maybe even the States.

'Yep. All set. I've invited all the couples that had successful matches, luring them with the promise of free champagne and luxury gift bags. I've ordered the most sumptuous canapés The Shelbourne offers and organised helium heart balloons with the events management company.' Bonnie

ticks a finger for every point. 'I also invited all our neighbouring businesses, both sides of Grafton Street, plus a few
bloggers. Though, given your brother is planning on attend-
ing, that should provide more publicity than we could ever
afford to pay for.'

'Brilliant. Thank you.' I might have given Bonnie this job
initially because she's my best friend, but she's proved her
weight in gold as my PA. 'Don't forget to plaster it all over
the socials.'

'The girls are on it as we speak.' She nods towards Cleo
and Violet who are both immersed in their computers across
the room.

'Fantastic.'

My spine shudders with a ripple of apprehension. I can't
wait for Wednesday night. And it has nothing to do with cele-
brating my first year in business, and everything to do with
seeing Cillian.

Our lives might be very different, but isn't that the precise
reason to enjoy this chemistry between us while we can?

I need him to give into this animalistic attraction
between us.

'We need to go to Brown Thomas at lunch. I need a new
outfit for Wednesday night. And I need it to scream "sex". I
also need a tonne of new lingerie, just in case.'

'Sex is my speciality.' Bonnie beams. She's not joking.
Bonnie treats sex like one of her five a day. She could be
Penny Jackson's long-lost love child.

It's late, and my feet are killing me when I finally get
home. I drop the mountain of Brown Thomas bags inside the
door, kick off my stilettos, and switch on the low lighting.

The open plan living area looks bare compared to the
twinkling Christmas lights on the street below. Putting up a
tree for an apartment that I live alone in seems pointless.
And considering I usually spend most of the holidays at my

parents' house anyway, it's an awful lot of work for just me. Don't get me wrong, I love Christmas, but it's one holiday that's geared around couples and families.

I pad through to the main bathroom, turn on the taps of the clawfoot tub and pour in a generous amount of jasmine scented oil. I didn't ask Nate to buy me a penthouse suite. I told him it was too much. But being the fabulous (if a little irritating) big brother he is, he insisted. And when I saw this Instagram-worthy freestanding bathtub, I had to agree with him.

Sinking beneath the bubbles, I check my phone for the millionth time that day. Twenty-two notifications light my screen, but nothing from the one person I'd like to hear from.

> Mam: How's Cillian? I think he could be 'The One.'

I roll my eyes. Sorry Mam. The only 'one' Cillian is going to be is 'the next one'– if I get my way.

> Natalie: Mam said your new man almost impregnated you on her doorstep last night. Details!!!!!

If only.

Nate: So, the boyfriend is real! Mam said he almost ate your face off for dessert yesterday. Yuck. Can't wait until Wednesday.

You and me both Nate.

Bonnie: Any word?

Bonnie's is the only text I reply to.

Nothing. Roll on Wednesday.

I close my eyes and let my hands wander across my chest, wishing they were Cillian's. I've never wanted anyone physically, the way I want him. I know he's no good for me long term. I've never dated a man where there was no possibility of a future before. But this is different. This is fake. There are no expectations. No pressure. It's not real. Apart from the carnal cloth-ripping attraction I feel for him, of course.

Will he give into it, though?

My phone vibrates with another text. One that makes my pulse quicken in my neck.

Cillian: I need you. Can you come over?
Unless you still feel awkward coming to a
strange man's house.

I pull myself out the bath and go in search of the Brown Thomas bags.

I know exactly what Cillian 'needs', because I need it too.

Chapter Fourteen

CILLIAN

'When am I going to meet her, Cillian? It's been a week, and there's been no sign of your "serious girlfriend".' Teagan's just put Phoebe to bed, now she's flouncing around my kitchen in another ridiculous sequinned dress.

Are her frivolous outfits supposed to entice me? All they do is remind me she picked partying over parenting.

The sweater dress clinging to Ava's curves yesterday was a million times sexier without revealing even a hint of skin. Another reason I haven't been able to get her out of my mind all day.

That kiss.

It's all I've thought about, along with her 'do you want to come up?'

I might not want a real relationship but I'm only human. A fact which Ava's stunning face and welcoming warmth worryingly reminds me of. Her sunny smiles infiltrate my cracks and lights the darkest corners of my cynical heart.

And if I were to think about her parents' relationship, and what I saw and felt yesterday, I'd have to re-examine everything I ever believed. And that's not something I'm anywhere near ready, or brave enough to do.

I lay awake all night imagining what would have happened if I could have gone up. If my life was different. If Ava and I weren't so radically different. But we are.

The last thing I need tonight is Teagan's mental games. As much as I hate her presence here, I'll never deny Phoebe the rare time she gets with her mother. Teagan made no secret of the fact she'd been preoccupied drinking cocktails all weekend with Dublin's movers and shakers. It won't be long before she gets bored and flits off again, but when she dropped in unannounced this evening, she scuppered all my plans of obsessing over Ava Jackson's long legs and luscious lips.

'She's actually on her way right now.' Texting Ava was a knee-jerk reaction to Teagan's arrival. One which I probably shouldn't have succumbed to. Especially given I didn't warn her that my ex is here. But if I did, Ava might not have agreed to come over, and with Teagan making herself increasingly comfortable in my house, I'm reminded of exactly why I need this fake-dating arrangement anyway.

Teagan's pale eyes widen. 'You'd have her over here while our daughter is asleep upstairs?'

'Would you rather I invited her over while Phoebe is awake?' I pour myself a glass of red wine without offering Teagan one. She's not staying.

'It's not right, having women over while our daughter is in the house. She could come down at any time.' Teagan glares at me and helps herself to a wine glass.

'It's not right that you left her for a man you met in Marbella.' I snatch the glass out of her hands and put it back in the cupboard. I want her gone.

'Left her, or you? Let's be honest Cillian, that's what really bothers you, isn't it?' Teagan jabs her index finger into my chest. 'That another man did it for me, when you couldn't.'

'Couldn't? Or wouldn't?' I bite, stepping back. 'We both know things were over long before you went to Marbella, but seriously, to up and leave your own baby, then just waltz back in here like it's the most natural thing in the world and have the cheek to judge my parenting?' I blow out a breath. 'Leave, Teagan. We all know it's just a matter of time anyway.'

A buzz sounds from the hallway and Teagan's head snaps in the direction of the front door. 'I'll get it,' she insists, strutting out of the kitchen.

'This is not your house. Nor ever will be.' I stride past her and hit the button to open the gate. Headlights swing up the driveway.

I hope Ava is ready for this. I should have warned her that Teagan's here with the claws out. But in fairness, it's what she signed up for.

A sleek midnight-blue Porsche crunches up the gravel driveway. I open the front door. Teagan loiters behind me. I don't have to look round to know her jaw is on the floor and she's probably salivating over Ava's car.

All I see is its impracticality. Another reminder we are worlds apart.

What Teagan sees is status. And a world she chose to be part of.

If she had any idea who Ava's brother is, she'd probably wet herself. While Nate Jackson is impressive, he has nothing on his little sister as far as I'm concerned. A fact that's both thrilling and worrying in equal measures.

Ava pulls up to the front door and steps out of the car. She beams at me with one of her trademark smiles. From the way she barely gives Teagan a second glance, I gather she has the measure of the situation.

'Hi, baby.' Pet names turn my stomach – previously at

least. Not tonight. The cavalry has arrived. Ava's hips swagger as she struts up to the front door like she's done this a million times before. She places her palms on my chest as her mouth crushes mine with a possessive carnality. My lips part as she steals the breath from my chest.

The rest of the world fades away. It's just her and me kissing on the step again. And it's even better than the replay that's been looping through my head all damn day. She smells like jasmine and tastes like sin. Her lips are soft and moist and loaded with promise.

Teagan clears her throat and Ava breaks the kiss, leaving me longing for so much more.

'Oh, sorry, I didn't see you there! You must be the house-keeper. Matilda, is it?' Ava palms her chest in a faux display of horror. Laughter bubbles in my chest. Oh, she is good.

Teagan's jaw clenches tight as her beady eyes rake over her 'successor', scrutinising her from her loose long dark hair to her heeled leather ankle boots. Ava looks as understated and sexy as ever.

'I'm Phoebe's mother.' Teagan juts her chest out with an air of self-importance.

Yeah, only by birth.

'Oh, I'm Ava, Cillian's girlfriend. I love your dress. Are you going somewhere special?' Ava beams, killing Teagan with kindness. Why does it not surprise me that Ava is trying to make Teagan feel good in some small way, even while she's putting her in her place?

Because she has the warmest heart of anyone I've ever met, that's why.

Teagan scrutinises Ava's casual jeans and chocolate-coloured jacket snidely and stares pointedly in my direction. 'More like seeing *someone* special.'

'It's a nice gesture. Really though, I guess it doesn't matter what a woman wears, when it's inevitably going to end up on the floor.' Ava winks knowingly at Teagan, whose temple is throbbing with rage.

'I'm honoured to meet you,' Ava beams again, before delivering the fatal blow, 'especially given you're rarely here.'

A wince creases Teagan's eyes.

'Come on in, sweetheart. I've just opened a bottle of red.' I take Ava's hand, entwining my fingers in hers. Electricity pulses between us.

Teagan's ashen features furrow into a frown. My sternum tightens. I might be cold, but I'm not cruel. If she does still have any feelings for me, this must be hard to take. Then again, if she had any feelings for me at all, would she have cheated on me and left in the first place?

An image of Phoebe's bloodshot eyes and snotty nose surges from the depth of my memory vault. All trace of guilt vanishes.

Teagan needs to understand she can't just waltz in and out of our lives when she feels like it. And if pretending Ava Jackson is my girlfriend is the only way to reinforce that point, then so be it.

'It was lovely to meet you.' Ava nudges past her and drags me into my own hallway. Teagan hovers for a split second before stalking across to her Mercedes.

I close the front door and slump back against it, exhaling a heavy sigh of relief. Ava swivels on her heels, taking in every detail of my home. 'You could have warned me.'

'Sorry. It was a dick move but you handled it perfectly. I thought if I told you she was here, you might not come.' When I'm certain Teagan's out of the gate, I push myself off the door.

'I meant you could have warned me that your ex is a supermodel.' Ava bites her lower lip.

On the surface she radiates confidence, reinforced by the understated dresses, smart casual clothing, and minimally applied make-up. But that's a mask. And beneath that mask the woman exudes a vulnerability. She's been hurt. The married man has a lot to answer for.

'Teagan is beautiful.'

I shrug. 'On the outside, at least. She's the life and soul of every party she goes to. People adore her. And that's what she lives for. The next compliment. The next ego boost. If I was looking for a life partner – and we both know I'm not – she's the last person I'd pick. She used to drag me to bars with her, then make me watch as everyone in the place fawned over her. It was like she wanted me to see how desired she was, then maybe finally I'd want her the way she wanted me to. I couldn't bring myself to dance with her. It felt fake. Forced. So, she'd dance with other men in front of me to get a reaction. I'd never give her one.'

'Jesus, that's mental fuckery at its best.'

'It was what it was. Now, how about that glass of wine?'

'I could do with it, after that. Just the one though. I'm driving.' Tension ebbs from Ava's torso.

If my daughter wasn't upstairs, Ava would be in serious danger of driving something else. The urge to take her in my arms and show her exactly how much more attractive she is to me than my ex consumes me. To worship every inch of her beautiful body until she sees her own worth. But then she'd be no better off in the long run when it didn't last. I'd only damage her further. Which is the precise reason I need to keep a rein on my attraction to her.

She follows me into the kitchen and slips off her jacket. A sheer shirt does nothing to conceal the flimsy lace bra beneath. Her perfect breasts are pushed up to perfection, the material is thin enough to reveal the outline of her pebbled nipples.

Holy fuck. She's trying to kill me.

How am I meant to rein in my attraction when she's flaunting those incredible assets in front of my face?

Finally, I manage to tear my eyes from her tits.

'Are you looking for trouble?' I will my dick down.

'What if I am?' Ava smirks, stepping closer. 'What are you going to do about it?'

My throat thickens. I spent all day imagining exactly what I'd do about it. Starting with bending her over the very island she's leaning on. Making a decadent dessert out of her, before slamming her into next week.

'I told you, Ava. This is business.'

'Do you kiss all of your business partners like you want to devour them?' She's a fucking mind reader. Her fingers graze the neckline of her blouse teasingly.

'No.' I fill a glass with wine and hand it to her. 'I only kiss stunning brunette business partners like I want to devour them. But that doesn't make it right.'

We want different things out of life. If we bring sex into our fake relationship, it will only complicate things. 'I'm never going to be what you want.'

'How do you know what I want?' She edges forwards until there's less than a foot between us.

'You own a dating agency. You want fairy tales and promises of forevers.' I'm talking myself out of a shag, but I can't let her think this thing between us will ever be anything more than just that. It wouldn't be fair.

'That's right. I do. One day.' Her tongue darts out over her lower lip. 'But right now, I just want to feel a man's body against mine. Lose myself in pleasure without the pressure of wondering if this is going somewhere. We might be fake-dating, but the attraction between us is real. I'm not asking you for marriage. I'm asking you to help me get back in the saddle.'

'Back in the saddle?' There's no controlling my dick now.

'Wouldn't we be a lot more convincing as a couple if we knew each other intimately?' Hooded eyes glint mischievously.

Knowing what I know – that nothing lasts, I've avoided intimacy, but on some subconscious level every cell inside me longs for it. Not just the sex but having a woman in my bed to hold. Someone who calls to say, 'how's your day?'

Would it be so wrong to let Ava in for a few weeks? Especially given we're going to be spending so much time together anyway.

Every nerve ending in my body crackles with need. Heat races through my veins. I drop my face to hers, our breath mingling. 'You're about to find out first hand that I'm not the gentleman you had me confused with.'

I take her glass and place it on the counter next to mine. When my lips capture hers it's with a burning urgency that makes me dizzy. I grab her waist, tugging her body flush with mine, moulding her around my frame. She exhales a low guttural moan of approval and grinds herself against me. My hands slide to her peachy ass, and I lift her onto the island.

Nudging her thighs open with my hips, I spread her out for my taking. Her nipples are like bullets beneath that flimsy shirt, begging to be worshipped. She cries out in protest as I drag my lips from hers and push her onto her back against the cold granite surface.

She's so fucking beautiful. I'm going to take my time with her. Make her come at least twice before I get inside her, because when I do, it could be a different story. It's been too long.

I push the sheer material upwards and drop my mouth to her stomach, licking a trail of soft skin to the waistband of her jeans. My fingers slide upwards to play with her nipples, and she exhales a breathy moan.

'I hope you know what you're letting yourself in for, Ava.'

I pinch her nipples and roll them between my fingers, popping off the button of her jeans with my teeth.

'I'm beginning to get the gist of it ...' She pants.

Just when I think nothing in the world would stop me a tiny voice calls from upstairs, 'Dad ...'

Chapter Fifteen

AVA

Cillian darts back as I bolt upwards, tugging my shirt back into position.

'I'll be up in a second, sweetheart,' he calls in a completely un-Cillian-like singsong voice, lifting me off the island and placing me gently back onto my feet.

Blowing out a heavy breath, he rakes a hand through his hair and shakes his head. 'I'm so sorry.'

'Don't be. Go up to her. Please.' I tuck my shirt back into my jeans and attempt to steady my hammering heart.

'She never normally wakes. She's unsettled with Teagan coming and going ...' His eyes linger on my lips as he adjusts his bulging trousers. My mouth practically waters wondering what he's got in there.

'You don't have to explain yourself. She's your daughter, for Christ's sake. She comes first.'

He rolls his lips into a wry expression. 'And I was so determined *you* would come first tonight. At least twice.'

'Another night.' I grab my jacket and follow him out to the hallway.

His huge hand catches mine sending tingles all the way to my toes. 'Stay. Finish your wine. I won't be too long.'

'No. It doesn't feel right.' I'm buying time.

Even though I want this, even though it's all my idea, I didn't expect to go all the way tonight. And if I stay, that's what will happen. 'We'll continue this on Wednesday.'

'You're damn right we will. I'll book that suite at The Shelbourne for us.'

'Perfect.' My fingers brush over my swollen lips. 'Promise you won't freak out between now and then and change your mind?'

'Only if you promise you won't.' His steely grey eyes bore into mine with an unwavering intensity.

'No strings sex, with my fake boyfriend. Sign. Me. Up.' I head towards the front door and blow him a kiss over my shoulder. As my hand finds the chrome door handle, his hand lands on top of it. He tugs me back round until my chest crashes into his.

He lands another lingering kiss on my mouth, raking his fingers through my mussed-up hair. My pulse pounds in my head, desire making me dizzier than any drink could.

'Dad …' That little voice calls from upstairs again and it's so cute I can't even begrudge the interruption.

'Coming!' He exhales a wistful sigh and whispers, 'Cockblocker.'

I fist my mouth to stop the laughter exploding out.

'I'll call you tomorrow.' He promises, opening the door for me.

'I'll look forward to it.' The damp drizzle has nothing on my lady parts. I've barely scratched the surface of the beast, but Cillian Callaghan is going to be a total animal in bed. And Wednesday can't come quick enough.

. . .

The traffic's quiet. Fifteen minutes later, I'm back at my apartment block.

Giles arches a wispy white eyebrow. 'That was quick.'

'It was over before it began. For tonight, at least.' I realise how that sounds and snort. 'Not like that!'

'The guy with the BMW jeep?' Giles cocks his head with interest.

'Yep.'

'Wow. Two days in a row. Do I need to tell the Mrs to buy a hat?' His weathered lips lift into a crooked smile.

'God no! It's not like that!' I swat the air in front of my face. 'We're just having a bit of fun.'

'That's how it starts.'

'Not this time, Giles. Not with him, anyway.'

A deep buzz in my back pocket signals an incoming text.

Did you get home ok?

Yes Dad ;)

We'll see how smart your mouth is on Wednesday.

I look forward to it.

He might be a grumpy, cynical, pessimistic divorce lawyer – but Cillian Callaghan is going to be dynamite in bed. He's got this repressed, serious, single dad thing going on, like he's been starved for adult affection for years. I can't wait to watch him unravel.

Chapter Sixteen

CILLIAN

Wednesday 6th December

I pull up outside the double gates of Phoebe's school, St Jude's. I didn't enrol her here because it's a Catholic school, or because it's an all-girl school, I enrolled her here because it's one of the best schools in the country. Even if one of the teachers went viral on TikTok for all the wrong reasons last Christmas.

Shit, now I think about it, that teacher then went on to get engaged to a Hollywood movie star. The very same movie star whose sister I'm currently fake-dating.

It's a small world, and Ireland's an even smaller country.

'Can I have a dog for Christmas, Daddy?' Phoebe asks in her sweetest voice. We've had this conversation a million times already.

'No, princess. We wouldn't be able to spend as much time with it as it needs and then it would bark the house down all day long. It wouldn't be fair on it. Daddy works and you're at school all day.'

'I'd mind it. And Matilda. And if Mammy's around ...' She trails off. Even at six years old she knows the score.

'Maybe when you're a bit older and you can walk it, okay?'

I twist my head to watch her unstrap herself in the back seat. 'Are you all set for school?'

'Yep.' She offers me a toothy grin as she grabs her backpack from the seat next to her.

I hop out the car into the crisp morning and help her out. 'Don't forget Nanny's going to collect you today. Daddy has to work late.' It's a lie. Daddy has to attend a party with his fake girlfriend. And hopefully a private party after that too.

'I remember.' Phoebe rolls her eyes. 'Don't work too hard, Daddy.' Her tiny hand grabs mine and tugs. I crouch to my knees and wrap my arms around her petite frame.

'I love you, princess.' I inhale the scent of her bubble-gum shampoo.

'I love you too.' A flicker of doubt crosses her silver eyes. 'You will come back tomorrow?'

It rips my heart out that she even has to ask. But is it any wonder, given Teagan's erratic behaviour?

'Of course, sweetheart. I'll see you tomorrow evening.'

Her teeth catch her lower lip, like she can't quite let go of that lingering uncertainty. 'Would you like me to take you to the Christmas market tomorrow evening? We could go on the Ferris wheel. Get some hot chocolate. You can tell me how your sleepover at Nanny's went, okay?'

'The Ferris wheel? Sarah Snowden went on it at the weekend, and she said it was awesome.' Sarah Snowden is Phoebe's new BFF. I'm just grateful it's not Cecilia. The one whose mother, Majella, was so keen to organise a playdate. With Stanley on business, it was me she wanted to play with.

Phoebe's doubt is replaced with a twinkle of excitement. 'Can I get marshmallows on my hot chocolate?'

'Extra triple marshmallows, sprinkles and cream.' I put my hand out for a high five and she slaps it as hard as she can.

'Ouch!' I pretend to wince and shake my hand as if she hurt me. 'My goodness, you're getting so big and strong!'

Phoebe's answering grin is one of triumph. 'See you tomorrow, Daddy.'

'Have a great day, honey.' I watch from my car as she links arms with twin girls in her class, Isla and Eden. The three of them skip safely inside the old Victorian building. The principal, Ashley Kearney, raises her hand in a curt greeting from the yard and I pull out into a long line of Dublin traffic.

My phone rings through the hands-free. My mother. She can't cancel on me tonight, of all nights, I need her to take Phoebe. My newfound obsession with Ava Jackson has only spiralled since she left my house two nights ago.

'Hello?'

'Cillian, how are you?' My mum's soft warm tone fills the car.

'Good, thanks. I've just dropped Phoebe at school. Is everything okay?'

'Everything's fine ...' She drawls out the last word, leading me to believe everything isn't fine.

'What is it, Mam?' I don't have time for small talk. I'm due in court in thirty minutes.

She clears her throat. 'Teagan called by here yesterday for coffee.'

Ahh. Now we're getting to the crux of it. 'And?'

'She said you're seeing someone.'

I sigh. 'Not that it's any of her business.' *Or yours.* I manage to hold my tongue.

'She's devastated, Cillian. Really devastated. I've never seen her like this before.'

'She wasn't nearly as devastated when she was shacked up with Marco from Marbella.' I scoff.

'I know I should mind my own business.' She pauses, and we both know that she never minds her own business and isn't about to start now, 'but I can't help but wondering if you thought about what we spoke about the other night. If it's not too late for you two to sort things out? For Phoebe's sake.'

'It's for Phoebe's sake that I won't ever give Teagan another chance.' That, and the fact I don't love her. Or trust her. 'It won't be my heart she breaks when she leaves.' Mine's frozen colder and harder than a lump of ice. 'I know you believe in sticking together through thick and thin, but Teagan doesn't, and neither do I. Even if I did take her back, she'd be gone again in a matter of months.'

It's Mam's turn to sigh. 'Okay, son. I just want to make sure you're doing the right thing.' More like Teagan asked her to have a word with me when she called for coffee yesterday.

'Trust me, Mam, I'm doing the right thing.'

She sighs.

'Are you still okay to take Phoebe for the night?'

'Absolutely. I'm looking forward to it. Your dad's going to some golf thing so he's away for the night. It'll be great to have some company.'

A golf thing? If he's heading away for the night, it's probably with another woman. And my mother doesn't even question him, as long as he takes his indiscretions out of town. Rage ripples through my gut. It's not right.

'Thanks, Mam. I'll see you tomorrow.' I disconnect the call before she can interrogate me about Ava, and before I can tell her for the hundredth time to kick my father out.

The day in court served to remind me why I don't believe in happy ever afters. Today I represented a woman who is married to a famous soccer player. While she was in hospital recovering from life-threatening surgery, he was hosting orgies in their family home. He didn't want to give her a penny, let alone one of the five properties he owns. It was a pleasure taking him to the cleaners.

I abandon the jeep outside The Shelbourne, not giving one iota that I'm singlehandedly holding up rush hour traffic in Dublin. I toss the keys to the porter and go in search of a shower and a neat whiskey.

I booked the penthouse. I could hardly ask Ava to leave hers for anything less. The navy and silver décor is traditional, oozing opulence and luxury. A huge sleigh bed punctuates the bedroom, dressed in plush pillows and expensive sheets. I hope Ava likes it.

I shower and shave in the huge mosaic tiled bathroom. The last thing I want to do is mark Ava with my stubble. Actually, that's not true. I'd love to leave a burning reminder of our night together. That is, if she hasn't changed her mind. I haven't heard from her since the texts we exchanged on Monday night.

Maybe she's been busy organising tonight's party.

Or maybe she's got cold feet.

Either way, I'm about to find out.

I dress in a black Tom Ford suit and white shirt, spray some cologne and head downstairs, too impatient to wait for the lift. A fifteen-foot white frosted artificial tree punctuates the hallway, and an open fire roars welcomingly as I pass.

The spacious bar is buzzing with chatter. No need to wonder if I'm in the right place. Huge red helium balloons in the shape of hearts sway from the ceiling, sporting the Heart-Sync logo I recognise from the sign-up form. Hard to believe that was just over a week ago.

Over a hundred people congregate in small clusters, picking canapés from the trays of passing waiters. In the corner of the room, a blonde woman in a black Bardot dress croons sultry jazz songs. My eyes home in on Ava. She's clutching a glass of champagne in one hand, while her other hand rests on the muscled arm of the mountain-sized man next to her. He has his back to me so I can't see his face.

What's very clear though, is the affection she holds for him. Her eyes sparkle up at him.

A rush of something unfamiliar whooshes through my chest and my molars grind together so hard they could crumble.

I strut across the room on instinct. Those hazel eyes flit away from Mr Muscle and her smile widens as I approach. The tension in my chest eases a fraction.

'Speak of the devil, and he arrives.' Ava shoves her companion aside and reaches out for me, throwing her arms around my neck in a dramatic PDA. Burying her nose in my neck she inhales deeply. 'I've missed you.'

Her acting skills are so convincing, if I didn't know better, I'd be utterly convinced her feelings for me are real.

'I missed you too.' I grit out, finding her waist with my hands. Mr Muscle hovers beside us quietly, but I deliberately don't look at him. Do I have to pee on her to make him go away? To make him realise she's mine, for tonight at least.

'Well, fuck me, you're real.' Mr Muscle lets out a deep belly laugh and slaps my back.

I turn to him with my steeliest stare. When our eyes lock, I inhale a sharp breath.

'Cillian, this is my pain in the ass of a brother, Nate.' Ava takes a small step back from me and slides her hands away from my neck. 'Nate, this is my boyfriend, Cillian.'

Nate's green eyes glint with amusement. He's normally so serious looking on the big screen. Then again, it would look a bit weird if he was smirking while saving the world. 'It's a pleasure to meet you.'

'The feeling's mutual.' The words come out stilted. Formal. I'm just glad they came at all. The guy's a Hollywood movie star. And as impressive as he is on the screen, in the flesh, he's even more remarkable.

Though, he still has nothing on his little sister, who looks dangerously delectable in a killer lace dress, the same shade of dark fuck-me red as the heart-shaped balloons.

A petite brunette dressed in a gold dress approaches. She's clutching a tiny baby to her chest. 'Hi, I'm Holly.' She shifts the baby onto her hip and offers her hand. 'We've been dying to meet you. Frank and Penny have been raving about you!'

'Actually, Holly. I think I know you.'

Holly blushes and Nate tenses, all trace of amusement evaporating from his eyes.

'My daughter goes to St. Jude's. You might remember her? Phoebe Callaghan. She was in your junior infant class last year.'

Holly clicks her fingers, and the tension evaporates. 'That's right. How is she?'

'She's great. Thank you.' I slip an arm around Ava's waist. It's not strictly necessary. We've already convinced them we're a couple. But the need to touch her is overwhelming. It took every ounce of willpower I had not to chase after her the other night.

Another woman approaches, introducing herself as Natalie, Ava's sister. She has the same dark hair as her sister, but shocking chartreuse eyes like her brother.

Natalie nudges Ava playfully. 'Did you check Cillian's ankle for tags?' From her teasing tone, she's joking, but Ava flinches.

Nate turns to me. 'We all thought it was hilarious when Ava started a dating agency. Especially given her own long list of dating disasters. How can she charge people extortionate amounts of money to set them up, when she couldn't even set herself up!'

Ava sucks in her lower lip. Her body tenses beside me, like she's waiting for the next onslaught. No wonder she's insecure when her own siblings aren't exactly supportive of her. Lillian and William might have preferred me to go into the family business, but they've always been supportive of my career choices, even when they haven't approved.

The itch to defend Ava scratches my throat. 'She had a run of bad luck.' I squeeze her tighter to me. 'Worse than you'll ever know. It takes guts to open a business. And blood, sweat, and tears to run it. Cut her some slack.'

Natalie puckers her lips, peering at Ava with an owl-like curiosity.

Nate opens his mouth like he's about to say something but then closes it again. He exchanges a surprised glance with his fiancé, then flashes his big Hollywood grin. 'Right, who's for a drink then?' He rubs his hands together and turns to the bar.

'Thank you.' Ava mouths up at me, her thick lashes dusting her chiselled cheekbones. My solid frozen heart officially begins to thaw.

The party is a huge success, primarily down to a few shared Instagram posts from my super famous brother. Nate and Holly are a walking, talking advertisement for true love. Which is why the HeartSync website crashed from an enormous influx of new clients.

This business is my baby, but I've always sought the support of my family. Asking Nate to invest was as much about having another adult to defer to, as it was for financial reasons. I'm the youngest of the Jackson siblings. The one they tease and rib for being naive. And because of that, it kind of became instinctive to look for an adultier adult when things got tough.

But tonight, I'm starting to see how much I've actually achieved on my own. And I'm proud.

'You must be pleased with the turnout.' Bonnie scans the crowded room, before returning to her iPad where she's tapping out an email to our IT guy.

'Of course.' Though all I can think about right now is the one man in the crowd who's 'turned out' better than most.

In a ridiculously well-tailored designer suit, Cillian emits wealth, power, maybe even arrogance to someone who doesn't know him. My eyes are drawn to him like a magnet. He still radiates the same presence that sucked the oxygen from my lungs when I used to watch him walk by my office window. Only later, I'm going to get the chance to suck it right back.

Though I get the impression that, no matter how much I breathe him in, I doubt I'll ever be right again. But it's a risk I'm willing to take because I've thought about nothing else since Friday night.

And when he defended me tonight, I realised it's not arrogance he emits, it's integrity. Sure, he's still a grumpy, cynical divorce lawyer, but there's also an underlying honourability to him.

He's loyal.

Lascivious.

And about to get laid.

No one has ever stuck up for me before. Even though my siblings' teasing isn't malicious, it hurts. Josh's ankle tag might be a long-standing joke. But the hurt on his wife's face when she arrived at my front door wasn't funny at all.

If my family knew the truth, they'd hunt Josh down and flog him.

I don't want that. I don't want their pity.

But I don't want their incessant ribbing either.

I have a feeling after tonight, I won't have to worry about either. Cillian's sizzling stare said more than 'cut her some slack'. It said, 'She's under my protection now' and it was hot as fuck.

If we hadn't already decided to take our fake relationship to a real bedroom, I'd be dragging him to one anyway.

'Cillian is hot as fuck.' Bonnie voices my exact thoughts.

'Yep.' I take a swig from my glass of champagne and watch as he converses with my mother and father like he's known them for years. While he's still unable to crack an actual smile, he appears at ease with them anyway.

'Are you going to sleep with him tonight?' Bonnie hits send and shoves the phone back in her metallic clutch bag.

'Yep.'

'Fan-fucking-tastic. It's about time your lady parts got shocked back to life. For a while there I was worried I was going to have to buy a defibrillator.' She snorts, grabbing a cracker slathered in caviar from a passing waiter. 'Just remember the plan. Do *not* get attached. He's the *next* one, not *The* One.'

'I know, I know.' I make a show of rolling my eyes to hide the fact I get a zinging sensation every time he so much as looks my way. Bonnie's right to offer caution. Because if I were to confuse this as something more for even a second, Cillian Callaghan would run a mile. With my foolish romantic heart tucked tightly in his possession.

'Nate's bought it anyway.' Bonnie's eyes follow Nate as he claps Cillian's back and joins the conversation.

'Good. We need that investment.' A ripple of guilt flares in my stomach. Then I remember my siblings' teasing and it subsides.

'Do we?' Bonnie gesticulates to the crowded room. 'After tonight, I'm not so sure.'

Cillian's silver stare stalks the room until he locates me. However cold he pretends to be, he can't hide the heat surging from his soul. Or the blazing sexuality he radiates like an inferno. One that I'm irresistibly drawn to, even though I know I risk suffering irreparable burns.

He swallows hard, those dark pupils flicker to my lips, then back to my eyes. 'Bed.' He mouths across the busy room.

It's not even a question. It's an order. One that I'm more than willing to follow. My work here is done. HeartSync's social media has exploded with new followers, new clients and the business is buzzing with interest. My family believe Cillian and I are together.

Now, it's time to actually be together.

Even if it is just physically.

I nod and turn away from my friend before she feels the need to offer any more worldly advice.

Squeezing through the crowd, I brush off congratulations on my business, and my new boyfriend.

Eventually, I reach the lift. Heavy footsteps approaching across the marble flooring set my heart thumping in my chest. I take a deep breath and a familiar intoxicating scent envelops me.

'Are you okay?' His deep voice rumbles into my ear.

'Yes, thanks to you.' I spin on my heel to face him. The lift doors open, and he nudges me backwards into the small, mirrored space. 'The night was a success.'

'Good, we should celebrate.' Grey eyes glint with a hint of mischief.

In the suite, housekeeping have already turned the satiny-white sheets down. A bottle of champagne chills in a chrome cooler, a plate of chocolate coated strawberries beside it. Moonlight filters through the open curtains, spilling shadows across the room.

Goosebumps ripple my arms. I glance at the bed, then back at Cillian, who's watching me. He's unwaveringly solemn as usual, but it's impossible to miss the desire raging in his eyes.

'Still want to feel a man's body against yours? Lose yourself in pleasure without pressure?' Only a cut-throat lawyer could quote my words back at me so precisely. Has he obsessed about Monday night as much as I have?

My throat thickens. The room feels hot. Or maybe that's just him. All I have to do is give him the nod. Yet I'm frozen like a lamb awaiting a sacrificial slaughter. My stomach twists with need. But the last person I let inside my body hurt me more than I've ever admitted out loud. He lied to me.

At least Cillian's been brutally honest from the start.

It's finally time to get back in the saddle.

One tiny nod is all I offer and he's on me in seconds. Hungry lips seek mine with a passion and urgency I've only seen on TV. Huge hands roam across my body with a surprising tenderness, like he can smell my caution, as well as my potent arousal. And he's here for all of it.

Deft fingers flick over the zip of my dress and it falls to the floor with a soft swish. Wolf-like eyes rake over my lingerie, a claret-coloured silk set with a matching suspender belt. It's the same shade as my dress, and my lipstick.

I wanted to wow him, and from the low guttural growl that passes from his mouth to mine, I think I've succeeded.

'So fucking beautiful, Ava.' He traces the silky material with his fingers and steps back to admire me like I'm a prize racehorse. His attention is addictive. It feels like too much, but not enough all at the same time.

I reach out for the buttons of his shirt, but he retracts, pulling his torso just out of reach. 'Not yet.' Huge hands reach round to squeeze my ass and I squeal as he lifts me, effortlessly wrapping my legs around his waist and carrying me to the bed.

He places me on the sheets. They're cool and soft against my rigid spine. 'Are you sure this is what you want, Ava?' His throat flexes, like he's barely keeping it together.

'I've never wanted anything more in my life.' It's the truth.

'You know I don't do fairy tales and forevers.' He's giving me the option to walk out of here right now.

As if that's ever going to happen.

My body thrums with nervous anticipation. Every cell hums, begging to be touched. Lust sweeps away logic. I might get burned, but given the attraction pulsing between us, the pleasure will be worth every second of pain. 'Just fuck me, Cillian.'

Finally, those perfect plump lips curl upwards into a wolfish grin. 'Oh, I'm going to baby. Believe me, I'm going to.'

His broad frame towers over me as he eats me with his eyes. 'I love your lingerie.'

I smirk. 'Don't be silly, Cillian. You don't believe in love.' I run a hand over the soft skin of my stomach as if to smooth away the nerves beneath.

Dark, knowing eyes bore into mine. 'I don't believe in a *lasting* love. And rightly so. Because this lingerie isn't going to last. In fact, I'd even go as far as saying it's ruined already.' He parts my legs, slips a finger inside my thong, and swipes through my wet heat.

A gasp slips from my lips. 'Cillian.'

He slides two fingers inside my core. I've died and gone straight to the most decadent heaven. 'So fucking tight, Ava.' He's still towering over me, watching as he wrecks my body with slow, languid pumps.

'That feels amazing.' I moan.

'I'm only getting warmed up, Ava.'

My core clenches. The urge to come builds like a dam ready to burst but I need more. I shift beneath him, wriggling to get the right friction but it's not enough.

An actual grin rips across his face. A real one. 'Tell me what you need.'

Pressure winds tighter in my thighs, my fingers claw the bedsheets, twisting them round my fingers as my back arches higher and higher off the bed. 'More.'

His thumb drags over my clit drawing small circles, until my orgasm rips through me so powerfully it shakes my soul. Hot hedonistic stars burst behind my eyelids as wave after wave of pleasure courses through every inch of my body.

Cillian watches the show, his own arousal apparent in the

bulge of his pants. Those gunmetal-grey eyes glaze and lighten with approval. 'Good girl.' His fingers still and slide out. My body aches for them the second they're gone. When he draws them up to his mouth and slowly sucks, my core clenches again.

'On your knees, Ava.' He reaches for his belt and another bout of greedy lust consumes me.

Chapter Eighteen

CILLIAN

Ava drops to the floor on her knees and reaches for my zip. She seems to have taken my whiskey and blow job comment literally. 'On the bed, face forwards.' The need to bury myself in her tight walls claws me from the inside out.

It's like she opened the door of the cage I've been trapped in for as long as I can remember, and the beast inside me is dying to unleash himself.

I pull a condom out of my pocket and watch as she crawls back on the bed, positioning herself on all fours. She rocks back and forth impatiently while I wrap up. From this angle I have a sublime view of her perfect pussy. Thank God I got her off already or this could be embarrassing.

'Are you sure, Ava. Last chance.' The last thing I want to do is hurt her. Physically or emotionally. It's only been a week, but already, I care about this woman more than what's good for me.

'I've never been surer.' She shimmies backwards and thrusts herself against my weeping cock. I yank her thong to the side and slide in, inch by glorious inch. My heartbeat pounds through my head. My senses are full of her. Her unique scent. Her heat. The sound of her breath hitching as I sink inside her.

I use one hand to guide her hips to meet my every thrust, and the other to worship her silky skin. Trace and chase the goosebumps that ripple across her stomach and beneath her decadent lingerie.

She glances over her shoulder, observing eyes scorch my skin as I drive into her again and again. She is electrifying. Her glossy, sex-mussed hair tumbles loosely around her shoulders. I grab it and wrap it around my hand, keeping her head angled towards me. Her pupils widen like saucers. I need her to watch me, like I watched her. I need her to see what she's capable of. Rid her of whatever stupid insecurities *he* put there.

I can't give her much, but I can give her that.

'Look what you do to me, Ava.' I pull back before thrusting deeper over and over again in a relentless sensory assault. Her lips part and she bucks back on my throbbing cock. 'You made me break the rules for you. You made me want this so badly, I couldn't think straight all week.'

'If it's any consolation, you're not the only one breaking your own rules.' Her tongue darts out, moistening her mouth.

'Some rules are made to be broken.' I reach round her waist and dip a hand inside the front of her thong. Her clit is swollen, pulsing with need again. I swipe through her slick folds, and she writhes beneath me, bucking and grinding. A vacant starry look clouds her eyes.

'Cillian, I ...' I increase the pressure and her fiery pupils roll into her head as she trembles and jerks and cries out through a second climax, shuddering and shattering over my cock.

Watching her come undone is almost enough to get me off. Her core clenches in a vice-like grip, the tiny electric pulsations jolting between us, and I explode inside her, riding the rippling, crippling ecstasy that has me both euphoric and exhausted.

I flop on top of her back, clinging to her like a koala as our ragged breath slowly regulates.

Her trembling body twists beneath me until she's on her back, propped up on both her elbows. Seconds pass as I gaze into her gold-flecked eyes in a manner that feels strangely more intimate than being inside her. Her expression is unreadable.

'Are you okay?' I ask tentatively.

'No, I'm not okay. I think I'm ruined for anyone else who comes after you.' She giggles and flops back on to the pillow, her dark hair fanning out across the white material.

Something lurches inside my stomach. My jaw locks. 'Don't talk about anyone else while you're still naked beneath me.'

'Careful, Cillian. A woman could get the wrong idea.' She arches her eyebrows and exhales a sigh of what I hope is contentment.

'The only idea you need to concern yourself with right now is which way you want it next.' Grabbing her wrists, I position them above her head, pinning her in position. 'You, Ava Jackson, are in for a long night.'

The soft gentle breathing of another human stirs me from a deep, satiated slumber. My arm is dead beneath the weight of the most beautiful body I've ever had the pleasure of exploring, but I can't bring myself to pull it away. Waking up next to Ava feels oddly natural. When she turns in her sleep and nuzzles against the smattering of hair across my pecs, something kindles in my sternum.

The permanent pang of loneliness has been plugged, temporarily at least.

I hadn't realised how starved of affection I'd been.

I starved myself, out of choice. Unable to risk bringing another person into my messed-up life, knowing that eventually a relationship will always lead to an expectation of taking 'the next step'.

Every woman I've dated has thought they'd be the one to change me. It always ends in disappointment – theirs. That's why I've abstained the past eighteen months. I don't enjoy hurting women. But I am what I am, and I'm never going to change. I don't know how.

This arrangement with Ava allows me to enjoy the short-term intimacy of female company, without any of the drama, anticipation, and ultimate heartbreak.

Last night blew anything before it out of the water. Ava Jackson is not leaving this room until I get a definitive answer to when we can do this again. Because it was transcendent.

We signed up to spend the month together. Which hopefully means we get to do this for the month too, by which point, this attraction between us will have run its course.

Teagan will be off my back.

Ava will have her investment, and enough confidence to get back in the saddle. The thought sends a hot wave of irritation surging over my spine, but I push it down.

All is good in the world.

Ava stirs, her palm brushes over my pec lazily. 'Morning,' she mumbles sleepily.

'Morning.' I press a kiss against her forehead. I tell myself it's because it would be a dick move to be cold towards her after exploring every inch of her flesh last night, but I'm not kidding anyone. Least of all myself. I kiss her head because I feel close to her. Closer than I've felt to any woman in a long time. I like waking up with her.

'Shall I order room service?' I trace lazy circles across her luminous skin.

'Yes please.' She peeps up from beneath those long ebony lashes. 'Order everything. I need pancakes. Eggs. Waffles. Fruit. Bottomless coffee. And get two of everything. I'm not sharing. You're not my boyfriend. And even if you were, which you never will be, I still wouldn't share. I'm starving after last night.'

'You're about to get a whole lot hungrier.' I yank her body on top of mine and position her knees either side of my hips. This is a short-term arrangement. I'd be a fool not to wring out every second of pleasure while I can.

Ava rocks up to a sitting position and grinds her hips against mine. I managed to tear that lingerie off her eventually last night. And as predicted, it's ruined. I should probably buy her more.

I palm her nipples and they pebble at the contact. 'You're a bad man, Cillian Callaghan. Just not in the way I thought.'

'A fact we can both agree on.'

Chapter Nineteen

AVA

Thursday 7th December

I haven't heard from Cillian since I left The Shelbourne this morning. Not that I expected to, given that he's not actually my boyfriend, but seeing as we spent eight hours physically joined at the hip and mouth, a text might have been nice.

'Still reliving last night's sexual awakening?' Bonnie teases, tossing a luminous yellow highlighter across the office at me.

I shelter my face from the incoming stationery and wonder why I ever thought it was a good idea to hire my best friend. She can read me like a book. 'Do you have to use such cringe-worthy vocabulary?'

'What? I could have said, "still daydreaming about Cillian's quivering member".'

'Urgh.' It's my turn to toss a pen back at her. 'Stop!' I eye Cleo and Violet across the open plan office and will Bonnie to shut up.

'Okay, how about, "still obsessing over Cillian's Super-soaker 3000"?'

I roll my eyes. 'It was more like a Supersoaker 10,000 if you want to get technical. The man is gifted.'

'So, he has the equipment.' Bonnie wiggles her eyebrows, 'But does he know what to do with it?'

'Oh yes.' My eyes drift to the window. Dusk decorates the sky in bright pinks and deep purples. The Christmas lights twinkle outside like millions of tiny shooting stars illuminating Grafton Street.

'Oh no!' Bonnie leaps out of her seat and over to my desk where she perches on top of a stack of new sign-up forms. 'You're getting all dreamy-eyed thinking about Mr Suave Suit Guy's six-inch subway.'

'Stop with the freaky euphemisms, will you? And his name's Cillian. He can never know I've been stalking him from afar for the past year.' I snap my focus back to her. 'And I'm not dreamy-eyed, I'm bleary-eyed. It's different.' I pinch the bridge of my nose and blink hard. 'It was a late night. Much alcohol was consumed.'

'Much spunk more like!' Bonnie grins wickedly.

'Enough!' I exhale a defeated sigh. 'Ok if you must know, you're right. I can't get Cillian out of my head, even though I know it's not one bit healthy. He was just so ...' I shrug and steal my friend's frighteningly accurate description, 'Dreamy.'

'I knew it! You've never had casual sex in your life. You don't even know how to.' She stands, smooths her skirt down and takes my hand, tugging me upwards. 'Come on.'

'Come on where?' I glance at the clock. It's three minutes to five. I still have a mountain of sign-up forms to get through, thanks to Nate's viral videos last night.

'We're done for the day. I'm taking you to the Christmas market. I have an hour before my date with James.'

Date's probably not the right word. Hook-up probably more accurately describes what Bonnie and James do, but who am I to judge?

She grabs her bag and slings it over her shoulder. 'Let's go find some mulled wine and music to distract you from the divorce daddy.'

I don't want to be distracted. I want to dissect every fleeting touch from last night. I want to divulge how he kissed my forehead so tenderly when he thought I was still asleep. How he traced tiny circles on my back. How his steely eyes turned to hot molten lava when he was inside me.

There's a tenderness about him that I wouldn't have deemed possible. But he said it himself, he doesn't do love. He doesn't do fairy tales and forevers.

Bonnie's right. I need to get out of here before I drive myself crazy. It is what is. A mutually beneficial pretend relationship, with sex that happened to be mind-blowing.

Earth-shattering.

Life-changing- for me at least.

I stand and grab my coat from the back of my chair. 'Okay, let's go.'

Bonnie claps her hands together with glee and turns to Cleo and Violet. 'Do you ladies want to join us for a glass of mulled wine?'

Cleo and Violet glance at the clock and then at each other. 'We're right in the middle of something here. Think we've found another A1 match.'

A1 is the best match a couple can score, based on their interests, aspirations, perfect first date, family history, and dating history. It's rare to get an almost identical sign-up form. Which is why we call it an A1. The only danger is the couple could be too similar, which is why we send out a second, more personal questionnaire before even considering matching them up. We've had six A1s over the past year. It's early days, but five of those couples are still together.

'Amazing!' Bonnie squeals. 'Well, if you want to join us afterwards, we'll be mooching around the Christmas markets with a vino in hand.'

'Sound.' Cleo gives us the thumbs up and Violet grunts, her nose still buried in the paperwork in front of her.

We step out into the chilling air, our breath pluming before our faces following the heat from the office. Grafton Street is bustling with commuters and tourists alike. Carol singers line the cobbled walkways crooning festive favourites. Shop window displays showcase intricate holiday scenes, elaborate decorations, and festive arrays of gifts for loved ones.

Bonnie links my arm as we soak in the dazzling lights illuminating the way to the glittering wonderland at St Stephen's Green.

Cabins flank the manicured lawns in a rectangular configuration. In the centre is a flashing display of illuminated snowmen, Santa on his huge sleigh guided by the reindeer, and Rudolph at the helm. The Ferris wheel towers in the starry sky in the distance, right next to the ice rink.

'Remember your mam used to take us every single year when we were kids?' Bonnie reminisces in a wistful tone. Her own mother passed when she was only five. Penny Jackson tried to fill that void as much as possible. Bonnie spent more time in our house than her own. Which is where she learned that sexual liberation is healthy, and where she harnessed the ability to read me like an open book.

'It was one of the highlights of the year.' A pang of something tinges in my stomach. Nostalgia maybe.

Or perhaps it's my weeping ovaries reminding me of my ticking biological clock.

My mother was twenty-two when she had my sister Faith. I always imagined being a young mum. Have three or four children. Sell my stunning, but solitary penthouse, and live in a house filled with love, like the one I grew up in.

'Yeah, that and the annual Jackson summer barbecue. Remember the year we stole the Pimm's punch?' Bonnie squeezes my arm and steers me out of the way of a bunch of rowdy teenagers fuelled up on candy floss and Christmas cookies.

'Oh, I've never been as sick in my life. What were we? Fifteen?'

'Fourteen.' Bonnie pulls me towards one of the small wooden cabins selling mulled wine and mince pies. The scent of roasted chestnuts and nutmeg saturates the air surrounding us as we get in line and order two large glasses of rich mulled wine.

I hand over twenty euros, and we continue browsing through the tiny festive stalls selling handmade ornaments, homemade fudge, and other seasonal treats.

Bonnie points out a stall where you throw rings around a teddy to win one. 'Come on, I'll see if I can win you a stuffed toy. At least you'll have something to snuggle up to tonight.'

We nudge our way through the crowd to the last stall lined with fluffy teddies. Next to it is a spinning carousel of prancing reindeer, festive white horses, and friendly polar bears. My feet root to the spot, I'm entranced by the flashes of colour and light as they rotate hypnotically in front of me. Age-old holiday melodies fill the air along with the joyous laughter from the children riding it.

My focus is drawn to a stunning little girl with long blonde hair and a smile that squeezes my heart. She clings to a rainbow-coloured unicorn as it rises and falls to the music. Her eyes are squeezed tightly shut in pure ecstasy. I watch her as she whirls through the air. When her eyes fly open, the startling shade of silver staring back at me is frighteningly familiar.

So is the bulky frame of the suave suit-wearing guy riding the red-nosed reindeer next to her.

And if I thought she looked ecstatic, he looks euphoric. Not to be on the ride. His white knuckles give that much away. It's the pleasure he's getting from watching the little girl who has him elated.

The small smirk he's offered me now and again has absolutely nothing on the broad face-splitting grin he offers his daughter.

The effect is utterly devastating on my ovaries.

His head cranes in my direction as if he senses my eyes on him. The smile freezes on his face as his eyes bore into mine. The ride slows to a stop, and the same hands that worshipped my body mere hours ago reach out for his daughter without breaking our stare.

Chapter Twenty

CILLIAN

I've been picturing Ava all damn day. It's like I thought about her so hard, I accidentally summoned her. Flashbacks of last night had me stumbling over my words in court today. Moonlit shadows spilling the most erotic images over those crisp sheets circled on repeat until I had no choice but to call for a recess.

Should I grab Phoebe's hand and run for the Ferris wheel, or say hello to the woman I'm pretending to be in a relationship with? The one who I both lost and found myself in last night.

I promised myself a long time ago that I'd never introduce a girlfriend to Phoebe. That I'd never bring another woman into her life. Never give another woman the opportunity to leave her like her mother did. And it's one promise I'll never break.

But I could introduce her as a colleague.

I step off the carousel and lift my beautiful daughter to the ground, holding her shoulders until I'm sure she's steady on her feet.

'That was so cool, Daddy. Wait 'til I tell Sarah Snowden

about that.' Phoebe adjusts her bobble hat and beams up at me.

Sarah bloody Snowdon.

I lift my head to the spot that Ava was standing in with her PA, but she's gone. My lips press into a grimace. It's probably for the best. I crouch, lavishing my full attention on the only girl I'm supposed to. 'You looked amazing on the unicorn! Now, do you want a hot chocolate, or do you want to go on the Ferris wheel?'

'Hot chocolate, then the Ferris wheel,' Phoebe squeals with glee and claps her pink gloved hands together with excitement. 'Thanks, Daddy. This is the best night ever.'

My heart inflates in my chest as I rise from my knees, then jumpstarts like a car being hot-wired as I come face to face with Ava Jackson.

'Hi.' She raises a hand in an exaggerated wave. 'Promise I'm not stalking you.' She glances to her PA, Bonnie. They seem to have a deep friendship, as well as professional relationship. Did she tell her about last night? And if so, what did she say? I'd have loved to be a fly on the wall for that one.

'Bonnie and I come here every single December without fail. We have done since we were kids.' She nods at the steaming cup of mulled wine in her hands. 'We used to drink hot chocolate, but we've evolved since then.'

'Well, rest assured, I'm not stalking you either.' Phoebe's watching Ava and my exchange with hawk eyes. 'Phoebe, this is Ava, Daddy's—' I'm about to say colleague when Ava says 'friend.'

I flinch. Still, it could be worse. Any second now, Ava will walk on. Other people's six-year-old kids tend to have that effect on people. Especially glamorous sexy twenty-somethings like Ava Jackson.

Phoebe's shining eyes glaze with a look of sheer adoration. I can't blame her. Dressed in a fitted woollen knee-length coat that nips in at the waist and kicks out over her hips, Ava looks like she's just stepped off the catwalk. And don't get me started on the knee-high boots she's paired it with. She's wearing that deep wine-coloured lipstick again. The same shade as last night's lingerie. Not helpful.

'Wow.' Phoebe doesn't even try to hide her awe. 'Daddy has a pretty friend.' She turns to me with an accusatory stare. 'Why haven't you invited Ava over for a playdate? I could have showed her my dolls.'

She turns back to Ava. 'I have an LOL doll that has boots and a coat exactly like yours.' Her tiny hands gesticulate over Ava's outfit. 'She has a matching black hat too. Do you have a hat? Daddy says we have to wear one, so we don't catch a cold.'

Ava drops to her knees to reach Phoebe's eyeline. 'Daddy's right.' Ava reaches for Phoebe's pink bobble and pats her head affectionately. 'I have a hat, but I left it at work. I better have another glass of this to warm me up.'

'Oh, we're just about to go for hot chocolate.' Phoebe's face shines beneath the Christmas lights. I know what she's going to say before she even says it. 'Do you want to come with us?' Her invitation is laced with hope, and a hint of a plea.

My heart breaks for her.

This is what's she's missing. A female role in her life. Sometimes I wish I had a sister. Someone I could trust to fill that role and never abandon her. Play with her dolls with her. Paint her nails. Take her shopping.

Teagan's been appearing before bedtime to read a story now and again, but what Phoebe needs is a female to play a stable part in her life.

Ava is not that woman. I'm sure she has a million better things to do than have hot chocolate with my daughter.

I grab Phoebe's hand, looking anywhere but at Ava. As

much as Phoebe would like to spend time with Ava and her friend, I'm sure they can't wait to escape. 'Sweetie, Ava probably—'

The weight of Ava's burning stare forces me to meet her gaze. There's an unspoken question in her eyes. Like 'is this okay?'

Why isn't she making her excuses and fleeing?

'Ava?' Phoebe persists, tugging the front of Ava's beautiful, belted coat.

'If it's okay with daddy, I'd love to come for hot chocolate.' Ava's pupils land on mine, flickering with uncertainty.

'I need to go anyway.' Ava's PA shrugs. 'I have something I'm supposed to do.' She downs the remaining mulled wine from her glass and deposits in a neighbouring bin. 'Well, someone.' She shoots Ava a wink and bids us goodnight.

I swallow hard. Ava spending time with Phoebe is not a good idea. She's not my girlfriend. But how can I deny either of them when they seem to have taken an instant like to each other?

'Daddy, please ...' Phoebe swivels on her heels and grabs both my hands, squeezing them. How can I say no to that face?

Ava taps her boot and takes a sip of her drink while I deliberate. 'If you're sure you've got time. You've probably got millions of other things you'd rather be doing.'

Ava places a protective hand on Phoebe's shoulder. 'Actually, there's nowhere else I'd rather be.'

'Yay!' Phoebe spins on her heels, and promptly drops one of my hands, only to slip it into Ava's so she's cushioned between us.

'I hope this is okay with you.' Ava leans into my shoulder.

It shouldn't be, but oddly, it is.

We follow the fairy-lit pathway until we find a stall selling crepes and hot chocolates. Ava stands with Phoebe while I get in line. I need one of those mulled wines. Hot chocolate isn't going to cut it for me tonight. Not unless it's laced with a double brandy.

The incessant chatter and laughter from Phoebe and Ava carries over the festive carols.

'I like your lipstick. You're so pretty.' Phoebe stares up at Ava awestruck, the two of them are still holding hands.

'Not as pretty as you, pumpkin.' Ava touches Phoebe's button nose with her index finger. 'If my lips were the same colour as yours, I'd never wear lipstick again.'

Phoebe bounces in her pink furry Ugg boots with glee. 'Daddy never had a female friend before, you know.' She has a knowing look about her. For six years old – the kid doesn't miss a trick.

'I'm sure daddy has loads of friends. Maybe you just haven't met them.' Ava's trying to play down the significance of our 'friendship'.

Good.

Because as lovely as it is to have both my girls together, ha, my girls – it can't happen again. I can't have Phoebe getting attached to any woman I'm sleeping with. Even if she is as amazing as Ava Jackson.

'No, he doesn't.' Phoebe insists, swinging Ava's hand back and forth like a skipping rope. 'My friend Cecilia's mammy asked Daddy over for a playdate and he said no.'

How the hell did the little mite hear that from where she was doing her ballet steps on the bar?

Ava stifles a snort with her free hand, her eyes landing on mine. There are no secrets when there are kids around. I shrug and bite back a smirk.

I return with two mulled wines, and one hot chocolate with extra marshmallows, sprinkles, and cream, just as Phoebe tells Ava she's playing Mary in the nativity play.

'You can come if you want.' Phoebe accepts the hot

chocolate and runs her tongue over the cream sloshing over the edges of the cup. 'Mam said she'll come.' Her eyes mist over like she's seeing something that isn't here. 'But she'll probably be gone again by then.'

My heart shatters into a million pieces.

Ava's stunning features soften into a sad smile. She strokes a strand of blonde hair that's escaped from beneath Phoebe's hat. 'I'm sure you'll be the best Mary that ever was.'

Good deflection. But I have a better one. 'Let's take these drinks to the Ferris wheel and get in the queue. Ava, are you coming? Or are you scared of heights?'

'Huh! I'm not scared of anything.' She thrusts her chin up.

Well, that makes one of us. Because I'm terrified right now. Terrified about how natural she is with my daughter. And even more terrified by how much I like spending time with both of them together.

I barely know the woman, and she's gotten under my skin.

The queue moves quickly and before I know it, the three of us are huddled into a cage like compartment, being hoisted up into the starry sky overlooking some of Dublin's most stunning sights. The river creates a shimmering ribbon as it winds its way enchantingly through the city below. Dublin Castle, Christ Church Cathedral, and the imposing façade of Trinity College are all visible in the distance. The cityscape is a brilliant fusion of warm golds, vibrant reds and cool blues as streetlights, cars and Christmas lights all contribute to the luminous display.

None of it is as stunning or luminous as the sight of Ava's arm draped over Phoebe's shoulders, pointing out the landmarks with awe.

Everything looks the same as it did last year. But nothing is the same. Because I'll never be able to unsee this night. Unsee how different mine and Phoebe's lives could potentially be if I wasn't the way I am.

If I could open myself up to the possibility of trusting another person enough to let them into our lives.

Trust them not to leave.

Trust that maybe some things can last.

After meeting Frank and Penny Jackson at the weekend, and seeing them again at the party last night, I have to reluctantly accept that it seems some relationships might last forever.

Which leads me to realise that the problem might lie with me.

Chapter Twenty-One

AVA

Phoebe has barely let go of my hand from the second I met her. She latched on to me like an orphan. If Cillian has a problem with it, he's not showing it. Though he doesn't exactly look ecstatic with this evening's turn of events either.

Then again, when does he ever look ecstatic about anything? He has the male equivalent of 'resting bitch face', which I suppose makes it 'resting bastard face'.

The more I see of him though, he's anything but a bastard.

He's a fucking teddy bear.

Especially when it comes to his daughter. He hides behind that stern exterior. It's a defence mechanism, of that, I'm certain.

The Ferris wheel slows to a stop and a burly guy in a bomber jacket opens the door for us. Cillian gets out first. When his feet are firmly on the ground, he reaches inside the compartment and grabs my waist, helping me out. Even through my thick woollen coat the sensation is electric. Those liquid metal eyes bore into mine with a heat that sears my soul.

Does he feel it?

How natural this evening has been?

Stop it, Ava. Don't make this into something it isn't. His exact words when he agreed to this were clear.

No touching.

No kissing.

And definitely don't fall in love.

Love? Oh my god, what is wrong with me? I barely know the guy. Unless you count the past year where I've been staring at his perfectly round ass every time he passed my office window.

It's not love. It's lust. But there's no denying the more time I spend with him, I fall a little bit more.

The way he took care of me when I was sick. Brought me pizza the next day. Stood up for me in front of my siblings, not to mention the tenderness he treated my body with, not just last night but this morning too.

And the affection and devotion he shows his daughter, who is absolutely adorable by the way, is nothing short of admirable.

Is it any wonder I'm a teeny tiny bit obsessed?

And seeing as he broke the no touching role, maybe there's hope of more ...

'Ava?' Cillian's voice is thick with concern. Probably because I'm drowning in his platinum eyes like a complete fucking idiot. 'Are you dizzy after the ride?'

Oh, I'm dizzy, alright, just with lust.

'I'm fine.' I lift Phoebe out of the carriage, and she wraps her arms around my neck, and it feels amazing. Yep, biological clock is well and truly ticking.

'It's probably time we got you home.' Cillian addresses Phoebe, prising her out of my arms. I feel oddly both bereft and envious for and of a child I only just met.

Phoebe places a hand over her mouth to hide her yawn. 'Ava, can we do this again sometime?'

I look at Cillian. The air buzzes between us. Despite the crisp cold night, heat kindles my core. I wish it was me who was in his arms. I wish things could be different. That I could go home with them and help tuck Phoebe into bed. Then carry on what we started in his kitchen the other night, and I'm not referring to the bottle of red wine.

Something flashes across his face. Regret? Disapproval? Did I overstep the mark with Phoebe?

It's impossible to tell.

'I'd love to, pumpkin. If it's okay with your dad.' I shoot him a tentative glance, but he's suddenly engrossed in fixing Phoebe's hat and smoothing down her coat.

'Maybe you could be my pretty friend, as well as Daddy's?' How could anyone in the world say no to that cute little face?

'Sure.' I reach into my coat pocket and pull out my lipstick and hand it to her. 'Here. This is for you.'

'For real?' She vibrates with excitement.

'Yeah.' I kiss her cheek, my heart as heavy as stone. 'I'll see you around kiddo.'

I hesitate for a split second before spinning on my heels. As I'm about to step away Phoebe calls, 'Wait!'

I turn slowly, oblivious to the crowds around us. Everyone else melts into the background.

'Yes?'

'You forgot to give Daddy a kiss.' Her upturned palms flounce in front of her face in an exaggerated gesture. Turns out with that level of dramatics, she really could be the best Mary ever.

'I – err ...' My feet are locked to the spot.

A small smirk tugs at Cillian's lips. He takes a step forward with Phoebe still in his muscular arms and presses his lips fleetingly against my ear. 'And I thought she was a cock-blocker after the other night.'

Laughter gurgles in my throat.

'I'll talk to you soon,' I say, and this time when I turn around to leave my heart feels slightly cheerier in my chest. Though the thought of going back to my empty penthouse isn't an appealing one.

Hailing a taxi, I give the driver my parents' address. I don't need to call ahead; Penny and Frank Jackson have a schedule like clockwork. They'll have had their dinner and are probably arguing good-naturedly about who's going on top tonight. God help me.

Outside the house, I ring the buzzer, I've been caught out with those two nymphomaniacs before. Not an experience I'd ever want to repeat. Even if it is 'what makes the world go round'. Yuck.

It's one thing knowing your parents are still sexually active, and a completely different thing to walk in on them on the job.

I stare at the mistletoe wreath responsible for kick-starting things between Cillian and me. There are some benefits to having super-open parents, at least.

When the front door swings open, it's my brother, Nate, who's standing in the doorway.

'Hey, sis, how are you?' He pulls me into his burly frame for a bear hug and ruffles my hair.

'If you like your balls where they are, don't ever ruffle my hair again.' I elbow him in the ribs.

Nate sniggers and releases me. 'So, last night was a success, huh?' He motions for me to walk in front of him towards the kitchen.

'It certainly was.' In more ways than one.

'You disappeared kind of quick.' Nate winks knowingly.

'I told you things were absolutely randy.' The heat of

Mam's new Aga slaps me in the face as I open the kitchen door. Holly, Nate's fiancée, is sitting at the table with their baby girl, Harriet, on her knee. Mam and dad sit either side, cooing like Harriet's their first grandchild, not their fifth. I can't blame them. My brother and Holly made a beautiful baby.

'Ava. This is a pleasant surprise.' Mam stands back from the table and welcomes me with a hug.

'Drink?' Dad holds up an open bottle of red.

'I'd love one, thanks.' I lean over the table and reach out for my gorgeous niece. Even at barely three months old, she has us all wrapped around her little finger. She gurgles and offers a drooly smile as Holly hands her over.

Nate watches on, arching an eyebrow. 'It'll be you next.'

Not with Cillian, it won't.

'One day, hopefully.' Harriet wraps her chubby fingers around my pinkie.

'If the way Cillian looks at you is anything to go by, it'll be sooner rather than later.' Holly chimes, a glint in her topaz eyes. 'He didn't take his eyes off you for a second last night.'

'Really?' I bite back my surprise.

'Oh, come on! The man is smitten.' My mother announces gleefully.

He must be a seriously good actor. I wonder if his parents sent him to stage school as a kid. 'Now, what's he like in bed?' Mam rubs her hands together, dying for the juicy details.

'Eugh, Mam.'

'I need his phone number,' Nate announces, sliding his hand across Holly's shoulder.

Alarm prickles my spine. 'Why?'

'Well, for one, I want to invite him on my stag night next week. And two, I want to fly both of you over in February for the premiere of *Ruthless Redemption*.'

Thankfully, Nate's gone back to his usual movie genre,

after an eventful attempt at a Hallmark movie last year. It was too weird watching him trying to be cheesy and romantic on the big screen.

Cillian won't keep up this farce between us into next year as well. We agreed to fake-date for December. Not indefinitely.

'I'll forward it on to you later.'

'Great.' Nate picks up his wine glass and raises it in my direction. 'You know, I thought you were telling fibs on the phone a couple of weeks ago. I'm so happy for you, Ava.' He shakes his shaggy hair from his earnest eyes and a ripple of guilt rips through me. 'It's great you've finally met someone decent. If only we could hook Natalie up with someone now too.'

'Natalie has no interest in being hooked up with anyone.' I readjust Harriet on my chest. 'She works such long hours at the hospital she's too exhausted to go out and find a man.'

'That will change.' Nate shrugs.

'Look at you, wanting everyone to settle down now you have.' I tease.

'It's working out for you, if your glowing cheeks are anything to go on.' He winks again.

Oh, it's working out in some ways alright. But what will happen after December? I'm only two weeks into this fake agreement and already I don't want it to end.

My phone chimes with an incoming text from my coat pocket.

Nate slips his hand in and grabs it, glances at the screen as he passes it over. 'Oh, it's lover-boy. *Phoebe loved you.*'

'You met his daughter?' Mam shrieks. 'It's official! I need to buy another hat!'

If only.

But the thought still sends a hot thrilling flush through me.

Chapter Twenty-Two

CILLIAN

Friday 8th December

Beth grabs my arm as I'm about to breeze out the door with today's case files. I like to start my mornings with a stroll along Grafton Street to Steamy Fix. Though its name makes it sound like a brothel, it's a coffee shop that just so happens to serve the best espresso in Dublin.

Popping to Steamy Fix also gives me an excuse to walk by the HeartSync office, something which I've been doing unwittingly for almost a year with no idea of the beauty of the woman working behind the high brick walls.

'How's the love life, boss?' Beth wiggles her eyebrows.

'I already told you, Beth, it's a business arrangement.' I flash her my sternest stare; one that would have the rest of my staff scurrying. Beth sniggers and thrusts her phone under my nose. Her Instagram account is open on the HeartSync page. A picture of me with my arms wrapped around Ava lights the screen. Her head is tilted back to rest on my chest and she's gazing up at me with gold-flecked fuck-me eyes. The attraction between us sizzles from the screen.

'Well, I'm glad to see you're so invested in this "business

agreement".' Beth snatches the phone away from me. 'You know I think there might actually be hope for you yet.'

'There isn't. Trust me.' Even though, there's a part of me that would like to believe it. Especially given what a hit Ava was with my daughter last night. But even if I wanted it to be more than what it is, it's too risky. It's not just me who could get hurt. I have Phoebe to consider too.

I attempt to make my escape through the open doorway, but Beth blocks the way.

'Are you taking Ava to the Christmas party tomorrow?' She demands, planting a hand on her hip.

'Tomorrow?' I trawl my fingers through my hair wondering how I could have forgotten the most expensive night of my year.

Every year at Christmas I hire out Huxley Castle for the staff and their partners. Huxley is the finest five-star castle in the country. Owned by a rock star and his wife, it's utterly lavish, and has really limited availability since the couple moved back into it, but that only adds to its popularity. Patrons get to literally live like a rock star, for a night at least.

I suspect this annual trip is one of the reasons I have such a low turnover of staff, despite being a grumpy bastard.

'Don't tell me you forgot?' Beth's hand swats the air in an exasperated gesture. 'It's been booked for months.'

'Which is precisely *why* I forgot about it.' Hopefully Matilda won't mind taking Phoebe. I can't ask my mother. Her and dad always tag along, making use of the fact I don't have enough staff to fill it.

'Does being away from my daughter for two nights in the same week make me a bad dad?' Beth is the only person I'd dream of voicing my parenting concerns aloud to.

'No. It makes you a busy dad. Trust me, Phoebe is lucky to have you. Matilda already agreed to mind her on Saturday.'

Beth is a godsend. 'I've arranged everything, from your child-care right down to the menu, and the optional Santa Run.'

'A Santa Run? You've got to be kidding me?'

'It's taking place on Velvet Strand at midday on the Sunday. Like I said, it's optional.' She arches a wry eyebrow. 'But it's run by Savannah Kingsley; you know the celebrity blogger "Single Sav." It's a fundraiser for the Single Parents Society.'

I exhale a weary sigh. I know Savannah. She's the mother of the twin girls in Phoebe's class, the same ones she sauntered into school arms linked with the other day. Single Parents Society is the one charity I always try and support, and Beth knows it. I'm lucky I don't struggle to support my daughter financially, but I'm painfully aware that for many single parents the fight is real.

'Can I just sponsor it and not partake in the run?' Thoughts of running the beach in a fucking Santa suit is ludicrous. Though, Phoebe would get a great kick out of watching it. And the twins will probably be there too.

'You already are sponsoring it, but taking part will make you look more human to the staff.' Beth leans against the door frame, examining her rainbow painted nails.

'Who says I want to appear more human to the staff?' I quite like that most of them avoid me like the plague.

'Oh, come on! That hard-ass front doesn't work on me. You have a huge heart beneath that steely exterior, why not let them get a glimpse of it? It's Christmas after all.'

I've deliberately avoided getting too familiar with my staff. At one point my father could name almost every single one of his employees. He knew their kids' names, what football teams they supported, and what they ate every day for lunch.

He also knew what colour panties his PA wore, because

they were usually round her ankles before lunchtime while he bent her over his desk.

She sent photographic evidence to the house. That's when my mother introduced the 'no shitting on the doorstep' rule.

I shudder at the memories, grateful for Beth's incessant chatting.

'And I think you should bring Ava.'

'But the entire office will be gossiping about us.' Which is something I despise, though the prospect of taking Ava for another dirty night away is pretty enticing. And if Teagan does have any little birds, it's the perfect opportunity to send them fluttering back to her.

'They've been gossiping about you since she waltzed in here last week looking like she'd just stepped of the catwalk. How she's snagged your miserable ass has the entire building intrigued.'

'Haven't they got anything better to do? Like work?' I scoff.

'Cut them some slack! Our hot, brooding boss hooking up with the owner of the hottest new dating agency is the story of the century! I use the term "hot, brooding boss" objectively of course.' Beth grins, stepping aside, finally allowing me to pass. 'You do absolutely nothing for me.'

'Thankfully.' I mutter. 'Fine. I'll ask her.' The prospect of Ava's stunning body spread out across one of Huxley Castle's four-poster beds has seared itself into my mind. 'Also, I need to take a few days off the week before Christmas.'

'What?' Beth's jaw practically hits the floor.

'Ava's brother's getting married. It's on one of those islands off the west coast. He's trying to avoid paparazzi. I'll need most of the week off.'

'But what about your cases?'

'You know as well as I do it's the quietest month of the year.' I roll my lips.

I never take holidays. Except when Phoebe's off school. 'Give them to Alex. It might keep him busy enough to leave the girls in the office alone.' Alex Benedict is like a younger, better-looking version of my father. He has the same voracious appetite for the opposite sex. And they have the same appetite for him. As one of my best attorneys, his statistics are only a fraction below mine. Worrying, given he specialises in criminal defence.

When he's not defending the bad guys, he can be found cruising Dublin in his brand-new Ibis-white Audi R8, like the playboy he is, picking up women. A taste of family law might calm him down a bit.

'Consider it done.' Beth singsongs, strutting out of my office. 'I told you there's hope for you yet.'

I type out a text to Ava.

> Any chance you're free tomorrow for an overnight trip?

Her reply is instantaneous. Thank God she's not one of these game players.

> Depends where ... my own bed is really comfy. You should try it out sometime ...

> Huxley Castle

> Hell yes! I was there last Christmas with my brother. I've been praying to get back there ever since.

'Daddy, can we go ice-skating tomorrow? Sarah Snowden went last weekend, and she said it was awesome.' Phoebe asks from across the dinner table.

Matilda left cashew chicken and rice for us, one of Phoebe's favourites. She has the sand-coloured sauce smeared across her chin as proof.

'Not tomorrow sweetheart. Remember Matilda's coming to mind you? It's Daddy's work party.' I place my cutlery together on my plate.

Phoebe pouts, and my dad guilt strikes my stomach like a tsunami. 'I promise I'll take you next weekend, okay?'

'Do you think Ava could come too?' Phoebe's little face looks so optimistic. She has a full-on girl-crush on Ava, and I can't blame her.

She's mentioned her name at least twenty times this evening and she's been carrying around that claret-coloured lipstick like it's her most prized possession.

'No sweetheart. I don't think Ava can come.' I hate to be the one to burst her bubble, but I don't want her to get notions about something that will never be.

Phoebe's face falls. The urge to distract her is overwhelming.

'Shall we put up the Christmas tree tonight?' Every year I let her decorate the house with fairy lights and tinsel whichever way she likes. It usually looks like a bad taste party gone wrong, but if she's happy, I'm happy.

When she was only two years old, she took a shine to a white Christmas tree in Arnott's Department Store. Kicked and screamed the place down until I bought it. At six, she still adores it, insisting it can only be decorated with pink baubles, and pink striped candy-cane sticks, but if it makes her happy, then I'm happy.

It's like flipping a switch. The smile is back, the light in her eyes is blinding. 'Will you put on the Christmas songs? And can we open the Celebrations?'

'On one condition.'

She fist-pumps the air and lets out a squeal. 'Anything.'

'You have to wash your face and put your pyjamas on first, okay?' Last year she conked on the couch before we finished. I had to put her to bed in the clothes she'd been wearing all day.

'You're the best Dad ever.' Phoebe flashes me her goofiest grin and blows me a kiss across the table. A warm rush of love inflates my heart.

A loud knock on the front door rapidly deflates it.

It can only be Teagan. No one else would get past the gate.

Phoebe leaps up from her seat at the table. I follow close on her heels.

'Mam.' Phoebe squeals. 'This is perfect timing. We're just about to put up the tree.'

I force down my irritation at Teagan's arrival. It makes my daughter happy, so I'll suck it up for tonight, but these erratic arrivals can't continue. 'You could have called to say you were coming.'

'Why? It's not like you'd be anywhere else at this hour of the evening.' Teagan's pushes her way into the hallway, a ridiculously bright smile plastered across her face. Yet another stylish party dress peeps out from her open coat. This one's cut indecently low on the front. Either she's on her way to a hot date, or she still hasn't got the memo that we are over.

'Last night, we were.' Phoebe pipes up, pulling Ava's claret-coloured lipstick from her pocket and thrusting under Teagan's nose.

Teagan's smile dies on her face. Accusatory eyes fixate on mine. 'Where did she get that?'

'We met a friend of Daddy's at the Christmas market. She was so lovely. And so pretty. You'd really like her, Mam.' Phoebe coos at the memory.

This is precisely why I would never have dreamed of introducing Ava to my daughter if it hadn't have happened organically. Not because the hurt on Teagan's face is too much to bear, but because the optimism on Phoebe's is.

'Is that right?' Teagan tuns back to Phoebe. 'And are you seeing Daddy's friend again?'

'Don't.' I whisper to Teagan's ear. 'It's not fair to put her in the middle.'

'I hope so.' Phoebe kisses the lipstick like her most precious possession. Teagan's nostrils flare.

'Go get changed for bed.' I smooth my palm over Phoebe's silky soft hair. 'I'll tidy up and get the decorations down from the loft.'

'Mam, will you come up with me?' Phoebe tugs Teagan's hand but Teagan brushes her off.

'I'll be up in a minute, sweetie. I just want to have a quick word with daddy.' Her sickly-sweet tone makes me nauseous.

Phoebe hesitates, glancing between the two of us. 'It's okay, Phoebe. Just go get changed, and I'll put on some Christmas songs.' I rub her back, gently nudging her towards the stairs.

Teagan's presence here is becoming problematic. And tonight's the night I stop pussyfooting around and tell her.

The second Phoebe's out of earshot Teagan tears into me. 'You introduced *her* to my daughter?'

'No. I introduced *Ava* to *our* daughter.' I signal for her to move into the kitchen. Phoebe's been through enough without listening to this shit as well. 'It wasn't planned. We happened to be at the Winter Wonderland at the same time. Not that it's any of your business.'

'Like I'm meant to believe that.' Teagan fumes.

'Look, Teagan, I've been exceptionally tolerant of you rocking up like this, but it stops tonight. Do you hear me? For the sake of our daughter, I won't throw you out right now, but know this, going forward, if you want to see Phoebe, you text and arrange a time in advance where you can take her, because you showing up like this, pretending everything is normal, is confusing for her.'

'Confusing for her, or for you?' Teagan slips off her coat, along with her frown and tries a different tack, pressing herself against me.

'For her.' Stepping back, I hold out an upturned palm. 'Give me the fob for the gate or get out. Your choice.'

Teagan tsks, fishing the fob from her coat pocket.

'And one more thing. I want you out of here before nine. Ava's coming over.' If I wasn't planning on inviting her over, I am now.

I tell myself it's just to make a plan for tomorrow but deep down, I know it's because I haven't seen her in twenty-four hours, and it feels like twenty-four days.

Chapter Twenty-Three

AVA

Sipping on a chilled glass of Riesling, I sift through my walk-in wardrobe, trailing my fingers over dress after dress, wondering what to pack. The prospect of a night at Huxley Castle is almost as exciting as another night with Cillian.

If things were different, Cillian could be my match made in heaven. Spoken like a true dating agency CEO. My parents love him. My sister Natalie thinks he's a ride. My brother has finally stopped tormenting me. And Cillian's daughter is an absolute dote.

If this thing was real, it might look promising.

But it's not.

So, I fully intend on making the most of the situation as it is, for however long it lasts.

My phone chimes from my bed. The same way I felt it when he walked into the bar, I just know that it's Cillian.

> Help. Teagan's here, being Teagan. Are you free to come over?

. . .

After how well he played Wednesday night, and I'm not just talking about the HeartSync anniversary party, I can hardly say no.

Sure. Give me an hour.

I hop into the shower to freshen up, smothering myself with jasmine scented oil, just in case my presence is required for anything extra. Looks like I am well and truly back in the saddle ...

I take a taxi to Sandymount, not just because I had a glass of Riesling, but because I brought another bottle hoping Cillian will be persuaded to open it.

Instead of buzzing the gate, I send a text to say I'm outside. If Phoebe's asleep, I'd hate to be the one to wake her.

The electric gates slide open, and I amble up the lantern-lit driveway to the front door. The grounds are stunning. So well maintained. A tree house and swing set punctuates the left side of the lawn. Pretty flower beds line the periphery of the property. It really is the perfect family home.

The front door opens, and a dishevelled but distinguished looking Cillian appears. Beneath the moonlight, his chiselled cheekbones could pass for marble. That square jawline oozes masculinity. And those liquid metal eyes were made purely to define the word piercing. The man is a living breathing piece of art.

Or ass.

Or both.

He places his right index finger over his lips in a shh motion and uses his left one to point upstairs.

'Where's Teagan?' I mouth.

Relief flickers in his pupils. 'Gone, thankfully.'

'Do you want me to go?' Clearly, I'm no longer needed. Well, not for the original purpose anyway.

'Don't you dare.' Those full hot lips brush over the sensitive skin of my earlobe. He steps aside and yanks me against the strong smooth planes of his torso.

He's still in his suit pants and a crisp white shirt but the top two buttons are undone, revealing a hint of tanned chest and a wispy tuft of delicious dark chest hair. He looks positively delectable, but he smells even better, that fancy cologne tinged with his own masculine scent is intoxicating.

I follow him through to the kitchen where he uncorks the wine and pours two glasses. 'How was your day?' he asks in a low voice, but with enough interest to make me think he actually cares.

'It was good. Busy. After the pictures of the party went viral, we've been swamped with new sign-ups.' I take a sip of the cold, crisp wine but it does nothing to soothe the burning yearning growing inside. The physical pull to Cillian Callaghan is beyond magnetic. It's a gravitational force of its own.

'I saw the photo.' He raises his glass to his lips, his eyes locking with mine over the rim. He doesn't need to say which one. It's obvious. It helped that my movie-star brother shared it on his socials, but I'm pretty sure that thing had the potential to go viral all on its own. Despite both of us being fully clothed, the image was unmistakably pornographic.

A hot blush streaks my cheeks. 'With that image circulating, no one will ever suspect this thing between us is a business agreement.'

'With benefits.' He drinks and my eyes are drawn to his.

'Is that why you lured me over here? To cash in on those benefits?' I don't mind. In fact, I might even be flattered.

'No. I really did have company, though I was contemplating inviting you over anyway.' He places his wine glass down on the gleaming kitchen counter; his hands gravitate to my waist before sliding over my hips. 'Is this okay?'

'I suppose I can tolerate it.' I place my glass next to his.

'The other night was ...' Huge black pupils study my face like he's searching for the right word but struggling. 'Unexpected.'

'In what way?' I would have thought given what happened in this very kitchen, it was utterly expected, if not inevitable.

'Unexpectedly mind-blowing.' He draws my body flush with his, peppering my neck with tiny teasing kisses that pebble my nipples beneath my cashmere midi dress. I was aiming for winter chic. I know how much Cillian hates the over-the-top way his ex flaunts her body at him, that's why I opted for understated. I don't want to have anything in common with her. I already hate that I ogled him from afar for a year, the same way she did.

He hands me my glass, picks up his own and steers me out the kitchen, guiding me into a large, double-height hallway. Thick coving frames the ceiling. One wall is comprised entirely of bookshelves, filled with everything from a collection of Encyclopaedia Britannicas to Dan Brown's latest novel.

I drift towards a weathered-looking copy of Stephen King's *Misery*, open the pages and sniff. 'Told you I couldn't help it.'

'Enough of that.' He takes the book from my hands and places it back on the shelf. 'My life is anything but misery with you here, looking like that.' His perusing gaze sends chills across my skin.

I follow him into the main living area. The walls are painted a deep shade of grey, giving the room a masculine feel, but there's nothing masculine about the extravagant fairy lights adorning the thick mantlepiece, or the pink and white Christmas tree flashing on a slow repetitive cycle in the big bay window.

'Not exactly what I'd have imagined.' It's a testament to him that he lets his six-year-old daughter have the final say on the Christmas decorations. Just as I suspected, the man is a teddy bear beneath the sharp suit.

'Phoebe's favourite colour is pink.' He slips that arm around my waist again. Does he feel that same gravitational pull? The one that urges me to touch him at every single opportunity. 'Well, it was pink until you gave her the lipstick. Now she wants her room painted a deep devil-red.'

'That particular shade is technically called Plum Passion Addict.'

'Sounds about right.' He motions for me to sit on the leather couch in front of the roaring open fire. I sit and place my glass on the coffee table.

'We always put the tree up early in December. I know it's a bit of an eyesore, but traditions are traditions. Did you put yours up yet?'

Nervous laughter bubbles in my throat. 'You invited me over to clarify if I put my tree up yet?'

'Indulge me.' He drops to the couch next to me, his fingers trailing circles on my stockinged thigh. 'I'm killing time until I'm one hundred percent certain my daughter is unconscious, then I'm going to devour you.'

My insides somersault. I press my legs together but Cillian's quick fingers wedge between my knees.

'I don't put a tree up in my apartment. I spend Christmas at my parents' place.'

'What?' Cillian's face scrunches into a more sullen expression. 'You have to put a tree up.' A low whistle resounds through the air between us. 'And people call *me* miserable.' He shakes his head.

I shrug. 'It seems kind of pointless, just for me.'

'Nothing is pointless, just for you, Ava Jackson. Don't ever forget that.' There's that surprising tenderness again. It's almost as much of a turn on as the hand snaking beneath my dress, blazing a trail of fire all the way to my flaming lady parts.

'Careful, Cillian, you're ruining your divorce-enforcer reputation.' He finds the top of my stockings and brushes over the lace.

'No, I'd have to smile for that to happen. And my smiles are rarer than an eclipse.'

'I noticed.'

'This makes me happy though.' He taps the lace part of the hold-ups. 'Even if I don't show it.'

My eyes fall to the significant bulge in his crotch. 'Oh, you're showing it alright, just not with your mouth.'

'I'm about to though.' His eyes bore into mine with an intensity that should emit actual steam. He drops to his knees on the carpet in front me, sliding the coffee table back to give himself more room. Nudging himself between my legs, he parts them to accommodate his beautiful body, hitching my dress higher at an agonisingly slow pace. 'Let's have a look what you're hiding under here tonight.'

The lace band of the hold-ups come into view. I watch as he drinks me in with a low hiss of approval. 'So fucking sexy, Ava. Did you put these on for me?'

'Would it make you happy if I said I did?'

'Very.' He growls, inching the cashmere higher until it's rumpled around my waist and the lace panties I picked up in Brown Thomas are on full display.

'These look amazing on you.' He tugs them down with an

appreciative moan. 'But they'd look so much better on my floor.' He slides the lingerie over the stockings, slipping them off, and into the pocket of his suit pants. 'These are mine now.'

It's not a request.

He stares appraisingly at me down there. 'That's better. So pretty. Tomorrow, at Huxley Castle, I expect to find you in this same state, okay?'

'Knickerless and spread out on the living room couch?'

'There goes that smart mouth again, Ava. Let's see if I can quieten you once and for all.' His face dips to the most intimate part of me and he offers a long slow lick that has me salivating for more. 'Divine.' He mutters and continues to torture me in the most hedonistic way with that expert tongue.

He's too good. It's too much. My thighs shake and shudder beneath the huge hands that pin them in place. 'Cillian,' I whisper.

His chuckle vibrates against my sex, and he works me harder, swirling maddening strokes around my clit until I explode on his tongue in a burst of flashing fireworks and rippling, paralysing waves of pleasure.

He rocks back on his knees, still fixated on my pulsing pussy. 'I have been dreaming of doing that all day.'

'Funny, it's not what you put on your sign-up form.'

'Well, I didn't want the women of Dublin beating my front door down.' He slips a finger inside and my head rolls back against the couch. 'I see your smart mouth has recovered. Let's see how you recover from this.'

He pumps me with his fingers, working me where I'm already so sensitive. I'm drowning in my own arousal.

'Not so smart now, are you?'

Another orgasm builds in my core. He adds another finger and swipes his thumb through my folds. The man is seriously talented. If he ever decides to give up his day job, he could definitely moonlight as a porn star.

His fingers slow to a stop and he stares at me. 'What are you going to wear under your dress tomorrow night Ava?' The glint in his eyes is pure wicked devilment.

'Whatever you want me to wear.' I pant.

'Wrong answer.' He pumps me once and stops again.

'Nothing.' I cry.

'Good girl.' He works me until I reach the next delicious starry oblivion.

Chapter Twenty-Four

CILLIAN

I could play with Ava Jackson all night long, and all damn day too. The way her body responds to my touch is like it's made for me. Which is a very dangerous thought for this divorce lawyer to entertain.

I slide my fingers from her flesh and lick them while she watches on with wide eyes. My suit pants are strangling my cock, but he'll have to wait until tomorrow. I don't mind playing around, but I can't take Ava to my bed. No matter how much I want to. I pull her dress down from around her waist and smooth it over her lap.

'Cillian, I ...' She tugs at my belt, but I shake my head and drag myself into the seat next to her and pass her wine from the coffee table.

'Tomorrow. Tonight was all about you.'

'It's a shame you don't believe in marriage because after that, I'd be tempted to propose this instant.' She accepts the glass of wine with a snigger.

Thank God we've both been crystal clear from the start. There's no awkwardness. No reading into this. Her wondering if it's going anywhere. Me knowing it's not, because nothing ever could for me.

Could it?

Imagine doing this whenever we wanted. For as long as we wanted. With no end date. No labels.

But she wants a label. She wants the fairy tale and the forever.

If she didn't, maybe we could reach some sort of compromise where we could carry this thing on between us. Because I've never experienced attraction like it, and the more time we spend together, the more I realise the month of December isn't going to be anywhere near long enough to get it out of my system.

And realistically, it won't be the month of December. Her brother's wedding is the nineteenth. She could finish with me before Christmas, find herself a man who *will* give her the fairy tale, now I've got her 'back in the saddle'.

The prospect sickens my stomach.

'Are you okay?' She takes my hands and squeezes it.

'Fine.' Why did I use the one word that translates to 'anything but'?

'You know I was joking about the proposal.' Those honey-flecked eyes colour with concern.

'I know.' *Worse luck.*

'I'm just going to get cleaned up. Which way is the toilet?' Ava wobbles to a standing position. I point her out to the hallway, grateful for a minute alone.

What has gotten into me? This woman and her long legs and luscious smiling lips has seeped well and truly under my skin.

When Ava returns smelling of the floral soap Matilda stocks the downstairs bathroom with, I broach a safer topic. 'It's my work Christmas party tomorrow. Every year, I hire Huxley Castle for an office blow-out. I need you to play the role of adoring fake girlfriend, if that's okay. Teagan has eyes and ears everywhere, and I need to make sure she thinks you and I are the real deal. She's already hanging round way longer than I thought she would. If she's staying, I need her to respect that we're never getting back together, and therefore establish a proper routine with Phoebe.'

'Adoring girlfriend with no panties on?' Ava draws a big tick in the air with her finger. 'Check.'

'Well, don't feel you have to show my staff the lingerie situation. If my friend Alex gets even a hint of the lingerie situation, he'll dry hump your leg like a Doberman with two dicks. Speaking of which, so will my father. I'm not sure how my parents started wangling an annual invite, I blame Teagan from years ago, but they like to tag along and play the proud parent card. They don't dine with us, but they do take the opportunity to stay in the castle.'

Ava cocks her head to the side like she's waiting for further explanation.

'My mother is a dote. My father is a dog. He humps anything that moves, while Lillian Callaghan turns a blind eye and plays the well-behaved wife.'

'I'm so sorry you've had to live through all that.' Enlightenment dawns in Ava's eyes. 'Your sign-up form hinted your father was a bit of a man about town.'

'That's the understatement of the century. He's the sole reason I specialised in family law, primarily divorce, so I could free my mother from him. Sadly, she's in it for the long haul. Unless he does something exceptionally unforgiveable, because apparently being unfaithful for the past thirty years isn't it.'

Ava pats my leg and opens her mouth like she's about to say something, but she's interrupted by a voice from the doorway.

'I knew it was you!' Phoebe charges into the sitting room

and straight onto Ava's lap, which thankfully, is now covered and clean. This is the exact reason I couldn't chance taking Ava to bed, despite having painfully blue balls.

Phoebe's smile could be spotted from space. 'I knew you'd come to visit! I just knew it!'

'Hi, pumpkin.' Ava glances at me with wide eyes and mouths the word 'sorry' over Phoebe's head, which she cradles against her chest.

'Phoebe Callaghan, what are you doing up again?' She was out for the count an hour ago. I blame the Celebrations. Too much sugar before bed.

'I don't know. I just woke up and heard voices, so I came down.' Sparkling eyes peep from under her long, light lashes. I know I am biased, every dad probably is, but my kid is beautiful. And curled into Ava like that, the two of them are an absolute vision.

'Bossy, isn't he?' Phoebe says to Ava, stifling her giggle.

'He is a bit.' Ava drops her voice to a whisper-shout.

'Come on now, back to bed, little lady.' I open my arms and motion for Phoebe to climb into them, but she shakes her head with a definitive no. 'You know Matilda's coming for a sleepover tomorrow and she'll want to let you stay up late. You'll be exhausted if you don't go back to bed now.'

'Can Ava put me up? I need to ask her something.' Phoebe wraps her little hands round Ava's neck while metaphorically wrapping her round her little finger.

Ava's shoulders shrug, 'If it's okay with your dad, I don't mind.'

Phoebe leaps to her feet and drags Ava by the hand. 'Come on, I'll show you my bedroom. I've got dolls. LOL ones. Barbies. Even Baby Annabell. She's my favourite.'

Ava shoots me an apologetic look over her shoulder as she leaves the sitting room. 'Show me your dolls, and I'll read you a quick story. That should make you nice and sleepy.' Ava's tone is warm. The way her palm rests on Phoebe's head is warm. Everything about her is warm. And she's heating the cold cracks in my life that I hadn't even noticed were present until now.

Is it healthy that the woman I'm having casual sex with is upstairs in my house putting my daughter to bed?

Probably not.

But something about it feels so natural. Because truthfully there's nothing casual about the sex, or anything else we do together. And that's probably something I should be worried about. But right here, right now, with the fire roaring, the tree twinkling, and the tinkling laughter of my daughter and Ava drifting from upstairs, a strange but welcome sense of contentment seeps in around me.

My head flops back on the couch, my shoulders sag and I sip the glass of wine, safe in the knowledge that Phoebe is happy, for now at least. It's a relief to let Ava take charge tonight. She can give her something I can't offer. Girl time. Friendship. Fun.

Again, my mind conjures up images it has no business conjuring. Ava and Phoebe hanging out Phoebe's stocking on the mantelpiece on Christmas Eve.

Ava and Phoebe sitting together beneath the Christmas tree opening presents on Christmas morning.

Ava and Phoebe sitting at the dining table while I carve the turkey.

What is wrong with me?

I never imagined a future with anyone.

Why her? Why now?

Ava tiptoes down the stairs half an hour later. 'She's asleep.' She creeps across the varnished flooring and perches on the couch next to me. 'I hope you didn't mind me putting her to bed.' She wrings her wrists. 'I know this is an unusual situation.'

I swallow. 'Let's not complicate it. Or overthink it. Let's just enjoy it for what it is. Phoebe clearly adores you.' She's not the only one.

'The main thing is that she doesn't get confused about the situation. I don't want her thinking this is something it isn't.' Bad enough I'm starting to think that way.

'Of course. Sorry if I overstepped. I was only trying to help.' She stands to leave, smoothing down her dress. 'I should go.'

'You don't have to.' I pat the couch next to me, motioning for her to sit.

She gazes at me pensively. 'You look tired.'

'I'm not tired. I'm relaxed.' And I mean it. Truthfully. When Teagan puts Phoebe to bed, I'm on edge, waiting for her to leave. Wondering what false hope she might be filling our daughter's head with. Waiting for her next advance.

Ava sits tentatively on the couch, like she's about to make a confession or something. 'Phoebe asked me if I'd like to go ice-skating next weekend.'

'I bet she did.' She might only be three-and-a-half foot tall, but she knows an opportunity when she sees one. 'What did you tell her?'

'I told her to ask you.'

Great. Now I'll be the bad guy if I say no. 'Can you skate?'

'Like a pro.' Ava tilts her chin upwards like she's daring me to challenge her.

Would it be awful if I let her come? It would make Phoebe's day. And mine if I'm honest.

'Looks like you've got yourself a date.' I shrug.

'That was the premise of our entire agreement.' Our eyes meet, and something unspoken passes between us.

A question? Or a reminder that that's all this thing between us is supposed to be?

She stares at the pink and white flashing lights in the corner of the room. 'You know, it's actually really pretty.'

'Not nearly as pretty as you.' It's out before I can stop myself. 'I'll get us another drink.'

We spend the rest of the evening curled up on the couch flicking through Hallmark movies and polishing off the wine.

It's oddly more intimate than the fact her panties are tucked in my pocket.

Chapter Twenty-Five

AVA

Saturday 9th December

I spent last Christmas Day at the Huxley Estate, so its grandeur isn't new to me, yet the sight of the pristinely manicured lawns and the majestic castle towering ahead still steals the breath from my chest.

Last year, Nate's crazed fans had camped outside our parents' house, along with the country's most shameless paparazzi. Spending Christmas there simply wasn't an option. Nate's agent, Jayden Cooper, invited us all here instead. Jayden's brother, Ryan, and his wife, Sasha, own this castle. They live in it most of the year, but the weeks it's empty, they hire it out for a ludicrous amount of money. Which only reinforces what I already suspected: Cillian's law firm must be doing pretty damn well.

'It's something else, isn't it?' Cillian murmurs, blowing out a breath.

'It really is.' The castle's main entrance comes into view. Two suited porters flank the wrought iron doors. A thick, red carpet lines the entrance to the atrium inside. 'I think I might get married here.'

Cillian offers me a wry glance and shakes his head. 'Not today, you're not, sweetheart.'

I slap his thigh playfully. 'Duh. I'm still looking for my perfect match.'

Thick dark eyebrows raise skywards. 'You really think he exists?'

'I know he does.' *Because he's sitting right next to me*.

I can deny it as much as I like, but the more time I spend with Cillian-Can't-Crack-A-Smile-Callaghan, the more I think he's as close to perfect for me as they get.

Apart from the teeny tiny fact that he doesn't believe in love, marriage, fairytales or forevers. That aside, beneath his stern sturdy exterior he's kind, considerate, generous, hot as hell, and utterly gifted.

Life can be so unfair. I exhale a heavy sigh.

'Are you okay?' His palm brushes my thigh, concern etches into those huge swirling twin pools. 'Are you nervous?'

'No.' Cillian mentioned his parents would be here, as well as every employee on his payroll and their partners but that doesn't faze me. Peopling is a skill I've perfected over the years. Though I *would* like Cillian's parents to like me just in case this thing between us blooms into something more.

Eugh! There I go again. I need to push this daftness out of my head. Cillian doesn't want me. Not like that, anyway.

I force a smile. 'I'm good, thanks.'

'Did you do as I asked?' His fingers slide higher up my thigh, skimming just beneath the hem of my dress. I swat them away playfully.

'You'll have to wait and see.' Who am I kidding? We both know how this is going to end. Especially after last night. The scales are seriously unbalanced, but I spent this morning formulating a plan to even them out.

Cillian parks beside the dolphin water feature and struts round to my side to open the door for me.

One of the porters greets us heartily and takes Cillian's car keys and ushers us up the steps, insisting he'll take our luggage to the room.

Inside the huge, dome-shaped atrium, we're greeted by the crackling and hissing of a log fire and a festive piano soundtrack. A sixteen-foot Instagram-worthy Christmas tree punctuates the centre of the room. Every silver and blue bauble is evenly spaced. There isn't a pine needle out of place. Tasteful white lights twinkle to dim before brightening again.

The scent of cinnamon swirls through the air.

Soft velvet couches and wing-backed chairs are scattered around the atrium, but the place is empty.

Cillian heads to reception to check in, while I soak up the magnificent architecture. The deep wooden panelling. The mosaic flooring beneath my Louboutins. The ornate staircase covered with the same thick red carpet as the steps. It's not hard to believe this is the home of a rock star for most of the year.

I swivel slowly on my heels, so busy looking up at the intricate coving that I don't see the glamorous older lady next to me until I crash into her, knocking her to the floor.

'Oh, my goodness! I'm so sorry. Are you okay?' My right hand flies to my mouth. I offer my left to help the woman sprawled across the ground. With flawless make-up and a tailored dress, she's immaculately put together. If I had to hazard a guess, I'd say she's in her mid-fifties.

'Watch where you're going.' She uses one of the wing-backed chairs to pull herself up, pointedly ignoring my extended hand.

'It was an accident. I'm so sorry.'

She eyes me with an owlish curiosity, smoothing down her dress.

'Mother?' Cillian appears besides me, scanning the woman from head to toe. 'What happened?'

Ground swallow me whole. Thank God I'm not Cillian's real girlfriend. What a way to meet the prospective mother-in-law.

'Ahh, Cillian, there you are.' There's no mistaking who the man swaggering in from the bar is. His silver eyes are the exact same shade as both Cillian's and Phoebe's. Salt and pepper hair flops across his forehead, thick on top and cropped short at the sides. His sharp grey suit screams wealth. The smarmy way in which his gaze grazes my chest screams wanker.

Cillian's mother's mouth drops open into a small O. 'Is she with you?'

Cillian splays his hand across my lower back and tingling sensations zip up my spine, despite our current situation. 'Mam, this is Ava Jackson, my girlfriend. Ava, this is my mother, Lillian.'

I don't miss the way his body tenses as his focus shifts to his dad. 'And this is my father, William.'

'It's a pleasure to meet you.' Unlike his wife, William Callaghan has no problem taking my hand. He raises it to his weathered lips and holds it there for longer than is appropriate, all the while absorbing every inch of me in an overfamiliar gesture.

I snap my arm back and force my brightest smile. 'It's wonderful to meet you both. Cillian's told me so much about you.' I address Lillian again, 'And I'm so sorry again for knocking you. I was so engrossed admiring the interior, I didn't see you.'

'Hmm.' The icy façade thaws a fraction. 'I suppose it can be distracting when it's your first time somewhere like this.' Her pupils roam over my dress and narrow.

Good job she can't see what I'm wearing underneath it. Or not, as the case might be.

'Actually, I spent last Christmas Day here.' I'm not one to

brag that my brother is a mega famous movie star. In fact it's something I never usually mention to anyone who doesn't already know, but it's a great ice breaker, and I want her to know I'm not just after Cillian for a free ride.

'Christmas Day?' Lillian takes the bait.

'Yes. With Ryan and Sasha, and Jayden and his wife Chloe. My brother's a good friend of theirs.'

'Oh, is your brother in the music business too?' William touches my hand again, completely unnecessarily. A small but unmistakable growl rumbles in Cillian's throat. Lillian pointedly glances away. The poor woman. How does she put up with him?

'No, he's an actor.' I retract my hand again, placing in on Cillian's rock-solid pec and offer my sweetest smile.

'Oh, how interesting. Has he been in anything we might have seen?' William's tone is so patronising I almost laugh in his face.

'Probably. His name is Nate Jackson.' I suck in my lips to stop myself laughing.

William splutters, masking it with a cough. 'Wow, that's impressive.' He gives Cillian a knowing nudge in the ribs, but Cillian doesn't spare him a glance.

'The others will be arriving any minute.' He presses a kiss to my temple in a convincing show of affection. 'Let's go up and get settled.'

I hope that's code for 'let's go up and get ruffled'.

'How about a drink in the bar?' William claps his palms together noisily.

'Give us an hour.' Cillian reluctantly agrees.

'It was lovely to meet you both.' I lie.

'You too.' William's wandering eye lingers a beat too long again. The man has zero shame and zero integrity. No wonder Cillian can't stand him.

'See you shortly.' Lillian says. I'm pretty sure the jury's still out on me. And for some reason, that bothers me more than it should, given that the relationship I have with her son isn't even a real one.

We take the cherry wood stairs to the upper floor. With a huge four-poster bed and resplendent red velvet drapes, the suite is every bit as stunning as the rest of the castle. Cillian locks the door behind us and puts his hands on my waist, tugging me towards him. His crisp cologne is my favourite scent. Its musky tones are subtle, deep, and rich, just like the man wearing it.

Deft fingers sweep my hair back from my face, tucking it behind my ear.

For a man who doesn't believe in love, he's ridiculously affectionate. 'I'm sorry my mother was a little off.'

I glance at the floor, but he cups my chin and forces my face up to look at his. Those stunning silver eyes bore into mine, sizzling with heat and promise.

'Don't be. I'm just grateful we're only faking this thing between us. My fairytale ending doesn't involve a mother-in-law who hates me.' My jovial tone is fooling neither of us.

'She doesn't hate you. Trust me.' His reassurance is kind, but unnecessary. 'She's never seen me with a woman other than Teagan. She was probably just shocked. Dad leering over you wouldn't have helped, but it's not your fault you're stunning and he's a sleaze.'

'It doesn't matter either way.' It shouldn't at least. Though truthfully, her disapproval stung. I wanted Cillian's parents to welcome me with open arms, the way Frank and Penny Jackson welcomed him. I wanted them to approve of me enough to root for me.

Stupidly, I thought maybe if they did, then Cillian might see we could be a real love match after all.

When will I ever get these stupid romantic notions out of my head? Bonnie was right; turns out I don't know how to have casual sex.

Cillian's palladium eyes fixate on mine like he's trying to physically laser his assurance. 'My mother's a big Teagan fan. They both are. Mam, because she believes parents should stay together through the good, the bad, and the ugly. Dad, because Teagan likes to party as much as he does. They also move in the same circles as Teagan's parents. It's not personal, I promise.'

It makes sense, I suppose.

'If my mother was to get past the idea that unhappy couples should stay together because they have children, she'd be much better off. Can you see why I'd love her to kick him out?'

'Absolutely.' I arch a single eyebrow. 'It wouldn't work for Penny Jackson, that's for sure.'

'Now, enough about our parents.' Cillian's hands glide from my waist over my backside, a rare playful expression lifts his features. 'Show me what you've got under that dress.'

'Not so fast.' My fingers trail across his chest. 'I just need to check something.'

'What is it?' He glances towards our luggage which the porter set by our bed.

I motion between us. 'Is this a date?'

'Is that a trick question?' His head inclines to the side.

'No.' I bite back my smile.

'A date. A fake date. Why do we need to label it?' He rubs a thumb across his smooth-shaven jawline suspiciously. 'Call it what you like. The end result is the same. I'm going to spread you out across that queen-sized bed, like the queen you are, and worship every inch of your beautiful body.'

Is it any wonder my brain keeps confusing him as my perfect match when he comes out with lines like that?

Energy pulses like a live wire between us.

'I look forward to it. But first, it's my turn to take care of you.' Something I doubt anyone has done for him in a very long time.

Chapter Twenty-Six

CILLIAN

Ava pushes me backwards towards a huge throne like armchair in the corner of the room.

'Sit.' She demands, a cat-like smile lifting her luscious lips.

I hesitate. This isn't part of the plan.

The plan is to worship her.

To build her up.

Especially given my mother's aloofness earlier. The first chance I get, I will pull her up on it.

I can't give Ava what she's looking for long term, but I can give her what she needs right now. Show her how beautiful she is. Teach her her worth. Repair her self-esteem since the last twat she dated shattered it.

Her worshipping *me* never came into it.

Backing away from me, she points her finger motioning me to stay, like she's training a puppy.

Opening her suitcase, she pulls out a bottle that looks suspiciously like a 1999 Middleton Very Rare whiskey. It must have cost hundreds of euros.

'Ava ...'

'Indulge me.' She pleads, but I get the feeling it's me who's about to be indulged.

Scanning the room, her focus lands on two small glasses. She opens the whiskey and pours even measures into the tumblers.

'I figured I owe you, after last night.' She struts across the room and hands me a glass.

'You owe me nothing.' Despite my protests, my heart rate doubles, and blood pulses furiously to my pants.

'What if want to repay the favour though?' Neat, white teeth nip at her lower lip as she drops to her knees in front of me.

'There was no favour. What happened last night was as much for my benefit as yours.' Getting her off gives me a different kind of kick. One I can relive in the shower with my right hand long after this comes to its inevitable end.

Perfectly manicured fingers reach for my buckle. 'You described your perfect date on your sign-up form. That's what you're going to get. So, sit back, sip your whiskey, and let me do this for you.' Lust lights her eyes as she tosses my own words straight back in my face, 'It's for my benefit, as well as yours.'

'Can you just do me one favour?'

'Anything.' Her voice is low and husky.

'Take your dress off. You're so fucking beautiful, Ava, it's a crying shame when you're covered.'

She lifts her dress, revealing another set of those stunning lace hold-ups. As requested, she's not wearing any panties. I inhale a ragged breath, exhale it slowly and watch as her nipples harden beneath lace so transparent, it might as well not be there.

'Stunning.' Without taking my eyes from her beautiful body, I take a sip of amber-coloured liquid. It's exquisite, but it has nothing on the woman who's on her knees for me. The one who I've known all of two weeks but knows exactly what I want.

What I need.

Who I am.

'Let someone take care of you for once, Cillian.' She places her own drink on the floor and pushes my torso back until my spine is flush with the chair.

My shoulders drop. I give in to her.

The breathy moan she utters as she undoes my trousers zips straight to my already weeping cock.

'I've wondered what you tasted like for months.' She rolls her tongue over my tip and our groan of pleasure is simultaneous. She takes me into her mouth and sucks.

It's heaven.

It's hell.

I don't stand a chance of lasting. Her provocative purrs and heady hums of satisfaction are enough to make me blow on their own.

'Ava.' I caress her thick glossy hair and scrape my fingers over her scalp. 'Fuck, that's perfect, baby.'

Goosebumps ripple across her flesh. She tilts her head up, her lust-filled eyes snap to mine. Desire thrums between us. I've never experienced intimacy like it.

She glances at the whiskey in my hand, arches an eyebrow and halts her mouth. I gather she wants me to drink. She's determined to give me the full 'perfect date' experience, but nothing is more intoxicating than watching her mouth wrapped around me. She's so perfect it's practically painful.

I pull the glass to my lips and take a mouthful. The alcohol has nothing on the blood burning its way through my veins right now.

Seemingly satisfied, Ava continues working me. From her breathy little moans, I'd swear she was relishing this experience the same way I am. Savouring every second. Memorising every detail.

My legs tremble and tighten, I'm hanging on by a thread. I want to finish so badly but I don't want this to end. Holding my breath, I arch backwards but Ava grips my thighs tighter, digging her fingers in to my skin, pinning me in place. Watching on from under those thick fluttering lashes, she silently pleads me to let go. As if she needs to taste me, as badly as I need to taste her.

My release tears through me, so powerful I feel like roaring. Rippling waves of ecstatic relief flood every single cell. I'm drowning in the most hedonistic experience of my life.

Ava watches on with smouldering eyes. We're sealed in a stare so powerful it's like we're connected as one. My pleasure is hers. I stroke her jawline as her mouth slows to stop.

'That was transcendent.' *And so are you.*

She kisses my cock before rocking back onto her knees and picking up her whiskey glass, clinking it against mine in a toast. 'To your perfect date. Cheers.'

Worryingly, it's worse than that.

I think she may be my perfect woman.

I down the remainder of the whiskey like it's a twenty-euro bottle of Jameson available in every Tesco in the country, instead of one of the rarest whiskeys around.

The only thing I want to savour right now is Ava.

Dropping the glass on the carpet beside me, I lean forward and swipe a finger through her wet heat. She's saturated. Blood crusades to my greedy cock again.

'You're soaked.' I slide my fingers through her slickness and her head rolls back with pleasure. I love how she's still on her knees for me, but not nearly as much as I'm going to love getting her on her back, spread-eagle across that bed.

'What do you want Ava? What do you need? Just say the

words.' My lips blaze a trail across her clavicle, and she whimpers.

Her hand covers mine. 'That's perfect.' The urgency in her voice is palpable. My girl needs to get off. So, I'm going to get her off, then I'm going to worship her.

'Swap seats with me.' I stand from the chair. She cries out in an animalistic protest as my hand leaves her body. I lift her into the seat and get on my knees. And not because anyone owes anyone anything. It's because the need to watch her unravel is addictive.

I part her legs and bury my face between them, rolling my tongue over her sweet spot. Her pelvis arches and I slide one hand beneath her peachy asscheek and squeeze. I slip a finger in her centre, pumping her until she cries out my name like a prayer.

'Don't stop.' She watches on, through hazy eyes.

We have a connection. It's primal. But it's so much more than that. There's something way bigger than I've ever experienced blazing between us.

A mutual respect. A deep knowing. A tenderness that I never dreamed I was capable of.

When she shakes and shudders and clenches on my fingers, her undoing is my undoing.

I'm not sure I'll ever be the same again.

When her body finally stills, I pepper her inner thighs with tiny feather-light kisses.

We don't speak. We don't need to. I carry her to the bed, place her gently on the cool, smooth sheets and unbutton my shirt. Those glazed eyes blink and then refocus. Good. She's ready for round two. Or is it round three? Who cares. The need to bury myself inside her is all-consuming.

I pull a silver square from my pocket and tear it open, sheathing my throbbing cock.

Her legs fall open giving me the most stunning view. I

drop my trousers and boxers and crawl up the bed towards her, kissing, licking, and sucking as I go. That lace bra might be transparent but it's in my way. I tug it down until her flawless breasts spill over the top. Taking her nipple in my mouth I suck, and she gasps.

I smile. Really smile, without holding back. It's the first real one I've ever offered her. She's given me more of herself than any woman ever has. It's time I give her some of me. The part I normally keep stowed away behind that clipped exterior.

Ava Jackson makes me happy, and it's time she saw it.

Our eyes meet and her lips lift into a dizzying grin. 'Hold it right there.' She teases. 'This is a Kodak moment if ever I saw one.'

'Baby, if this moment was captured on camera, they'd call it porn. And I'd have to rip the head from any man that watched it, because I don't share.' I inch myself inside her, careful not to hurt her.

Her hands reach round to my backside and wrench me closer. 'Best we keep this scenario to ourselves then.'

Her thoughts mirror my own.

But it's not the scenario I'm compelled to keep to myself.

It's the woman starring in it.

It's several hours later by the time we reach the majestic bar. Lillian Callaghan watches curiously as Cillian guides me across the room, his hand once again positioned protectively on the base of my spine, stirring a million butterflies in my stomach.

'There you are.' William Callaghan's beady eyes flash between Cillian and me, and it doesn't take a genius to work out what he's envisioning.

The seminal smile that's been present on Cillian's face since our adult Kodak moment evaporates. It's becoming crystal clear why he has such a negative impression of lasting relationships.

Thankfully, William and Lillian aren't the only familiar faces in the bar looking for our attention.

'Cillian!' Beth, Cillian's stunning PA, slides over with an equally attractive auburn-haired woman in tow. Both are dressed to kill in sculpted midi dresses, but where Beth's is more conservative in its cut, the redhead's is almost completely backless. It makes the slit cutting up the thigh of my floor length Victoria Beckham dress look subtle.

Cillian's posture relaxes as Beth greets his parents, introduces her wife, Carly, and provides a general buffer between the Callaghan family.

'What do you want to drink?' Cillian's lips graze my earlobe, his hot breath sending goosebumps rippling across my skin.

'Surprise me.'

He orders me a glass of champagne and buys everyone in the bar a drink as well. Members of his staff trickle in, clustered in groups of three and four, timidly making their way over to greet us. From their hesitant approach, I gather most of them are nervous of their gorgeous grumpy boss. Little do they know that grump is a tiger/teddy bear in disguise.

By seven o'clock the place is packed. Christmas music fills the air. The alcohol's doing a stellar job of breaking down the icy wall which Cillian hides behind from his staff. One of them even musters the courage to ask if he wants to partake in this year's Secret Santa.

I'm about to excuse myself to go to the ladies when a tall, athletic-looking guy with dirty blonde hair and an even dirtier smile struts in. In a black tuxedo and brilliant white shirt, he looks smoother than silk. Startling blue eyes scan the crowd, and a smirk settles on his full lips as he makes a beeline directly for us.

Cillian steps forward to greet him but the blonde-haired Adonis ignores him and grabs me instead, dropping a hand on my hip and a kiss on my cheek.

'Well, well, well.' Bright eyes sparkle with interest. 'I'd heard the rumours; I mean the whole building's been talking about Cillian's new woman. But words failed to capture exactly how exquisite you truly are.'

Cillian's jaw ticks as he glares at the hand on my body and removes it.

Our new companion chuckles as Cillian slides possessively closer.

'Is that right? Well, at least you had access to *some* information. I haven't heard a word about you.' I wink at Cillian.

'I'm Alex Benedict, criminal defence lawyer at your service.' His hand raises to his head in a salute. 'I'm also Cillian's oldest friend. Our mothers were in the labour ward together.'

Cillian's words from a couple of weeks ago float back through my mind. 'Oh, you're the guy who sold his soul to the devil?'

Cillian leans forward and whisper-shouts, 'No, baby, he is the devil.'

A deep, surprised laugh bites from Alex's mouth. 'Touché, *baby*.' He arches a fair eyebrow at Cillian.

Alex turns his attention back to me. 'You know Cillian hasn't brought a woman to a Christmas party in years. Which makes you pretty special.'

I'm foolishly flattered for all of about five seconds before remembering I'm here for a reason, and it's not because I'm special. It's because someone here is reporting back to his ex.

Which I suppose at least gives me the perfect excuse to give them something to report. 'Is that so?' I tilt my head round to Cillian's and our eyes deadbolt. 'I plan on being brought to the next fifty Christmas parties too. Especially if they start the way today did.' The memories of earlier rotate freshly through my mind.

A satisfied smirk touches Cillian's lips as a loud bell chimes through the castle. It's time to move into the ballroom for dinner.

Alex looks up and sighs. 'We'll continue this conversation later.'

'We won't.' Cillian assures him reassuming his resting bastard face, but it doesn't fool me. Not anymore.

The ballroom is as spectacular as I remember with high ceilings, gilded oil painted landscapes, and thick velvet drapes.

There's also another Christmas tree, even larger than the one in the atrium. Fresh flowers and designer candles decorate the tables. I follow Cillian to ours and am relieved we're sitting with Beth and Carly. I'd like to get the opportunity to spend time with Lillian to win her over, but not with William being sleazy, rendering both of us uncomfortable.

Alex is nowhere to be seen, which is a blessing for Cillian's molars, and his blood pressure. He was clearly vexed by Alex's flirtation, but was it because it was an insult to him, or because he's starting to feel something real for me?

The conversation flows effortlessly around us. For once, I sit back and don't say much. Watching the subtle movement of Cillian's lips as he talks is far more entertaining than anything I could come up with.

Oh, God. I've got it bad.

What will I do when this is all over?

When I have to go back to life without Cillian?

When Teagan leaves and he no longer needs me?

A warm hand glides across my thigh beneath the table, caressing my skin with delicate strokes. It's not sensual, it's reassuring. I peep sideways and our eyes meet in a brief but blistering exchange.

How did I ever mistake this man for cold?

Course after course of gourmet delicacies are placed before us.

The food is sublime.

The wine is divine.

But the company; the fleeting touches and lingering glances is what really makes my Huxley Castle experience one of the best evenings of my life.

After dinner, the tables are cleared and stowed away. The room is transformed back into what it's meant to be, a ballroom. A band take to the makeshift stage and blast a mix of modern music and Christmas favourites. The dancefloor fills fast. People sway and jump to the beat.

Cillian does the rounds, making a point of speaking to every one of his employees, even if it's brief. I stick close to Beth and Carly. They're easy company.

A light tap on my shoulder sets the fine hairs on my neck standing. 'May I have this dance?' Alex Benedict's smooth voice soars into my ear from behind.

I swivel on my heel and meet six feet of lean muscle.

'You absolutely may not.' Cillian appears at my side. 'This one is mine.'

'You never dance.' Alex's eyes glint with mischief.

'I do now.' Cillian's tone is final as he pulls me into his chest and nudges me towards the dance floor.

'The next one then?' Alex calls to our backs.

Cillian flicks him the birdie over his shoulder. 'I said she's mine.'

My insides are doing victorious somersaults. He told me himself he never danced with Teagan. He refused to claim her as his, but he just claimed me in the sexiest, most possessive, public way. And I am so here for it.

Lillian and William waltz by us, Lillian's jaw falls to her knees as she takes in Cillian spinning me around the floor. Her dull eyes light with a newfound understanding. She pauses mid-dance, shell-shocked. Her tight lips crack open in an authentic smile. She offers a very brief but very definitive thumbs up before resuming her waltz.

Thank God. It would be awful if we couldn't form some sort of friendship, given how much we both adore her only son.

The beat changes to a slow festive favourite and I snuggle into Cillian's sturdy arms. It feels so right. So perfect. So natural. He dances like a pro. Is there anything he doesn't excel at?

Oh yeah – fairy tales and forevers.

But he's doing a damn good job of pretending.

Chapter Twenty-Eight

CILLIAN

Sunday 10th December

I wake with Ava's lithe body in my arms and her leg draped over my thigh. Worryingly, I could get used to this. Those long lustrous eyelashes flutter like she's dreaming.

Is it me she sees when she's fast asleep? Does she think about me as much as I think about her? For something that's supposed to be fake, this thing between us is starting to feel very real.

Could it ever be?

Ava's parents are living proof that there is such a thing as a love that lasts.

Maybe, just maybe ours could too.

Though her comments in the car yesterday rattled me. '*I want to get married here.*'

Marriage was never part of my plan.

Ever.

But the thought of Ava marrying someone else makes my stomach bottom out. Because she's mine. Whether I intended for it to happen or not. I have feelings for her. Big feelings. Ones that devour me. Ones that are too early to voice out loud. Ones that I'm not sure I'll *ever* be able to say out loud.

Alex flirting with Ava last night only served to further prove what I already know. I want her, for real. I publicly claimed her with zero hesitation.

But how can I keep her, when I'll never be able to give her what she wants? The fairy tale and forever.

Even if I could bring myself to risk my own heart, my own life, I have another person to think of. One whose heart's been through too much already.

'That's a very pensive expression.' Ava murmurs, snuggling closer. She's unbelievably affectionate. Even in her sleep.

I never realised how lonely I was, how ravenous for tenderness I was, until she ploughed into my life and filled the fissures of my fragile heart.

I've never been one to beat around the bush.

'I was thinking this thing between us is starting to feel very real.' I bring her fingers to my lips and kiss them, rolling from my back onto my side to face her.

She blinks hard and reaches for my torso, tracing the line between my pecs with her fingers. 'Wow.'

My chest tightens. 'Did I read it wrong?'

Huge doe-like eyes flick up to meet mine. 'No.' She pauses, like she's considering her next words carefully. I'm sensing a 'but ...'

A big one.

Instead, she opts for, 'I've never been very good at casual sex.'

'There's nothing casual about the sex we've been having.' I place my palm on her hip, brushing circles over her silky skin. 'This thing between us, it's different. It's more.'

More than anything I've experienced before.

More than anything I ever wanted to experience before.

And possibly more than I'm able for.

Ava is ridiculously in tune with my deepest inner thoughts. 'But you never wanted "more".' She wets her lower lip and waits for me to disagree with her, but I can't.

'And "more" is all you've ever wanted.' It's not a question, but yet it is.

She nods. 'It's true. I've never made a secret of it. I want the kind of relationship my parents have. I want a husband who's my best friend, but who also wants to bend me over the kitchen counter while the kids are out.' Water forms in the whites of Ava's eyes.

'Kids?' I check.

'Yep. I want it all.'

My heartbeats like a drum. 'And you deserve it all.'

Her head bobs in another nod and the column of her throat flexes as she swallows thickly. 'But I also want you, Cillian. You're the most amazing man I've ever met. Even though you try and hide it behind a façade of being a sullen, scary lawyer, you're sweet, and kind and tender.'

'Please don't ever call me sweet again. Or I'll have to bend you over and bang you into next Christmas.'

The corner of her mouth angles upwards in a wry smile. 'At least we can both agree we want "more" of that.'

I trace her lower lip with my thumb. 'I don't want to lead you on, but I don't want to let you go after your brother's wedding either. I don't know if I can ever give you what you want. But the thought of another man giving it to you makes me sick to my stomach.'

'I understand. We come from very different families. Different life lessons.' She reaches for my hair, tousling it with that tenderness again.

'Look, Ava, I don't make promises I can't keep. Ever. So, the only thing I'm going to promise you is that if you are willing to give this thing between us a go, I'll try.'

Light flashes in her pupils. 'You mean, a real relationship?'

I swallow hard. 'Yes. But can we take it slow? Really slow? We've raced to this point in only a couple of weeks, and I'm fucking terrified if we keep up this momentum where we might be in another few.'

'Okay, baby steps.' She presses her lips to mine gently, then pulls away. 'I better put a t-shirt on. If we're going to take things slowly, we should probably go back to second base, which, I think, means you can feel my boobs over my shirt, but not under.' Her eyes sparkle with mischief. 'Tell me if I'm wrong.'

Pushing her onto her back I pin her wrists above her head and nudge myself between her thighs. 'You're wrong. The only base we're going back to is bas-ics. Basic instincts that is. Now open your legs wider. I'm starving for something they don't serve in the dining room.'

'Do I seriously have to do this?' I moan to Beth as she hands me a Santa suit, the winter wind whipping from the beach to my face. Velvet Strand is packed with spectators and racers alike, sporting crimson Santa hats and silly smiles, including many of my staff who are also nursing hangovers this morning.

'Yes.' Beth chucks a Santa suit unceremoniously at me. 'We're one of the main sponsors of this event.'

'Precisely!' I throw my hands up in the air in exasperation. 'I've done enough.'

'Not as far as your daughter is concerned.' Beth points to across the street where Matilda's car is parked. Phoebe's button nose is pressed up against the foggy window as she peers back at me and waves. My lips crack open with a smile at the sight of my daughter.

'She can't wait to see daddy dress up as Santa for the race,' Beth coos.

'Why did you have to mention it? She'd have been equally happy to spend the day ice-skating and drinking hot chocolate instead.'

'Because it's a family fun day! And I thought it would be nice for her! Besides, Matilda has to go to her son's birthday later, so I told her to bring Phoebe here. She has met Ava, right?'

Beth knows she has because I spilled my guts about it the second I walked in the office the morning after the Ferris wheel night, agonising over whether meeting a 'friend' of Daddy's could be detrimental to my daughter's mental health.

Beth assured me it wasn't, especially given she's never been introduced to any other female 'friends' along the way.

'What's wrong? Frightened you're going to embarrass yourself in front of your girlfriend?' Beth nods towards a nearby coffee cart where Ava's ordering her caffeine fix.

I'm about to open my mouth and say "she's not my girlfriend" when it hits me square in the chest that she is. And it's one label I'm very comfortable with.

'Phoebe might buy the 'friend' shit – but I saw the way you looked at Ava last night.' She wiggles her eyebrows. 'And my room is next to yours.'

'For fuck's sake.' I don't get embarrassed, but if I did, my face would be on fire right now.

'Oh, look.' Beth's gaze travels towards the coffee cart where Alex is sidling up to Ava in a fucking Santa suit ready for the race. 'Alex isn't afraid of embarrassing himself. You know, I heard he's a really good runner.' Beth knows exactly where to poke to get a reaction.

'Fine.' I glance down at the ridiculous outfit in my hands.

There's no way Alex is going to beat me. Not at this race. Not with his annual case statistics, and not when it comes to impressing Ava.

Alex and I have been friends as long as I can remember,

but there's always been a sibling-like rivalry between us. Where my father was absent a lot, his mother was too. It was something we bonded over in our formative years through school, and then later college, many moons ago. The competition between us has always been playful, but ferocious. I know if I truly needed a friend he'd be there. But I also know, if he thought he had half a chance with my woman, he'd probably take that too.

He interprets the saying 'all is fair in love and war' literally.

'I'll go get Phoebe from Matilda.' Beth offers.

'Thanks, I'll get changed.' And get my woman away from the second biggest womaniser I know. 'I'll meet you back here in two minutes.'

Ava looks up as I stride towards her, grasping a steaming Styrofoam cup. Her entire face lights like Phoebe's as she spots me. 'Oh my god, are you entering the race?'

'I'm going to win the damn thing.'

Alex sniggers from beside me. 'Not a hope. I beat you in college, and I'll beat you today.'

I ignore the smug look on his face. 'Ava, do you mind if Phoebe watches with you? Beth has to sort out the paperwork for the sponsorship.'

'Sure.' Ava doesn't hesitate. In fact, if her tone is anything to go by, she's thrilled to be asked.

'She's over there with Beth.' I point to Matilda's car. 'I'll just get changed, then I'll be over in two minutes.' I press a kiss to Ava's temple, not just to mark her as mine in front of Alex, but because the urge to touch her overwhelms me.

Ava strides towards Phoebe who whoops in delight at the sight of her.

'Wow, she's met your daughter?' Alex's eyebrow hitches. 'Must be serious.'

'It is.' Seriously worrying how natural this feels.

Seriously fast how things are moving.

Seriously scary how fast I'm falling for Ava Jackson. Because that's exactly what's happening and even as the knowledge terrifies me, it's exhilarating too.

'Just be careful, man. You know I love to stir the pot and get your back up, but seriously, you've got more than just you to think about.' His stare flicks to where Phoebe is throwing herself into Ava's arms.

'Careful, Alex, anyone would think you care.'

'For some weird reason, I actually do,' Alex mutters.

I don't win the Santa race. But neither does Alex. I beat him by three seconds. It's enough for me. Especially when my daughter and girlfriend are screaming and clapping at the side of the finish line with Savannah Kingsley, and her twin daughters.

Alex shakes his head as we both pant for breath. 'You win some you lose some, I guess.'

Today, I feel like a winner. And it has nothing to do with a run and everything to do with the beautiful brunette holding hands with my daughter.

Chapter Twenty-Nine

AVA

Wednesday 13th December

Even though we agreed on baby steps, nothing is infantile about the way this thing is unfolding between Cillian and me.

We spent hours on the phone last night, talking until two a.m. about everything and anything. Tonight, we're taking Phoebe ice-skating as soon as he gets out of court.

It's going well, but perhaps not the way we agreed on Sunday morning.

I glance at the clock. It's almost five. Cleo and Violet are still trying to catch up on the influx of sign-up forms. The way things have transpired financially, I don't need Nate's investment.

Bonnie's meeting our first ever marriage match to see if we can sponsor their wedding. Their love story has been picked up by a local radio station and they're being interviewed live tomorrow. It would be great publicity for us to get on board as a sponsor, and it would mean they could have the wedding of their dreams. I'm really hoping they'll go for it.

My phone vibrates on my desk.

Cillian.

Outside

I leap to my feet, waving at the girls as I pass their desks. 'Don't stay too late. There's nothing that can't wait until tomorrow.'

'Sure.' They smile and wave me off.

The moon hangs low in the midnight sky, a silvery orb almost the same shade as Cillian's stunning irises. He waits with Phoebe, clutching her hand in his. Both their faces light as I step out of the building.

'Ava!' Phoebe throws herself at me while Cillian watches on with an expression I can't read.

I pull the little girl into my arms. She's bundled up in a pink puffer coat and matching woolly hat and gloves. 'How are you, sweetheart?'

'I'm so excited. Sarah Snowden said the ice rink is twice the size as it was last year. Can you skate? Will you hold my hand?'

Cillian's lips touch my cheek, heating me from the inside out.

'Yes, I can skate, and yes, I'll hold your hand.'

'How was work?' Cillian asks, running a palm over my lower back.

'Great. If things keep going the way they have since the party, I won't need Nate's investment.'

'Wow. That's amazing.' That palm drops to my ass and squeezes. A million volts of electricity soar across my spine.

We stroll along Grafton Street towards St. Stephen's Green and through the Christmas markets. Phoebe slips one hand in mine and the other hand in Cillian's. She swings her arms back and forth with glee. People glance at us, offering smiles and nods. Phoebe's grin appears to be infectious to just about everyone we pass.

They probably think she's my daughter.

She's so adorable, I wish she was. My ovaries are still ticking like a time bomb, especially given the hot mate I've found, but he made no promises for the future, only that he'll try. I know how he feels about marriage, but how does he feel about having more kids?

It's ridiculously early days to even be thinking this way but Penny Jackson always maintained that when you know, you know.

And I know. The knowledge beats like a familiar base through my body.

But I need to be careful not to scare Cillian off, because even though he seems every bit as smitten with me as I am with him, we agreed to take it slowly. Outside of the bedroom, at least.

Phoebe continues to chat incessantly with the enthusiasm that only a six-year-old can muster as we collect our skates. 'So, the nativity play is next week. I'd love you to come but we're only allowed to take two people and Dad and Mam are already going, but I'll make sure Daddy takes loads of pictures and maybe he can even video the bit where I have the baby Jesus.'

Cillian whispers over Phoebe's head and shrugs. 'Speaking of Teagan, it looks like the message has finally ben delivered. She hasn't showed up unannounced since last week and she texted to ask if she could take Phoebe to stay at her parents' house tomorrow night.'

'That's good, isn't it?'

'It's progress. It's been a long time coming.'

I nod. I can only imagine how hard it is being a single parent, running a business, and trying to explain to a six-year-old where her mother is.

'Teagan is taking her Friday night too.'

'For Nate's stag night?' My eyes widen. After Nate's inces-sant texts, I finally caved and gave him Cillian's number. Not for a second did I expect Cillian to agree to go on the stag. Then again, that was before things got real between us.

'Yes. For Nate's stag. Though, I could think of a million other things I'd rather be doing with you, especially in my big empty house.'

'There's always tomorrow, isn't there?' I don't want to force myself on him two nights in a row.

'Absolutely. I took the liberty of booking a table at Prestige.'

Prestige is one of the fanciest restaurants in the city. The venison is to die for.

'Oh, you did, did you?' These baby steps are more like giant leaps.

'Pack an overnight bag.' He shoots me a wink that makes me dizzier than the circles he's skating round me on the ice. 'I want you in my bed.'

Phoebe is a natural. Some kids just are, especially if they're used to roller blades. Within minutes she's skating like a professional. Festive music blares. Multicoloured disco lights rotate and flash on a rapid seamless sequence cascading across the slick white ground. The scent of candy floss and crepes fill the air. We laugh and spin and slide around. I almost lose it when a teenager bumps past me, but Cillian grabs my hand, steadying me before I can fall – to the ground, at least.

Our eyes collide. His brim with a display of euphoria I wouldn't have dreamed he was capable of. When our time is up and we hand back our skates, Phoebe turns to me.

'Are you coming home with us? Matilda left a pot of chilli. Do you like chilli? It burns my mouth but I kind of like it.' Phoebe adjusts her hat on her head, lifting it from where it keeps falling over her eyes.

'No, sweetie, I—'

'Do you have somewhere else you need to be?' Cillian's eyebrows hike together.

'No, but I ...' Going home with him and his daughter isn't taking it slow.

'Well, it's settled then.' He nods and Phoebe jumps in the air with glee.

As Cillian crunches up the driveway, I imagine what it would be like to live here. To live with them. My chest twinges with a longing so acute it physically hurts. I love my apartment, but I've always known it's not my forever home.

Cillian would probably run a mile if he had any idea of the stuff going through my head right now. Especially if he had any idea I've watched and wanted him for months from afar.

'Are you okay?' he asks quietly as he pulls to a stop at the front door.

I unclip my seat belt. 'Perfect. Thank you.'

'That, we can both agree on.'

'Ava, want to come and play in my room while daddy heats the chilli? I've got two more dolls since you were last here.' Phoebe pipes up from the back seat.

'Sure, if that's okay with your dad.' Cillian nods, opens the driver door, and hops round to open mine, then Phoebe's.

'They're both LOL dolls. Mammy bought them for me. And she bought a huge bag of treats.' Phoebe explains.

'Guilt.' Cillian mouths at me as he unlocks the front door and ushers us in. The delicious aroma of roasted tomatoes tickles my nostrils.

Phoebe shows me her dolls and we dress them up in their different outfits until Cillian calls us down for dinner. The table is set for three, an open bottle of red wine sits in the centre next to a plate of steaming buttery garlic ciabatta.

Cillian carries over our plates, his rolled-up shirt sleeves reveal strong, deft forearms that I want to grab onto while ...

'Sit next to me.' Phoebe insists, patting the huge oak table.

'Thank you.' I inhale the steaming hot food placed in front of me. It looks and smells divine.

Cillian pours two generous glasses of wine into crystal glasses and hands me one.

'Cheers. Thank you for having me.' I lift my glass up to clink Phoebe's glass of water.

'I've got a feeling it's us who should be thanking you for having us.' Cillian murmurs.

The buzzer sounds from the front door and Phoebe throws her fork down and leaps to her feet. 'Mammy?'

'No sweetheart,' Cillian stands, following her out into the hallway. 'It's probably a delivery. Mammy's coming tomorrow, remember?' Cillian sighs, 'Phoebe don't open the gate. It could be anyone.'

The beeping noise that follows suggests she'd already pressed the button.

I put down my fork and listen as Cillian lectures Phoebe on the dangers of opening the gate. That it could be anyone out there.

'But it could be Mammy.' The hope in her voice is heart breaking.

'Mammy isn't ...' Cillian's voice stops mid-sentence.

'Mammy!' Phoebe squeals.

'Teagan, I told you, you can't just turn up unannounced like this.' Cillian's stern voice travels closer.

'Don't worry, this is the last time. I'm leaving tonight. I came to say goodbye.' Teagan's voice cracks with emotion and I feel guilty for listening, but it's not like I've got any other choice.

'Why bother this time? You don't normally.' Cillian bites.

'What about the nativity?' Phoebe wails. 'Mammy you promised you'd stay. Please don't go.'

My chest cracks wide open. I choke back a sob.

'Is *she* here?' Teagan demands, footsteps approach the kitchen. A deep sense of unease washes over me even though I've done nothing wrong.

I stand as Teagan enters the kitchen. She's wearing jeans and a grey hoody. Her face is pale and tear-streaked.

'Teagan, I—' It's the first time I've seen her since things got real between Cillian and me, and for some reason, I don't know what to say to her. Because there are no words. If I was her, if I'd had a man like Cillian and lost him, I'd be devastated too.

But then again, she didn't lose him. She never had him in the first place.

Chapter Thirty

CILLIAN

Every time I dare to hope for some sort of normality, some sort of lasting stability, Teagan blows in like a gale and destroys everything. I was a fool to think this peace would last. Nothing ever lasts.

'I was talking to your mother. I heard you two had quite the night at Huxley Castle. I heard you were *dancing*.' She spits the word like it's poison. 'I'm the mother of your child. You never once even sat next to me in public, and yet you're canoodling on a dancefloor with some floozy you've just met.'

'That's enough, Teagan.' It's not about the dancing and we both know it. It's what it represents. That I put my hands on Ava and claimed her as mine.

Teagan scoops a sniffling Phoebe up and places her on the kitchen counter next to her, rubbing her little legs in what's supposed to be a soothing gesture. If she knew her own daughter at all she'd know the best way to soothe her is to play with her hair.

I exhale a heavy breath and reach my arms out to Phoebe, but she shakes her head, staring only at her mother.

Teagan tilts her face towards Phoebe's. 'I need to go away for a while.'

'You don't *need* to!' Phoebe shouts. 'You *want* to!' Her astuteness is shocking. I thought I'd done a fairly good job plastering the cracks but, clearly, I was wrong.

'No, sweetie, this time, I need to. Mammy has to go and do a bit of soul-searching.' Teagan turns to Cillian. 'Alone.'

If you believe that, you'll believe anything. It's on the tip of my tongue to ask what his name is, but firstly, I wouldn't do that in front of Phoebe, and secondly, I don't care.

'Seriously, I need to sort myself out. I'm getting too old to flit around like a used to.' Teagan's blue eyes well. 'I had hoped things might have been different.' She glances between Ava and me. 'But it's clear they never will be. I know I only have myself to blame but it still hurts.'

Ava watches on, wringing her hands, discomfort etched into every fine line of her face.

Welcome to my messy family. If this doesn't put her off, nothing will.

Teagan stares at Ava with a cross between envy and curiosity and says, 'He never looked at me, the way he looks at you. Not even before I got pregnant.'

'That's enough.' I eye Phoebe pointedly. I've made it my mission to protect her from Teagan's toxicity and I'm not about to expose her to it now.

Teagan takes Phoebe's two hands in hers. 'Mammy is going away for a little while to think about where I'm going to live.'

Phoebe sobs harder and Teagan wipes her tears.

'I'm going to buy my own place. I'm not sure where yet, but I'm going to make sure you have your own room there and you can come and stay whenever you want, as much as you want. I just need a bit of time, okay?'

When I reach out for Phoebe a second time, she drops

her mother's hands and lunges for me. Tears streak her tiny cheeks and my insides twist in agony for her. Smoothing her hair behind her ear I 'shhh' her, rocking her gently back and forth in my arms. 'It's okay, princess. It's okay.'

'It's not okay,' she cries, thumping my chest. 'She always does this. She always leaves.'

'I'll call.' Teagan promises.

'You'd better this time.' I warn her with a growl.

Teagan makes her way towards the doorway, glancing back over her shoulder at a shell-shocked looking Ava. 'Take care of them', she says, sashaying down the hallway without looking back.

The front door slams shut, and I return to my seat at the table, positioning Phoebe on my lap. She curls into my chest, her tears soaking my shirt. I wrap my arm around her, and pick up my fork, motioning for Ava to eat. There's no point in ruining a perfectly good meal. It's not the first time Teagan's done this and, sadly, it won't be the last.

'I'm sorry,' I say both to Phoebe and Ava, but for very different reasons.

'Should I go?' Uncertainty flickers in Ava's huge hazel eyes.

'No!' Phoebe protests. 'Please don't leave as well.'

Ava reaches across the table, caressing Phoebe's white-blonde hair. 'Okay, pumpkin. I'm here. I'm not going anywhere.'

Ava resumes her place at the table. The previously care-free atmosphere has been replaced with a dark subdued one, and I can't shake the feeling that I'm responsible.

Is it my fault? Did Teagan go because of my relationship with Ava?

And if she did, wasn't that the whole point?

But what's the alternative? Let Teagan back into our lives

and wait for her to do this a month or two down the line anyway?

Guilt eats at me as I shove my fork around my plate. Eventually, I abandon it in favour of the wine. It was a no-win situation. But at least I didn't give Phoebe or Teagan hope it would ever be any different.

'She always leaves.' Phoebe says repeatedly. 'Did I do something wrong?'

'It's not you, honey.' Ava leans across the table and strokes Phoebe's hair from her face. 'I promise, it's not you. Sometimes people have to do things in their lives before they can truly settle. It's like they haven't found what they're looking for, or something. But shall I tell you a secret, Phoebe, darling?'

Phoebe nods, her watery eyes peeping up from my saturated shirt to meet Ava's.

'Usually, what people are looking for is actually inside of them the whole time. They just need to work it out for themselves. So, whatever happens, you mustn't think it's you. It's your mam. And when she finds that thing that she's missing inside of herself, then she'll be able to be there for you. But until then, you've got daddy. And you've got me, sweetheart, okay.'

'You won't leave us?' Hope lifts Phoebe's tone and she wipes her tears with the back of her hand.

Tumultuous emotion swirls in my stomach as my gaze meets Ava's, her gold-flecked eyes brimming with concern.

'I'm not going anywhere.' Ava offers Phoebe her baby finger. 'Pinky promise.'

I'm utterly torn, terrified of the size and meaning of the promise Ava just made my daughter, and unreservedly impressed that she did.

I rock Phoebe on my lap while Ava clears the dishes away like she's done it a million times before, while making small talk with my daughter in a bid to distract her from Teagan abandoning her once again.

'Did you hear that Santa's going to be at Hollybrooke Hall on Saturday night?' Hollybrooke Hall is a stunning mansion on the outskirts of the city. Every year they put on a fabulous Santa experience for both kids and adults alike.

'It's probably not the real Santa.' I doubt anything in the world would lift Phoebe's spirits tonight, but I appreciate Ava's effort all the same.

'What do you mean, not the real Santa?' Ava puts her hand over her mouth to mask her surprise.

'You know he has a load of helpers who dress like him, coz he can't be everywhere at once,' Phoebe explains glumly. 'I did meet the real one once though. His beard was real, it was definitely him. It was the right colour, and it didn't wobble when he talked.'

'If I made sure it's definitely the real one, would you like to go?'

'Sure.' Phoebe shrugs noncommittally. 'Do you think if I ask him to send my Mam back, he'd be able to work it?'

Anguish crushes my windpipe.

Ava bites her lip and continues to stack the dishwasher.

Eventually, Phoebe's eyelids flutter closed and her breathing settles into a slow even rhythm. 'I'm sorry you had to see all of this. Thank you, for what you said.' We both know I'm not referring to her offer to go see Santa at the mansion. I pinch the bridge of my nose. 'It's important Phoebe knows it's not her fault Teagan breezes in and out like the wind.'

'I'm glad I could help. My heart breaks for her,' Ava whispers, taking the seat next to me and tops up our glasses.

'It gets harder each time.' I exhale a weary breath. 'How can a mother leave her child like that? Nothing in the world would persuade me to leave my daughter.'

'And that's just one of many reasons that you're a brilliant father.' Ava's palm brushes my bicep.

I wet my lips, thinking out loud. 'You really want a family?'

Ava doesn't hesitate. 'Yes.' She picks up her glass, staring thoughtfully over it. 'I hope me saying that doesn't terrify you. It's such early days and I know how you feel about relationships, but I'd be lying if I said anything else.'

Again, I'm torn. Ava's warmth, her empathy and compassion, and the way she listens so attentively when Phoebe speaks leave me in no doubt, she's made to be a mother. But I never envisioned having any more children. Just like I never envision myself getting married. But that was before Ava Jackson hijacked my life with her succulent lips and amorous approach.

My guts knot. Panic flares in my chest.

'Hey.' Ava traces a finger across the back of my hand. 'Baby steps. Don't freak out on me, please.'

It's uncanny how well she can read me already. She pushes back her chair and stands. 'I should go.'

'I'll get you a private hire car if you want to go, but please, don't feel like you have to.' After an announcement like that, she probably thinks she'd better give me a bit of space but selfishly, I don't want to commit to anything, but I don't want to let her go either.

'It's probably for the best. It's been an eventful evening.' She kisses Phoebe's forehead tenderly, before her lips find mine. She pulls away all too soon leaving me hankering for something.

It's that word again.

The one we spoke about in bed last Sunday morning.

More.

But I'm still not sure I'm able for it. No matter how badly I want to be.

Chapter Thirty-One

AVA

Friday 15th December

'Another hot date?' Giles arches a white eyebrow as my heels click across the marble flooring.

'Yeah, with my future sister-in-law and her friends, unfortunately.' I hesitate at the glass revolving doors, drawing my coat tighter around my waist.

'I thought you liked your sister-in-law?' Giles' weathered forehead crinkles further.

'I do. A lot, in fact.' I shrug. 'But not as much as I like the divorce daddy.'

I haven't heard from Cillian all day and an anxious knot is starting to form in my stomach. I'm giving him space after what happened with Teagan on Wednesday night, and the subsequent conversations we had.

Giles sniggers. 'Divorce daddy has a nice ring to it! He's going to the wedding with you, isn't he?'

'Supposed to be.' If Phoebe is okay. She might panic about him going away given what happened on Wednesday. And who could blame her?

'Well, you know what folk my age always say.' Giles tips

his head forward and winks knowingly. 'Going to a wedding is the making of another. Make sure you catch the bouquet!'

'Oh God, I swear Cillian would run for the hills, seriously.'

Giles exhales a deep belly laugh. 'The man would be a fool not to lock you down if he had the chance.'

'Ah, thank you, Giles. It's a shame you're already married.' I grin. 'Though with lines like that, it's not surprising.'

'Have a good night.' He bows as I step out into the dark frosty night. 'I'll see you later.'

'I'll get extra chips if it's before two a.m.,' I promise.

'If that's not wife material, I don't know what is.' He winks and waves.

Holly's friend Savannah, the same celebrity blogger who organised Sunday's Santa Run, is in charge of the hen night. Which is why a gang of Magic Mike lookalikes are currently delivering our cocktails. The tiny black square material tied over their private parts would hardly pass as a handkerchief, let alone an apron.

Once upon a time, I would have ogled. Now, if it's not Cillian Callaghan's, it's not worth a wank.

We're in the VIP area of Heaven On Earth, an upmarket wine bar in Dublin's Temple Bar. It's absolutely packed with Christmas parties, but we're cordoned off from the main area, spread out over a long rectangular table decorated with heart-shaped balloons and cock-shaped confetti.

I know a few of Holly's friends, but not all of them. Savannah is a celebrity in her own right. She started a blog a few years ago, documenting her journey as a single mother to twin girls. Fast forward six years and 'Single Sav' is a household name. She has her own kids clothing brand, numerous luxury properties that she rents out, and is paid thousands to advertise prams and other baby items.

Ashley, Holly's other best friend is the principal of an all-girl Catholic school, St Jude's. Now I think about it, Phoebe goes to St Jude's. Ashley must know her. And Cillian. It's a small world.

Holly's mother isn't invited, not in a mean way, but she is a self-professed pearl-clutcher. She asked if she could do an afternoon tea with Holly, my mother, and Holly's pregnant sister-in-law, Clarissa instead. Looking around now, it was the best decision for everyone.

My mother sits to my right, fanning herself with a napkin as she ogles our waiters. Judging by her glassy eyes, she's hit the sherry hard tonight. 'My oh my, Frank Jackson is in for it when I get home! I must text him and tell him to pop a Viagra now, so he'll be good and ready the second I get in the door. It doesn't make him James Bond, but it does make him Roger Moore.'

She snorts, slapping the table and I roll my eyes, entirely unsurprised. However liberal my parents are when they're sober, they're a million times worse when they've been drinking. 'Jesus, Mam. Too much information.'

'Don't be daft!' She swats the air in front of her face, 'It's what we were put on this planet to do.'

If I had a euro for every time I'd heard that line, I could start a million dating agencies with no investors.

My sister Natalie sits to my left. She's texting someone underneath the table. It must be a man. A hot one, because why else would she be looking at her phone, and not the naked granite glutes giving my mother hot flushes.

'Who are you texting?' I nudge her ribs and she jumps.

'No one.' My sister throws her phone into her hot pink clutch bag and flicks her pristinely blow-dried hair from her shoulder.

'Liar!'

She trails her fingers over her lips in a zipping motion, twists, then pretends to throw an imaginary key across the room.

'How's lover-boy today?' She leans in closer to be heard over the cackling hens and eclectic Christmas music blasting from the speakers.

'Good, I think.' I haven't seen him since Wednesday, but I suppose it's only Friday. With everything that's happened I'm sure he has his hands full reassuring Phoebe. 'Bar a couple of texts yesterday, I haven't spoken to him.'

'Is he at Nate's stag tonight?' Natalie asks over the rim of her salt-crusted margarita glass.

'No, he didn't want to leave Phoebe after everything.' I'd already filled Natalie in on the events of Wednesday night over coffee yesterday lunch time.

'It's a lot to take on. I know you're mad about him,' she smooths down the cerise satin dress rising over her thighs beneath the table, 'but I'm not sure I could handle all that baggage.'

'We all have baggage, whether it's in the form of small people relying on us, or distasteful exes who leave scars on our soul.' My words come out harsher than I intend, probably because her comments hit a nerve.

After witnessing Teagan leave the other night, I can fully appreciate Cillian's caution at letting another person into their circle. The pressure feels all too real.

Natalie raises her palms like a white flag. 'Chill, I didn't mean it like that.'

'Sorry, I didn't mean to snap. Let's get another cocktail.'

'Great idea. But no more for Mam.' Natalie jerks her head towards our mother who's accosting one of the 'waiters'.

'Get up on the table and give us a dance, will you? Ripple those abs! Show us what your mama gave you!'

Holly, Savannah, and Ashley are doubled over across the table, clutching their stomachs. Holly's wearing a white dress, complete with a pink sash bearing the logo Bride To Be and she has actual tears streaming down her cheeks.

I turn to my sister, 'Imagine Holly is willingly signing up to be part of this fucking family.'

'That's love for you, right?' Natalie and I watch our mother cheering as two nearly naked guys get up on top of the table.

'That's it, I'm ringing Dad. He needs to come and get her before she drinks anymore.' I pull my phone from the pocket of my bronze-coloured shift dress and glance down at the screen. No messages from Cillian. I hope I didn't overstep the mark by offering to take Phoebe to Hollybrooke Hall. My intention was to calm, not complicate things.

Then he had to go and ask if I wanted children of my own.

'Good idea.' Natalie nods, keeping her eyes on our mother. 'Go outside where it's quieter.'

I glance at my phone as I pass through the throng of people, bopping along to the beat. A tall, blond hunk of a guy in a Santa hat pulls my hand as I pass. 'Dance with me!' He begs, tugging me towards his friends.

A powerful arm slides around my waist and locks me backwards against a rock-solid torso. 'Sorry pal, she's spoken for.' Cillian's familiar gruff tone bursts past my ear.

I spin on my heels to face him, drinking in those chiselled cheekbones and razor-sharp eyes. A small smirk lifts the corner of his lascivious lips.

'What are you doing here?'

'I came to see you.' His palms roam round to my back, tracing over my spine.

'But it's a hen night.' My mouth drops open, staring in wonder at this gorgeous man in front of me. The one I've spent all day obsessing about. Ok, who am I kidding, all year, truth be told.

His low chuckle permeates the air between us. 'I won't stay long. I just had to see you.'

Relief trickles through my core.

I didn't terrify him the other night.

'When you didn't call, I wondered ...' Hot lips crash against mine, halting me from finishing the rest of my sentence. His tongue swipes through my mouth dancing, teasing, possessing me. The rest of the bar fades away. It's just him and me.

When he does tear his lips from mine, regret spins in his silver eyes. 'I should let you get back to it.'

'Wait, who's with Phoebe? How is she today?'

'She's at Sarah Snowden's for a sleepover. When I picked her up from school today and she said she'd been invited, I swear I've never been happier to hear that name.'

The cogs whir in my brain as a plan formulates. 'Did you drive here?'

'Yes.' His eyes fall to my lips, then up again.

'Is there any chance you could take my mother home? She's had one too many and she's about three minutes away from tearing the apron from Magic Mike's crotch with her teeth.'

'Why does that not surprise me? Let's hope her daughter is better behaved.' He tightens his grip on my ass and squeezes. 'I was hoping to take you home, but I suppose I'll settle for your mother.' He teases, and it's my turn to squeeze his ass.

'Well, if you play your cards right, you could do both.' I lift my eyebrows suggestively.

A low, carnal rumble sounds from the base of his throat. 'Have you got any underwear on beneath this poor excuse of a dress?'

'Yes.' I pout indignantly.

'Good, but now I'm here, we'll have to rectify that imme-diately. Go get your mother. The quicker we get her home, the quicker I can get you home.'

I crane my neck to the VIP area just as two Magic Mikes hoist my gyrating mother on to the table with them. Oh. My. God. If anyone had any idea that she was the mother of one of the most famous actors in Hollywood, the paps would be crawling all over this. It's not the type of publicity Nate needs before his wedding.

'Get her down.' I mouth to Natalie, who's laughing and clapping along with the rest of the hens. Penny Jackson needs no encouragement.

Cillian spots her and lets out a long whistle. 'Wow. It's not hard to see where Nate got his flair for drama from.'

'You're telling me.'

Chapter Thirty-Two

CILLIAN

'Are you sure you won't come in for a drink?' Penny asks for the hundredth time. She stumbles across the doorstep.

Fuck my life. I could be wrong, but it looks like Ava's father is sporting a serious wigwam in his chinos.

Could this family get anymore inappropriate?

And why am I so okay with it?

'Don't be ridiculous, Penny.' Frank pulls his wife into his arms, steadying her.

Penny eyes widen as she slams backwards into him. She giggles and reaches round to his crotch. I'm mentally scarred for life.

'It's Friday, the kids have plans. Just like I have for you,' Frank says.

'Gross.' Ava spins on her heels. 'Make sure she drinks some water, Dad, or she'll be like a grizzly bear tomorrow.'

I grip Ava's hand in mine as we saunter down the drive-way. Penny wasn't the only woman drinking, though Ava appears to be holding her alcohol much better than her mother. 'Your parents are hilarious.'

'They're not right in the head.' Ava sniggers, shaking her head. 'But I wouldn't have them any other way.

I open the door of the X5 and slap her ass as she climbs in. 'My place or yours?'

'Mine. But we need to make a quick stop on the way.'

Twenty minutes later, we arrive at Ava's apartment block in Ballsbridge.

The white-haired door attendant manning Ava's hallway is the same guy who let me in a couple of weeks ago when I arrived with the pizza. His entire face lights when he spots Ava approaching through the revolving doors. Wordlessly, she hands him the white bag she insisted we stop for.

The scent of vinegar fills the air, and he sniffs appreciatively, his hearty laugh echoing off the marble flooring. 'I told you – wife material.'

She pats his arm. The woman has a heart of gold. 'We'll have to save the chat for another night.'

'We surely will.' Aged blue eyes blaze into mine with an unspoken warning. *Treat her right. She's one of the good ones.*

I nod and follow Ava into the cold chrome lift. We don't speak. I wouldn't know where to start.

I spent the last forty-eight hours either comforting Phoebe, or comforting myself, just for very different reasons.

Life as I know it is changing.

I'm changing.

To the point I don't even recognise the guy grinning back at me in the mirror.

The guy who's thinking about his girlfriend and laughing like a lunatic. Wondering what he can possibly buy her for Christmas, something that will show her how much he cares because he's not great with words, and too much talk of the future terrifies him.

I barely slept a wink on Wednesday night. Not because

Teagan left, but because Ava didn't leave when Phoebe asked her not to. She stayed for my daughter, a girl she's only met a handful of times yet was so desperate to comfort and reassure.

Did I freak out a bit at the talk of her wanting kids?

Absolutely.

No one can do a complete one-eighty overnight.

But am I open to the possibility of it at some point in the distant future?

Yes, I think I am. Because one thing's for sure, Ava Jackson is one in a million. There's no way I'm going to stand back and let another man give her all the things she deserves because I was too chicken shit to even try.

She's like no one I've ever met before. Or am likely to meet again.

As long as we take it slowly, it'll be okay.

Ava opens the door to her apartment. Moonlight shines in through the balcony doors casting a luminous glow on Ava's pristine home. Its decadence is unquestionable, but it's devoid of any decorations, or any of Ava's warmth or personality.

'I can't believe you didn't put the decorations up. I thought we talked about this.'

'We did talk about it.' Ava kicks off her heels by the door and rubs her right heel. 'Not everyone wants a pink sparkly tree cluttering their home, Cillian.'

'You can't fool me.' I hoist her up on to her kitchen work top and take over the foot massage she started to give herself. 'I saw the way you were staring lustfully at those metallic baubles.'

'No, I believe it was you I was staring lustfully at, thinking about your "metallic baubles" while you had your face between my legs.' Her head rolls back as I knead the balls of her feet with my thumbs. 'Besides, I told you, it's pointless just for me. Christmas trees are for couples and families.'

'And aren't we a couple?' I cup her chin and angle her face towards mine. 'Besides, I told you, nothing's pointless "just for you". You're the warmest person I've ever met but your apartment is cold. I hate the thought of you sitting here alone.'

'I'm not alone. I have you here now.'

'Tonight, you do, but when I have to get back to my responsibilities, when I'm in my house, I want you to have some light on these dark December nights. I'm going to buy you a Christmas tree.'

'I have one.' She points a finger to a small square loft entrance above the front door. A small smile plays on her lips. 'It's in the attic.'

I roll my eyes. 'Of course it is. That's why you didn't put it up, it's too much work. Please tell me you have something up there to decorate it with.'

'I do, but you don't have to do this.' She says that, but there's no missing the excitement sparking in her eyes. Christmas brings out the inner kid in all of us.

There's something magical about this time of year. It feels like a really coupley thing to do, decorate a tree together.

'I want to do this with you. Let's start our own tradition, like your parents.' By hiding behind my clipped, cold exterior, I've deprived myself of so much fun. That stops now. 'Then we're going to find that lustful stare of yours again, deal?'

Her lips curl upwards exposing neat white teeth. 'You're like a dog with a bone.'

'Couldn't have put it better myself, baby.' I grab her hand and brush it over my ever-ready erection.

A tiny squeal of delight surges out from between her parted lips. 'You big tease.'

'It'll be worth the wait.' I promise. 'Get the drinks.'

'I have a bottle of champagne in the fridge. It's been screaming "pop me" all week.'

By the time I wrestle the tree out of the loft I'm sweating like a criminal in court and covered in a thick film of dust.

Ava takes one look at me. 'Take those clothes off, will you, you'll destroy the place! I'll wash them for you. They'll be dry by the morning.'

'Desperate to get my clothes off one way or another, aren't you?' I unbuckle my belt and step out of my trousers, watching as her greedy gaze drinks in my black boxer briefs.

I'd love nothing more than to take her on the couch right now but making her wait is all part of the foreplay. I unbutton my shirt and toss it on the kitchen counter. She drinks in the smooth planes of my torso, with a hum of appreciation.

'Let me get you a t-shirt while I wash this.' She turns on her heels, heading in the direction of her bedroom.

'I doubt you've got one that fits me,' I call after her.

'You'd be surprised.' She returns a minute later wearing a red scoop-neck vest and Lycra flesh-coloured leggings that sculpt her ass into a perfect peach. Oh, this is definitely fore-play, but it was me who was meant to be teasing her.

She throws me a red t-shirt. 'What's this? His n hers?' I motion at her red top. 'And please tell me this didn't belong to your ex.'

'It did not. I bought it for you at the Santa Fun Run last weekend. I was saving it for Christmas but ...' She shrugs, and there's a distinct hint of mischief in her tone.

I unfold the cheap cotton material and snort at the image of a cartoon Santa crossing a race finish line, with the slogan 'The Big Man Always Comes First' plastered across the front.

'Hilarious, but not exactly accurate, in any shape or form.' I tug it over my head and spread my arms. 'What do you think?'

A blush flushes her porcelain cheeks as she reaches for the bottle of champagne she left on the counter. 'I think you bombing around my lounge in what looks like Christmas pyjamas makes this place look more homely and warm than any Christmas tree ever could.'

I assemble the tree in front of the window while Ava pours bubbly and lights the electric fire. Michael Bublé's velvety voice fills the air and I glance round to see Ava smiling into her glass. She looks like I feel, content, happy, peaceful.

We sip our champagne, while hanging the baubles, none of which are pink, by the way.

'So do you always go to your parents' on Christmas Day?' I stand back, looking for any bare branches we might have missed.

'Pretty much. Apart from last year when we had to hide out at Huxley.' Ava tucks a thick line of tinsel around the tree, biting her lips as she concentrates. 'What about you? What do you and Phoebe do?'

'We spend Christmas Eve at home in Sandymount. Santa always comes to our house. I usually make Phoebe chocolate pancakes for breakfast and let her play with her toys. Then we usually go to my mother's where we have an Instagram-worthy Christmas, as long as we all pretend we don't notice my father leering over my mother's youngest sister.'

'Oh.' Ava picks up her champagne flute from the coffee table. Is she wondering what I'm wondering? If we'll see each other on Christmas Day?

I'd like to see her, but my day isn't flexible, and I'm pretty sure she wouldn't come to my parents' house. And now I've gotten to know hers, I wouldn't blame her.

I step back from the tree and turn to Ava. 'Do you like chocolate pancakes, Ava?'

The question has nothing to do with chocolate pancakes really, and from the sparkle in her eyes she knows it as well as I do.

'I love chocolate pancakes.' She sucks in her lower lip almost shyly.

'Then maybe you'll join us for breakfast?'

'Well, I suppose I'll have to drop off your gifts anyway.' She shrugs nonchalantly, but we both know there's nothing meaningless about making plans together for Christmas Day. It's the most family orientated day of the year and choosing to spend it together is a huge statement, no matter how slow we're supposed to be taking things.

I pinch my t-shirt between my index finger and thumb. 'You mean this isn't my Christmas gift?'

She rolls her eyes. 'Duh, there's a matching jumper to go with it too.'

'We'll see how smart your mouth is in a minute, lady.' I nod towards her coffee table where the final touch of her tree waits.

She sets her glass down and picks up the gold-plated star. The air hums between us, both aware that once this tree is done, the real fun begins. 'You'll have to do it. I can't reach.'

In one swift movement I place my head between her legs and hoist her up onto my shoulders while she shrieks out every curse known to man.

'Stop wriggling woman and put the damn star on the top of the tree.' Pinning her thighs with my hands, I reach up on my tiptoes and wait as she places the star on the highest point.

'Ta-da.' Ava's jazz hands have nothing on what my hands are about to do to her.

'Finally! Now it's time to make you wriggle for all the right reasons.'

I wanted her to have some warmth, but while I'm here, I'm going to make sure she's on fire.

Chapter Thirty-Three

AVA

Saturday 16th December

Last night was magical. The time Cillian and I spent together. The laughter. Even our casual, comfortable attire seemed to take our relationship to the next level. As did the way Cillian pinned me down and worshipped my body, then held me all night afterwards. The way he's still holding me, like I'm the most precious woman in the world.

Something's changed between us. I'm not sure if it's directly related to Teagan's exit, or if it was my brutal honesty in the conversation that followed. It could have gone one of two ways, and I thank my lucky stars it went the way I wanted. It feels like his perception on love and lasting relationships might finally be evolving.

Cillian shifts, thick lustrous lashes prise open to reveal those twin silver lakes that I could cheerfully drown in. 'Were you watching me sleep?'

'Maybe.' I drop a shoulder in a shrugging motion.

'You know that's kind of creepy.' He flips me onto my back and nuzzles my neck.

'No creepier than being pinned down by the man who

thinks I'm creepy.' I nestle back into the plump pillow and watch as his tongue rolls between my breasts.

'You know what's truly creepy?' His mouth chases goose-bumps across my flesh, all the way to my nipple before clamping his lips around it.

'The fact that you can talk such nonsense and still turn me on at the same time?' I squirm beneath him, opening my legs in an unspoken invitation.

'No.' He sucks before releasing with a pop. 'What's creepy is that every time I close my eyes, I still see you. And every time I take your body with mine, the need to do it again only grows.'

It's not traditionally romantic, being called creepy, but I know what he's trying to say. This thing between us is grow-ing, blooming, and laying roots in a heart he previously wouldn't admit he owned.

My soul feels satiated. My body however needs more.

'Well, what are you waiting for?' I nudge against the rock-solid length digging into my inner thigh and he drags himself higher up the bed.

The need to feel him inside burns. He raises his face, lips brushing tenderly against mine, his tip sliding through my soaking flesh, teasing, and nudging my most sensitive spots.

'Cillian.' It's a warning to quit the teasing and give me what I want. 'I need you inside me.'

'Like this?' He pushes in barely an inch.

'More.' I beg.

He gives me another thick inch but it's nowhere near enough. 'How's that?'

'If you don't give me what I need, I'm going to flip you on your back and take it anyway.' I pant.

'Tell me what you need, baby.' He watches me writhe and buck beneath him with a mix of raw need and awe.

'I need you.' Physically. Emotionally. Every damn way.

Because the more time I spend with Cillian Callaghan, the more certain I am that he was made for me.

'You have me.' His voice rasps, his words seeping beneath my skin, scorching my soul. 'You have me, baby.'

He slides in, inch by glorious inch. My fingers follow his spine to the base, slide over his sculpted ass cheeks and drag him as deep as he'll fit.

His eyes latch onto mine, glazed with arousal and the promise of euphoria. 'Ava, I'm obsessed with you.'

'The feeling's mutual.'

He groans and halts his hips mid-thrust, catching himself without a condom.

'It's okay. I'm on the pill. I've been tested.'

He pauses for a beat, his lips roll into a troubled expression. He's been caught before. I understand, but I would never do that to him.

His rich husky baritone roughens with need. 'Promise me.'

'I promise.' I run my hands across the hard expanse of his chest.

'Thank God.' He drives into me slow and hard. 'Christmas has come early.'

'As long as you don't.' I smirk.

'I'm going to wipe that smirk from your face, baby.' His fingers dig between our hips until he hijacks that sensitive bundle of nerves and strokes. His sweat-sheened skin glides across mine, his thumb caressing while he thrusts into me, relentlessly driving me to the most decadent oblivion.

Hot white flames burst behind my eyelids, pure carnal pleasure shakes my limbs and sears my soul.

'Open your eyes, baby.' Cillian urges. 'I want to watch you. I want you to watch what you do to me.'

Turbulent titanium eyes bore into mine. I lose it, as he finds it. My orgasm detonates a second before his and wave after wave of ecstasy crusade through us as we cling and buck and deepen our bond.

It's official. I think I'm in love.

'I need to get up.' Cillian gathers my hair behind my ears as we lie, limbs entwined. 'I have to pick Phoebe up from her friend's house. Thank God you booked Hollybrooke, or I'd have to drag her away from Sarah Snowden's sleepover kicking and screaming.'

I reluctantly roll away, giving Cillian back the arm I was lying on. 'I'm looking forward to it. It's supposed to be as magical for adults as it is for kids.'

'What could be more magical than spending the day with my two favourite girls?' Cillian stretches into a standing position. 'Shall I open the blinds?'

I watch as he struts across my bedroom like a Greek god. Broad shoulders taper to narrow waist. His ass is the perfect bubble of solid muscle.

'Do.' I shimmy up the bed. 'Then you can stick the kettle on and bring me a cup of tea before you go.'

Cillian's lips curl upwards. 'I love a woman who knows what she wants.' His expression freezes on his face as he realises what he's just said.

'The blinds.' I remind him, pointing at the big bedroom window. The last thing I need is for him to freak out now, he's been doing so well.

'Holy fuck,' he exclaims as blind light bounces into the bedroom. 'It snowed.'

'What? No way! We couldn't have planned it better if we tried. It's the perfect day for Hollybrooke.'

'Any day with you sounds pretty perfect to me.' He saunters out of the room and I exhale a sigh of relief.

.   .   .

Four hours later, Cillian and Phoebe collect me outside my apartment block.

Phoebe's little face is paler than usual but I'm hoping that's because she had so much fun at last night's sleepover, and not because she's traumatised by Teagan's rapid departure.

Cillian said Teagan had kept her word for once, and called the next day, so hopefully this time she'll keep in touch.

'How was your night, pumpkin?' I slide into the back next to her, and she squeals with excitement. Cillian arches an eyebrow in the rear-view mirror but says nothing.

This evening is about Phoebe, not what he wants. Besides, I don't trust my hands not to linger on him longer than 'friends' should and the last thing we need is for Phoebe to get confused.

'It was great. We watched *Gabby's Dollhouse* until like nine o'clock and then Mrs Snowden let us watch *The Grinch*.' Her blonde hair whips round, 'And we had ice cream and popcorn.'

'Oh my goodness. That sounds like the best sleepover ever.' I strap myself in as Cillian negotiates the traffic.

'It was. You should come to ours for a sleepover some-time, shouldn't she Dad?' Phoebe places her tiny hand in mine, while Cillian battles to keep his expression straight.

'One day. If she's good.'

I swallow down my snigger and snuggle into Phoebe, listening as she chats about everything and nothing for the rest of the journey. It might only have been a few weeks but already, I can't imagine my life without either of them.

Hollybrooke is every kid's wildest Christmas fantasy on steroids. The Georgian manor house has been transformed into an opulent winter wonderland. The grand façade is adorned with thousands of twinkling white lights that cast a magical glow over the snow-blanketed gardens. Tall, majestic, evergreen trees line the winding entrance, furnished with glistening frost. Even the air we breathe in feels fresh and fabulous.

Real reindeer languidly munch on hay in the stables to the left of the main building, while children pet them in awe.

Phoebe isn't the only one who's utterly overwhelmed. Cillian flashes one of his real smiles, he's not nearly as sparing with them these days. 'Let's go in, see if we can find Santa.'

Inside the manor, the magnificent foyer is decorated with red velvet ribbons, and thick, lavish garlands embellish a huge mantelpiece. Flames lick the logs of the open fire, roaring and crackling, radiating a welcoming woodsy scent. Kids are toasting s'mores, leaving trails of dripping marshmallows across the original wooden flooring.

At the bottom of a sweeping staircase is a sign for Santa's Grotto. An overly enthusiastic elf with a clipboard takes Phoebe's name as she twirls her hair round her finger shyly. Mrs Claus appears with a tray of warm gingerbread cookies for the kids and steaming mulled wine for the adults.

A couple of minutes later, another elf descends the stairs and calls Phoebe's name. She glances at Cillian, then me, wide-eyed with anticipation. I pray to God that this Santa's beard is not only real, but the right shade to pass the Phoebe test.

I nudge her up the stairs, but she digs her pink Ugg boots into the spot and tugs my hand. 'You have to come in with us too.' She grabs my coat and pulls me with them and warmth sloshes through my stomach that has nothing to do with the mulled wine.

Santa's Grotto is a cosy room decorated with candy canes and piles of presents. The man himself sits in a throne-like chair in the corner.

'Welcome, Phoebe Callaghan, do come in,' He booms, and thankfully his thick white-grey beard doesn't budge.

Phoebe beams, seemingly satisfied. 'Hello Santa. I'm going to cut to the chase this year.' She puts a tiny hand on her hip. 'Is there any chance you could deliver me a second Mammy for Christmas? My one only works intermittently.'

Chapter Thirty-Four

CILLIAN

I'm not sure which of us is more shocked, Ava, Santa, or me.

The guy in the Santa suit glances between Ava and me, then returns his focus back to Phoebe. 'Hmm, I'm more of a toy type of gift giver, Phoebe, darling.' He adjusts himself in the chair.

'I know, but Christmas is about love and happiness and families, right?' My daughter would make a great lawyer. She certainly isn't giving up without an argument. 'So maybe you could sprinkle some of your Christmas magic about and make it happen for me?'

'And is there anyone you have in mind for this, ahem—' He clears his throat. 'Position.'

Phoebe stares pointedly at Ava, a blush colouring her neck. It has nothing on the colour of Ava's blazing face. She smothers the nervous rattle that bursts from her lips with her hand.

'Sarah Snowden's dad left, and her mammy married another man and gave Sarah a second dad.' Phoebe gesticulates wildly in front of her. 'He buys Sarah loads of presents, lets her stay up late at weekends and Mrs Snowden is always smiling now.'

'Is that right?' Santa chuckles, his eyes gleaming. I bet that man has heard it all.

'Yep.' Phoebe says matter-of-factly. 'They even go on family date nights to the pictures and for days out to the zoo.'

'And what is this, exactly?' Santa raises a white furry eyebrow in my direction. 'Isn't this a family date night?'

Phoebe's face furrows while she thinks about it. Like the flicking of a switch, her face lights. 'That magic, Santa, just sprinkle it here, now.' She attempts a wink but ends up blinking instead.

Santa exhales a huge belly laugh. 'I'll see what I can do.' A white gloved finger taps the side of his nose conspicuously before handing over a gold token. 'Take this for now. It's for the toy factory downstairs. Hand it to one of the elves and you can pick any toy in my workshop.'

'Thank you, Santa.' Phoebe squeals, hopping from foot to foot with excitement.

'No, thank you, Phoebe Callaghan. You made my day.' Santa shakes her hand, and she blows him a kiss before skipping out the door.

'Oh, and if you could throw in a dog, for good measure, Santa, I won't ask for a single thing next year!'

'Good luck with that.' He murmurs with another chuckle.

Helpful, Santa. Really fucking helpful.

I drop Ava home after Hollybrooke and promise to call her tomorrow. As she gets out of the car, every single cell in my body vibrates with a silent protest. I want her to come home with us so badly, but given Phoebe's romantically astute notions, it's better for all of us if we spend the rest of the evening apart.

Phoebe has been suspiciously quiet for a child who had plenty to say all afternoon and evening. She stares out of the window watching as Ava dips in through those revolving glass doors.

'I miss Ava already.' She pouts. 'Can we go see Nanny?'

I glance at the clock. It's almost seven but if we go this evening then that will free up tomorrow. I need to pack for Nate's wedding, that's if Phoebe is okay for me to leave her. Seeing my mother might be the exact encouragement she needs.

Fifteen minutes later we pull up outside the three-storey mansion I grew up in. I never call it home because it never felt like one. Mam was trying so hard to make it pristine enough for Dad to want to come back to each night, it was never a place any of us could relax.

Phoebe bounds up the white steps and leans on one of the heavy round pillars flanking the glass framed double doors.

Their housekeeper, Iga, answer the door. She's in her late thirties, slim, with long blonde hair, just the way dad likes them. Though if he's been stupid enough to get involved with her, he's been discreet about it, for once. 'Ah, welcome home Mr Callaghan and Miss Phoebe.'

Phoebe charges past her into the house. 'Where's nanny?'

'She's in the dining room,' Iga calls after her retreating back.

My father insists on having a formal dinner each evening, even though it's just the two of them.

In the dark, wood-panelled room, my mother and father flank each end of the mahogany dining table that could sit twelve. My father rises as Phoebe bursts into the room with me on her heels.

'Nanny!' Phoebe launches herself onto my mother's lap and they embrace like they haven't seen each other in weeks instead of days.

'How's my gorgeous girl?' Mam rocks Phoebe on her lap and examines her face. 'Would you guys like some dinner?'

Phoebe eyes the half-eaten medium-rare steak and steamed vegetables on the plate in front of her and shakes her head vehemently. 'I'm not hungry.'

'That's because you're full of gingerbread cookies and marshmallows from Hollybrooke.' I pull out a chair on my mother's end of the table, offering a curt nod at my father.

'We had the best afternoon out with Daddy's friend, Ava.' Of course, Phoebe outs me at the first chance she gets.

My mother's eyebrows almost hit the ceiling. 'William, why don't you show Phoebe the Christmas tree we put up today?'

'Yay!' Phoebe darts towards my father. 'Did you put an angel or a star on the top?' Their voices trail off down the corridor.

'So, you're allowing Ava to spend time with Phoebe.' My mother lifts her napkin from her lap and dabs the corners of her mouth. 'Things must be serious.'

'They are, Mam. Ava is a beautiful woman, inside, and out. She's a wonderful role model for Phoebe. She's kind. Considerate. Consistent. She runs her own business. I think it's amazing that a woman like her wants to spend time with a six-year-old who isn't hers. Phoebe adores her. She's the first woman to put a smile on my face for years, honestly Mam, she makes me happy.'

Mam jerks backwards in her chair, staring at me like I've grown a second head. 'Well, that's all fantastic. All I've ever wanted is for you to be happy, but what will happen when this thing between you runs its course?' Concern creases her forehead.

I swallow thickly. 'This feels different. It feels like it could be more.'

Thin fingers fly to her breastbone. She takes a mouthful

of wine and places her glass back down, tracing her index finger up and down its stem. 'I suppose I always put myself in Teagan's shoes, as a mother. She was so young when she had Phoebe. She came here a few weeks ago pleading me to help her get you back. I thought she'd settled over time. I know she was unfaithful, but when you're committed to someone, you work through these things.'

I roll my eyes. 'Mam, if you love someone, you don't repeatedly hurt them. You don't make a fool out of them. Just because you and Dad—'

'Enough.' My mother raises her hand silencing me. 'The last few years have been blissful between us.'

The only thing that's blissful is her ignorance.

'I've made no secret of my hopes for you and Teagan to work things out, for Phoebe's sake if nothing else. A child needs stability. Marriage and relationships take work. But if you think you and Ava can offer Phoebe that stability then that's wonderful.'

'The right relationships don't take nearly as much work as the wrong ones. You know how I feel about marriage. I've never entertained the notion in my life. But maybe I was wrong. Maybe with work – from both partners, maybe some can last.'

'You love Ava?' The faintest tinge of hope rings in my mother's voice. I'd say she had pretty much written off any remote chance of her only son ever settling down.

'It's early days, but I've never felt anything like it before. I think about her all day every day. I want to be with her all the time. And when we are together it's effortless, you know?'

She reaches across the starched white tablecloth and takes my hand. 'You know what, son? Life is short. If Ava makes you happy, and if she truly is a good role model in Phoebe's life, then grab it with two hands. Don't let her slip away. True love is hard to find.'

'Thank you.' Now to address what I really came here to say. 'Will you please make an effort with Ava? Make her feel welcome. It's enough for her to take on me and Phoebe, let alone a monster-in-law as well.'

Her hand clips me across the bicep. 'I'll give you monster-in-law, you cheeky ratbag.' Her eyes soften. 'I'm truly happy for you, Cillian.' She wrings her wrists wistfully. 'I'm sorry your dad didn't set the best example over the years. I'm just glad you're finally getting over everything.'

The doorbell chimes from the hallway. 'Who's that?'

'It'll be the Benedicts.' Mam smooths a palm across the tablecloth dusting a speckle of tiny crumbs on to the floor. 'Irene and Cyril usually call on a Saturday evening.' Alex's parents.

I'm just glad it's not Teagan's.

Perhaps this time, she really will stay in touch with Phoebe, but I won't hold my breath.

Chapter Thirty-Five

AVA

Monday 18th December

'Are you excited?' Cillian nuzzles my neck from behind, as the winter wind whips my hair into a wild frenzy around the two of us. We take in the scenery from the open deck of the tiny, dilapidated ferry that runs twice daily from Galway to Inis Emeraude.

My brother might have renovated an entire hotel in preparation for the wedding, but he certainly overlooked the transport situation. Thankfully, the stellar company and the mesmerising view of the snow-coated rocky cliffs and rugged tapestry in the distance compensates for the lack of luxury, and the bumpy crossing.

'Excited about a few dirty days away with you?' I tilt my face up to his and our noses bump. 'Absolutely.'

'Excited for your only brother's wedding.' He nips the sensitive skin of my earlobe with his teeth.

'Oh yeah, there is that too I suppose.' And the prospect of spending a few days with my family, and best friend is the icing on the cake. Bonnie practically grew up in our house. There was no way she wouldn't be invited to my brother's wedding. She didn't bring James, unashamedly admitting she's hoping to snag one of Nate's famous actor friends.

Inis Emeraude looms enchantingly before us, a hidden gem nestled twenty miles off the rugged west coast of Galway. At only twelve miles in length and four in width, it's going to make for a cosy few days. Let's hope no one falls out.

'It's stunning, isn't it?' Cillian's voice is thick with awe. The small ferry hits a wave and the spray from the crashing wild Atlantic Ocean blasts into the air. We jump backwards, giggling like school kids.

'It really is. Stunning and secure.' Nate paid the islanders a hefty price to vacate this week, which means the only people here are friends and family. No chance of smarmy paps gate-crashing.

'Coo heee, love birds!' My mother's blow-dried blonde bob pokes out on to the deck. 'The captain says we're docking in five minutes.'

'Great.' The quicker we get off this boat, the quicker we can get the celebrations started.

'I can't believe my baby boy is getting married.' Mam gushes, grasping her scarf as it thrashes in the wind. 'This time next year, it could be you too! Imagine that.'

Cillian stiffens behind me, and not in a good way.

'Give us a break, Mam, will you.' I swat her away with my hand. 'Bonnie was hoping you'd share your mince pie recipe with her, go find her before the madness starts.'

She wasn't.

Bonnie hates mince pies but it was the first thing I could think of to get rid of my well-meaning but pushy mother. Planning our wedding doesn't fall under the 'baby steps' category and I don't want my mother terrifying Cillian.

Several private hire cars await when we disembark, driving us the couple of miles along the coast to the only hotel on the island. We share with Bonnie and Natalie, while Mam and

Dad thankfully travel with my sister, Faith, and her husband, helping them to load the kids into the car seats.

'Wow.' Perched atop a rugged bluff overlooking the Atlantic, the hotel boasts breath-taking panoramic views of the ocean. Waves crash therapeutically against the rocks below. The shingled exterior, large windows and beautifully landscaped grounds combine a timeless elegance with the charm of a classic seaside estate.

No wonder Nate snapped this place up. It's like owning a tiny slice of heaven.

We make our way inside the grand lobby, welcomed by high ceilings and chandeliers. The coastal colours inside reflect the ocean's hues.

Holly and Nate are waiting for us. Harriet's sleeping in the pram next to them; Holly rocks it back and forth with one hand and clutches a glass of champagne in the other.

'Welcome.' Her complexion is flawless and glowing.

Nate's arm is tucked protectively over her shoulders, as he glances up from his fiancée and daughter with a look of pure wonder in his eyes.

'It's not too late to run, Holly.' I greet her with a kiss on the cheek. 'The boat is docked, I'm sure someone round here knows how to sail it.'

'Very funny, sis.' Nate ruffles my hair in that annoying big brother way. 'But I see you managed to bring a date, so unless *he* finds someone to sail that boat before one o'clock tomorrow, it looks like HeartSync has a new investor.' He extends a calloused hand.

'Actually, Nate, can we talk about that in the new year?' My brother's generosity knows no bounds. He already bought me the apartment. It's too much.

Him making me go it alone for the year was the best gift he could have given me – the ability to appreciate how capable I am and to grow into a confident businesswoman in my own right. The need to take my business to the next level alone has become an internal personal quest. I can do it, I know I can. I no longer need the emotional or financial support an investor brings.

'Sure.' He looks quizzically at me then shrugs. 'Let me show you to your rooms. The rehearsal dinner is at five. Meet back here for the drinks reception at four.'

'Where's Tom Hardy?' Bonnie peers past Nate's broad shoulder.

He offers her the same hair ruffle as he did to me. 'He's around here somewhere. I'll put in a good word for you.'

'Never mind Tom Hardy.' My mother ploughs into the lobby. 'Where's Jayden Cooper?' Oh God, Penny Jackson has always had a soft spot for Nate's agent.

'He's probably balls-deep in his wife, Mam.' Nate rolls his eyes. 'You'll just have to make do with Dad again. Let's hope he remembered to pack the Viagra this time.'

Sniggers ripple around the room. Even Cillian's smiling, something which he seems to do a lot more of this past week or two.

'Come on. Let's go unpack.' *Starting with your penis.* I lick my lips and his eyes flare with understanding.

We excuse ourselves to 'freshen up,' ignoring the whistles and cat calls from my family. If they don't scare Cillian off, perhaps nothing will.

Our room is on the second floor with a huge wraparound terrace and sweeping views of the ocean. The ensuite boasts marble counter tops, a deep soaking clawfoot tub and designer toiletries. A huge walk-in wardrobe provides ample storage space for the dresses I brought.

However luxurious the place is, the biggest luxury is having my boyfriend to myself for three days solid. I adore our time with Phoebe, truly, but this time together is a real treat.

The timing isn't ideal with Teagan leaving last week. A flash of guilt flows through me. Though, if Phoebe's Santa wish is anything to go by, she seems to be getting stronger every day where her erratic mother is concerned.

'How's Phoebe? Is she okay at your mother's house?'

'She's perfect, don't worry.' He stalks across the plush carpet to reach me. 'I didn't come up here to talk about her.'

'Oh, is that right?' I slip off my knee-length coat, revealing the dress I picked out this morning with specifically this – alone time – in mind. 'What did you come up here to talk about then?'

His eyes heat and flare as they roam over the sheer material clinging to my every curve. 'Who said anything about talking?' His lips brush over mine, owning them. 'Talking is overrated. Show me what you've got on underneath that dress.'

His hand slides beneath the material. He inhales sharply as he skims over the silk suspender belt I put on this morning.

I take a step back, tugging the dress over my head, revealing myself to him.

'So stunning, Ava.' His finger traces between my breasts. 'But I need you naked. I need your skin on my skin, every inch of it.'

He reaches round and unhooks the silk balconette bra, drawing its straps down over my shoulders until it falls to the floor with a gentle swish. My nipples peak at the cold, and under his hungry stare.

His mouth nips at my neck while his hands cup my breasts. I buck my hips against him and a low chortle echoes through his throat.

I nearly miss the sullen version. At least sullen Cillian got on with it.

'Patience, baby, what's the rush?'

'I need you.' My breath is heavy with want. 'My ovaries are about to explode.'

'And you'll have me at least twice before dinner.' His finger dips inside my thong, teasing and probing. I part my legs, allowing him better access. 'Did you touch yourself since I last touched you?'

My face flames and his eyes darken.

'You did, didn't you?'

I nod, suddenly shy.

'Did you pretend it was my hand?' He drops to his knees on the floor in front of me, his head is in line with my belly button. 'Or my mouth?'

I can barely breathe; I'm shaking with lust. 'Both.'

His mouth grazes my stomach, tracing lower, tugging at my thong with his teeth as his fingers reach round and unclip the suspender belt. 'Show me how you did it.' His head tilts upwards, his breath skimming my flesh as he takes my hand and guides it to where I need it. He slips two fingers inside me and pumps, watching as I work my clit.

'Good girl.' His praise sends a fresh hot wave of hunger through my veins. 'How does it feel?'

'It's not enough,' I admit.

'Why not?' He stills his hand.

'Because what I really need is you.' Admitting that fact out loud feels way more intimate than touching myself for him.

I don't want to sound desperate but that's exactly what I am.

I've been touching myself thinking about him for longer than he'll ever know, and now I have access to him, I want the real deal.

Chapter Thirty-Six

CILLIAN

Her openness and honesty are my utter undoing.

She's like no woman I've ever encountered. That's why I feel safe enough to lower my walls, lose the clipped tone and let her into mine and Phoebe's life on a permanent basis.

I lick my lips and swipe my tongue through her perfect pussy before rolling it up across her stomach. She tugs me backwards onto the king size bed clawing at my shirt like a wild animal.

My need consumes me, but it's so much more than just the physical. I need us to be one. I need to be inside her body, her head, and her heart. She's changed me into one of these fucking fairytale-loving fannies who dreams about forever, because the thought of not doing this for the rest of our lives doesn't bear thinking about.

We both tear at my shirt, the buttons popping in every direction. She tugs my belt and I undo my trousers until there's nothing between us. Naked never felt so good. Peppering tiny, teasing kisses across her slender neck and beautiful breasts, I slide between her long shapely legs, inching myself into her heat slowly. She grabs my ass, impatiently yanking me deep into her core, driving my dick home with everything it's got.

It's feral. But after years of aimlessly wading through life, it also feels like coming home. We moan and grind and slide, losing ourselves and finding ourselves in each other's lust-sheened skin.

'Cillian,' she murmurs into my mouth.

My breath hitches. I feel like she's going to say those three little words. The same ones that have been eating me up from the inside since Saturday morning when I woke up in her bed. Since I watched her hold my daughter like she wanted to take away her pain as much as I did. Hell, since she hurtled into my office all those weeks ago and hijacked my heart.

'I love the way your body fits mine.' She grinds against me slowly and deliberately to emphasise her point.

She's challenging me with her 'I love' comments. Testing the water to see if we can swim yet, or if my caution is still at risk of drowning us.

I grab her ass with my fingers and dig them into her supple skin. 'I love the way your thighs tremble when you're close to the edge.' They're vibrating like a musical instrument, one that only I know how to play.

Her lips curve into a smirk that says game on. 'I love that glassy lustful look you pin me with when you're about to come.'

'I love this game we're playing, but you know my views on love, and lasting, so please, come for me baby, because I'm not going to last another fucking minute buried inside you.' I slip my hand between our pelvises, caressing her sensitive nub until she clenches and convulses around me.

Her vice-like grip sends me spiralling over the edge into the most decadent oblivion, dragging me under until the two of us are shaking, shuddering, and sniggering.

'I love how you can make me come and laugh at the same time.' Looks like the game isn't over yet. I place my cheek on her chest, moving with it as it rises and falls.

'I love sharing a bed with you.' I admit. 'I just wish it could be mine.'

'One day maybe, you never know,' she edges, hopefully.

I'd love to tell Phoebe about us so Ava's presence in our house in the morning wouldn't be unusual. And given Phoebe's Christmas wish, I think she'd be more than happy with it. 'I know it's early days but maybe you could come for a sleepover on Christmas Eve and be there for the present opening as well as the chocolate pancakes? You'd have to sneak into the spare room before she got up, that's the only thing.'

Ava rocks up, resting her head on her elbow to look at me. 'But what will Phoebe think?'

'Well, I'm pretty sure she'll think she met the real Santa, and that he sprinkled that Christmas magic she was talking about.'

Ava looks at me coyly. 'I'd love nothing more, but only if you think it's right. I'm sticking around Cillian. Whatever happens between us, I'd never walk out on Phoebe. Ever. I'll never abandon her, she's the most awesome six-year-old I know. I'll be her friend for life if you let me. And so much more if you want.'

'I believe we already talked about "more" and we're living it right now.' I place my hand on her sternum, feeling the quick beat of her heart.

'Speaking of more,' she eyes me provocatively. 'I believe you promised me two rounds before dinner, so what are you waiting for old man? Do I need to text my parents and ask them to drop up some of those blue magic pills they pop like smarties?'

'Oh, baby, I've got you covered.' I nudge my thickening cock against the inside of her thigh.

'Halle-fucking-lujah.'

My mother FaceTimes us just as we're having dessert. Actual dessert, after the rehearsal dinner, not each other. Though I'm hoping that will be on the cards later too.

I swipe to accept, and my daughter's stunning face fills the screen. 'Daddy!' she squeals and my heart melts. She's still in her school uniform and she should definitely be in her pyjama's now, but I guess it's her little break away from normality too.

'Hi Princess, how are you?'

'It was The. Best. Day. Ever! We spent nearly all day practicing the nativity play. You will be home for it, right?' She sticks a candy cane in her mouth, and I try to not wince. If she's bouncing off the walls instead of sleeping, there's not a lot I can do about it from here.

'Of course, I'll be home. I wouldn't miss it for the world.' I promise, taking Ava's hand beneath the table. Her parents are sitting across from us watching everything like hawks.

'Is Ava with you?' Phoebe's nose comes so close to the phone I can see straight up both nostrils.

'Yeah, she's next to me. Want to say hi?'

'Hell, yeah!' my daughter screams.

'Language.' I scold, handing the phone over to Ava, shaking my head at a sniggering Frank and Penny Jackson.

'Ava, I've missed you so much!' Phoebe screeches across the phone. The fact Ava gets a more enthusiastic greeting than me flips the inside of my stomach, not with envy, but with excitement. This is real. This is happening. And for once in my life, I'm going to trust it.

'I missed you too, sweetheart,' Ava coos, beaming into the phone. 'Are you having a nice time with your granny?'

'Yeah. She doesn't force me to eat broccoli like dad, in fact she brought me to McDon—

'Phoebe.' My mother's fake-stern voice cuts across the line. 'That was supposed to be our secret.'

I lean over Ava's shoulder so Phoebe can see both of us. 'Mother ...'

'What? You were brought to McDonald's as a kid, and you didn't die.' My mother's immaculately made-up face appears on the screen next to Phoebe's. She smiles when she sees Ava.

'Mam, you remember Ava.'

'How could I forget? You're not the only one she's knocked off their feet.' Mam winks and blushes. 'Sorry, Ava, that I wasn't especially gracious about our unusual meet-cute.'

Ava flashes her pearly whites. 'I am so sorry about that. No wonder you were taken aback, literally.'

'Perhaps when you're home, you'd like to join us for dinner?' my mother offers Ava, but it's Phoebe who answers for her.

'Yes! She'd love to! And can I come?' Phoebe bounces around the screen excitedly.

'You never need an invite, pet.' My mother kisses Phoebe's head.

Ava presses a palm over her heart. 'I'd love to. Thank you.'

'And will you come to my nativity on Friday?' Phoebe asks, fiddling with her braids. 'You know it's supposed to only be Mams and Dads allowed in, but seeing as Mam has gone again ...' My daughter's voice trails off and my heart bleeds right out on the floor.

Ava doesn't hesitate. 'Are you for real? I'd love to come to the nativity! You'll be the star of the show. It's a privilege to be invited.'

Phoebe positively glows as she whispers, 'what does privilege mean?' to my mother.

'Okay you two, enjoy your evening.' My mother takes charge of the phone. Her tone is genuine and sincere.

Finally, she seems to have accepted Teagan and I are over, and that I'm moving on. This is turning out to be an epic month.

'Thanks.' And not just for the phone call. Or for minding my daughter. It's 'thank you for accepting Ava and inviting her to dinner'.

'Send us a picture tomorrow when you're all dolled up for the wedding of the year.' Mam waves and blows a kiss.

Phoebe's face fills the screen again. 'Love you, Daddy!' she shouts. 'And you too, Ava.'

I freeze at the enormity of what my daughter just said to my girlfriend, the weight of it trouncing me like a ten-tonne truck.

Seconds pass before we both reply unanimously, 'Love you too.'

I end the call and throw the phone on the table. 'Yeah so, I don't think Christmas morning is going to be a problem. Or any other morning for that matter.'

Chapter Thirty-Seven

AVA

Tuesday 19th December

Soft flickering candles create an enchanting glow throughout the chapel. Evergreen garlands with twinkling lights drape gracefully along the altar and the pews are dressed in plush white cushions. The place is packed with our family, friends, and Nate's Hollywood buddies, dressed to kill.

Not one of them looks as sharp as my date.

My eyes shamelessly roam over Cillian's broad frame. His sharply cut tuxedo emphasises the shape of his strong shoulders and narrow waist. His full lips are pressed into a studious line, one that I'd love to lick until it lifts. His dark brown hair is tousled to perfection, mostly by my own hands as I dragged my fingers through it not half an hour earlier.

Those silver eyes flick to mine and sparkle, like he can read my mind. Like he's replaying the same decadent memories as I am.

His throat bobs as if he's going to say something, but the organ sounds throughout the quaint old building. I slip my palm into his, watching earnestly as my soon-to-be sister-in-law walks up the aisle. Holly looks stunning in a simple silk dress. It's not hard to see how she captured my brother's heart.

When she reaches the altar, her father places her hand in Nate's. Emotion bubbles inside my chest. Water fills my eyes. Thank God for waterproof mascara. I'm a sucker for a Happy Ever After, and watching my brother get his will have me blubbering like a baby if I'm not careful.

I barely register the priest's words, watching Holly, wondering what it feels like to be up there, praying that one day it'll be me in a white dress surrounded by my friends and family.

Cillian's thumb brushes over the back of my hand with an attentiveness which makes me think he's still reading my mind. That one day it could be me and him up there, no matter what his previous views were.

We are 'more'.

So, hopefully we'll achieve more together.

The priest finally says, 'you may kiss the bride' and my big brother leans down to kiss his wife. The crowd erupts, clapping, whistling, and cheering. My mother and father are the loudest from the pew in front of us.

'That's the stuff!' My father yells as Nate's mouth parts Holly's in a kiss that's a little X-rated for a church.

My face aches from grinning so hard but I can't hold back my tears for another second. Cillian wraps his strong arms around me, cradling me against his chest. His face finally cracks open with a smile almost as wide as my own.

'You're such a romantic,' he murmurs into my ear.

'I never denied it.' I pull a tissue from my pocket and dab my eyes carefully so as not to smudge my make-up.

'It was a beautiful ceremony.' Cillian admits.

'There might be hope for you yet.' My palm roams over his chest, appreciating the smooth taut muscle beneath, but what I'm really searching for is the spot over his heart.

'Hope is the one thing you've given me since you walked into that bar four weeks ago.' He presses a kiss to my temple, nodding at Holly and Nate as they dance down the aisle together. 'So, who knows ...'

His words sink into my soul.

For the first time in my life the fairy tale feels like it might just be on the verge of becoming a reality.

A warm buzz crusades through my blood, heating me from the inside out. It could be the champagne, but I suspect it has more to do with Cillian spinning me round the floor like Michael Flatly. Yep, he has no problem dancing with me. We've been at it for hours.

'I never knew you could dance so well.' I laugh, gasping for breath.

'Baby, you know I've got rhythm.' Cillian lifts my arm and twirls me around before tugging me tightly back against his torso. His hooded eyes darken with desire.

'Look at the kids!' My dad yells to my mother, whirling her around next to us.

Anyone would think they were the kids.

'And you told me that love doesn't last?' I nod towards my parents, who are grinning at each other like they're the newlyweds. 'Forty years married next year.'

'They're a great advertisement for it,' Cillian concedes.

'Or a great advertisement for Viagra.'

'Both. But please, if you see your dad popping any pills can we leave because I'm still traumatised from the time we dropped your mother off after the hen night.'

I cover my mouth with my hand. 'Two pieces of advice I probably should have given you before bringing you home. Watch where you're sitting, and never look down.'

'I don't know if that's gross, or impressive.' Cillian snorts.

'I think it's both. Can we please get a drink?' I motion towards the bar.

'Sure.' He winds his arm around my neck as we weave and bob through the crowd.

My sister Faith is dancing with her husband, Dermot, but they don't share nearly the same level of enthusiasm as our parents. Faith glances up at him, but he's staring over the top of her head watching Holly's two bridesmaids Savannah and Ashley. Savannah must say something funny because Ashley clutches her stomach and guffaws.

'Isn't Ashley the principal of Phoebe's school?'

'She is.' Cillian raises a hand in greeting, but we keep nudging our way through the throngs of bodies in search of a drink.

Bonnie is at the bar, dressed to kill in a Shona Joy fluted-sleeve maxi dress. She's wrangled herself in amongst a cluster of Nate's Hollywood pals from his latest action movie. I met them at the premiere and they're the sleaziest players around. Bonnie is biting off more than she can chew.

They're lining up shots with zero regard for the headache they'll have tomorrow.

'Isn't that your PA over there?' Cillian raises his eyebrows as Bonnie licks the back of her hand, knocks back her shot, and then bites the lemon wedge in her other hand. She shakes off the sourness with a full body jiggle that has the men around her gawking at her cleavage.

'PA, friend, sister from another mister.' I shrug. 'Call her what you like, but from the glassy look in her eyes, the only accurate name for her is drunk.'

I lead the way, tugging Cillian's hand from behind until we're wedged into the bar next to Bonnie and the boys.

'Ava!' She wobbles as she grabs my arms like she hasn't

seen me in years instead of an hour. 'Have you met Dax and Carter and ...' She squints at the third guy and hiccups. 'Jackson?'

I smile at the boys. 'We've met. How are you all? Welcome to Ireland.'

'Such a beautiful country,' Dax says, resting his elbow on the bar counter.

'Yes, the scenery is outstanding,' Carter adds, leering at Bonnie.

Jackson steps forward, offering an arm out to steady my swaying friend. 'And the locals are so hospitable.'

'Oh, you haven't seen anything yet.' Bonnie wiggles her hips.

Cillian and I exchange a look of concern. Bonnie is unashamedly sexually liberated, but I don't think she's any match for these three, especially given how much she's had to drink. 'Bonnie, maybe we should go to the bathroom and freshen up?'

I reach for her but Jackson clings on tightly to her. 'She's fine, aren't you, babe?'

'You're the fine one,' Bonnie slurs, licking her lips.

'Hey! What about me?' Carter thumbs his chest indignantly.

'And me!' Dax tries to prise Bonnie from Jackson.

'Now, now, boys, there's enough of me to go round,' Bonnie says flirtatiously.

Yep. She's bitten off a tumultuous amount of trouble, with no idea she's about to be chewed up and spat out. Bonnie is all for casual sex, but she's not an advocate for orgies, or being used by three handsome hedonistic devils.

Cillian and I exchange a look of concern.

'Bonnie, let's go get some fresh air. We'll come back here in a few minutes. Trust me, you'll feel better for it.' I step forward, willing to frog march my friend out of here if necessary.

'Oh, come on, Ava. I'm fine. We're just having a bit of harmless fun. Stop being so judgemental!' She rolls her eyes like a petulant child.

Uh- oh. She's even drunker than I realised. 'Some of us are good with casual sex. Not all of us stalk our prey for a year before we pounce!' She gesticulates wildly towards Cillian. 'Mr Suave Suit Guy was a tough conquest, but he's yours. And I'm happy for you, but please, let me find my bit of happiness now, even if it is just for the night.'

Ground swallow me whole.

Cillian stiffens behind me.

Even in her drunken stupor, Bonnie realises what she's just let slip. She slaps a hand over her mouth, making the situation look a million times worse than it actually is.

'What is she talking about?' Cillian's eyes glint like cold, sharp metal.

'It's nothing.' I pull him away gently. We need to get out of here before Bonnie puts her foot any further down her throat. From the horror etching into her expression, she's sobering up fairly fast.

Good, because I've got bigger problems now. 'Let's get some fresh air and talk about this where it's quieter.'

Cillian stalks across the ballroom and out the French doors overlooking the ocean. The waves crash on the rocks below, each one sending plumes of salty spray into the air. An icy gust of wind slams into my chest but it has nothing on the cold horror creeping through my veins.

I can only imagine how it sounds, especially given what Teagan did to him.

'What did Bonnie mean when she said you stalked me for a year?' His shoulders are rigid, and the tendons on his neck look tight enough to snap.

'It's not how it seems, Cillian.' I reach for his bicep, but he flinches, shrugging me off along with any hopes I had for our future.

Chapter Thirty-Eight

CILLIAN

'Am I Mr Suave Suit Guy, Ava?' My voice sounds immeasurably calmer than I feel.

Her head bobs, her eyes falling to the ground as she nods.

'You knew who I was before we met at Elixir?' The heart that was so full it could burst shrivels and withers in my sternum. 'Have you and Bonnie been laughing at me this entire time?'

'No, we have not! It sounds way worse than it is, Cillian.' She reaches for me again, but I take a step back.

'You had your eye on me for a full year, stalked me from afar, lured me in with a false sense of security. Just like Teagan did.' The moonlight casts a sinister shadow across her pronounced cheekbones.

'I didn't! You came to me, remember?' Desperate eyes flash to mine, overflowing with despair.

'No, I approached a professional matchmaking agency, or so I thought.' My head is splitting. 'You must have thought Christmas came early. Tell me, why me? What is your end game?'

'This is the end game. You and me together. I swear. I

know it looks bad, but I promise I'm not trying to trick you or trap you like Teagan did.' She throws her hands in the air in a dramatic display of exasperation.

'I confided in you. I told you how she played me, and you've done the exact same thing.'

'I've done no such thing. This is totally different. I used to watch you walk by my office window in the mornings and I thought you were the hottest guy I'd ever laid eyes on. I had no idea it was you when your sign-up form came through.'

'How convenient.' My tongue clicks against the roof of my mouth. 'But that doesn't explain why you didn't tell me afterwards. After everything we talked about, after I confided in you that Teagan followed me around for a full year, you didn't think to mention that you had too.'

'I didn't follow you anywhere.'

'The Christmas markets? You just happened to be there, too?' She knew how I felt about her meeting my daughter. By bumping into us like that, she fast forwarded our entire relationship.

'That was a coincidence! Jesus, you think I slipped a tracker in your coat or something the night before? You really think I'm capable of that?'

'I have no idea what you're capable of.' Have I been so foolish? Duped again?

Though what would Ava want with me? Her family is far wealthier than my own.

'My ovaries are about to explode.' Her words from yesterday stab me like a stake in the stomach.

'Oh, God, Ava, please tell me you are actually on the pill?' The thought of more kids, Ava's kids was something that yesterday seemed like a distant dream.

But having the choice taken away from me again is an unforgivable nightmare.

It's like history repeating itself.

'How could you even ask that?' She clutches her chest like she's physically wounded. 'Come on, you know me.'

'Not as well, or for as long as you've known me apparently.'

The sounds of music and laughter drifts through the open doors mockingly.

I need to get away from here. I need space to process. But we're in the middle of fucking nowhere, with no way out until tomorrow at the earliest.

'Cillian, I—'

'Look, we made this arrangement because we needed something from each other. It was a success. Teagan thinks I've moved on. You brought a date to your brother's wedding. You'll get your investment, if you decide you want it. Everything else was ... a bonus.'

'A bonus? Is that what you call falling in love?' The pain cracking her face matches the one cracking open my chest.

'Don't go there, Ava.' We've danced around those three little words all day. I don't want to hear them. Not now. Not like this. My throat thickens. There's no denying it. That's exactly what this thing is between us. But now she's said it out loud, now she's breathed life into the ghost I never used to believe in, I'm not sure I'm ready for it.

'I'm going to bed.' I turn on my heel. 'Please don't follow me. It's your brother's wedding. Go dance. Drink. Do whatever the hell you like, just please, give me some space.'

I stare at the ceiling, forcing the oxygen past the knot that's formed in my chest. The ache from it extends all the way to the bottom of my stomach.

Memories from the last few weeks bombard my brain. Ava on her knees for me. Taking care of my needs. Putting me first. Then *I've wondered what you tasted like for months.'*

Mr Suave Suit Guy. Looks sharp but is fucking stupid.

I twist the sheets in my hands, squeezing out my frustration. If she'd have been honest that night at the bar. Said, 'hey, it's you.' Or even, 'funny story, I've noticed you around.'

Anything.

Though if she had, I would have pulled on my coat and raced out the door faster than a stolen Ferrari.

But she had so many chances to tell me after that and she didn't, and that's what feels like a betrayal. Especially given the way I opened up to her about Teagan.

The Ava I know wears her heart on her sleeve. Or I thought she did. I feel like our entire relationship has been based on a lie.

Am I overreacting?

Maybe. But I've been burned before, and I never want to feel that way again. It's not just me I have to protect, it's Phoebe too.

Though deep down, I can't deny it. Bonnie's comments have given me an out. I'm panicking. I don't know if I can do the whole relationship thing. The risk is almost as big as the reward.

I don't know how to fully trust another person.

All the comments from Penny and Frank and the rest of the Jacksons weigh on my mind.

'You guys are already a sure thing. Trust me. I'm never wrong.'

'It'll be you two next.'

'You guys are perfect for each other. Even if you don't know it yet.'

We were perfect for each other. At least it felt like it, for a while. Before I knew she'd been stalking me.

What if my original assumptions were right? That nothing lasts?

What if Ava's parents are the anomaly?

Hours pass before the door to the suite opens and Ava creeps in. I close my eyes and pretend I'm asleep, wishing to

God I was. The sound of metal unzipping slices through the air and every cell in my body yearns to look, to touch, but I don't trust her, and I don't trust myself.

She slips across the room and under the sheets beside me.

I don't reach for her.

And she doesn't reach for me.

The incessant buzzing of my phone wakes me from a fitful sleep. I snatch it from the floor, squinting at the time and the name Mam on the screen.

Worry slivers through my stomach. It's six am. Something must be seriously wrong.

I slide open the balcony doors and step out into the dark, freezing morning.

'Mam?' Panic taints my tone.

'Cillian, sorry.' My mother sobs across the phone.

Every hair on body pricks with an ice-cold fear that makes the winter morning feel positively tropical. 'Is it Phoebe?'

'No. It's your dad. He had a mini heart attack last night.' She hiccups. 'He's okay. Unfortunately. The rotten bastard took ill in Irene Benedict's bed.'

'Irene Benedict?' The words trickle out in slow motion.

Alex's mother?

My mother's friend of thirty odd years?

This is despicable behaviour, even by my father's standards.

'Cyril arrived home from the gentlemen's club to find an ambulance outside his house and his wife in her nightdress apparently. Oh God, son, I've been such a fool for all these years. They've been having it off for years.'

Being right gives me absolutely no satisfaction at all. The only thing that will give me satisfaction, is when I take him to court, and wipe the floor with him.

She swallows hard. 'She was my friend, Cillian. Well, I thought she was. I'm such a stupid fool.'

'You're not Mam. He's the stupid fool.' And I'm going to make sure you're free from him once and for all.

'They didn't even deny it. They've been sneaking around under my nose for years.' She sniffs. 'I want him gone, Cillian. Enough is enough.'

Finally.

Though it doesn't give me a fraction of the joy I thought it would.

'Consider it done.'

Is it possible Alex Benedict didn't get his womanising ways from the wind?

'Where's Phoebe? Did she get wind of any of this?' The poor child has seen enough instability to last her a lifetime. This would probably tip her over the edge.

'She's asleep. She's fine. She has no idea.' My mother inhales a shaky breath. 'Can you come home? I can't give her the attention she needs. My head is spinning.'

'Of course.' I gaze out across the port. 'I'm on my way. Hang on in there, Mam.'

'That's what I've been doing for years, hanging on.' She scoffs bitterly. 'No more, Cillian. No more.' She disconnects the phone.

I creep back inside, blowing my breath onto my hands in a bid to warm them up. The glow from the phone casts a dim light on Ava. She's curled into the foetal position on the other side of the bed. My chest tightens.

Was I too hard on her last night?

I don't know.

Bonnie's words shocked me more than I'd care to admit. But the truth is, it's the depth and strength of my feelings for Ava that shock me the most. She used the L word when I wasn't brave enough to.

I don't know if I'll ever be brave enough.

I have to go but I hate leaving like this with everything up in the air.

I wanted space, maybe this is the Universe delivering.

Maybe in a couple of days things will feel different. Clearer, perhaps.

I toss my belongings into my small suitcase, throw on some casual clothes, and open the door as quietly as possible. Taking one last glance backwards over my shoulder, I exhale a heavy sigh. I'll call later. Explain.

Just as soon as I get my own head around everything.

Chapter Thirty-Nine

AVA

Wednesday 20th December

I wake to an empty bed.

Cillian's gone.

His stuff is gone.

Bonnie and her big fucking mouth.

No, that's not fair. I had ample opportunity to admit to Cillian that I'd had my eye on him for the best part of a year. Though the guy I used to fantasise about wasn't real. The guy who used to walk past my office window was perfect, in my mind at least. And in real life, there's no such thing.

We're all flawed.

Wounded in some way.

Wearing invisible scars that only we can feel the pain of.

And unfortunately, something as innocent as failing to mention I'd been harbouring a crush for the best part of a year sliced Cillian's trust-wound right open. Given what Teagan did to him, it's no wonder.

But I am not Teagan. Nor anything like her.

Which is why I'm going to give him the space he asked for.

It's been a crazy few weeks. Things moved ridiculously

fast between us. He's right. My family took one look at us and assumed this was it. That we'd be the next ones down the aisle, and given the background Cillian's come from, it's understandable he's panicking.

Part of me even expected it.

Though that doesn't plug the planet-sized hole in my chest when I pat the cold sheets beside me. I pat the bedside table and locate my phone.

There's a message from Cillian, sent an hour ago.

I had to go. We'll talk when you get back.

Does 'we'll talk' mean it's over?

Or that he thinks we can talk through this stupid misunderstanding?

I roll out of bed, pull back the thick velour curtains and step out onto the wrap around terrace. The waves roll in a relentless rhythm, their peaks crowned with frothy white crests. They rise, they fall, just like the rest of us.

The ferry disappears into the distant horizon where the sea and sky meet. All I can do is pray that a little space from me and my overfamiliar family will make Cillian realise we're meant to be together.

I throw on a shirt dress and flat pumps and go in search of coffee. Between yesterday's alcohol and today's uncertainty, the thought of food turns my stomach.

Breakfast is being served in the main restaurant and although my heart is heavy, I'll hide it so as not to ruin my brother and Holly's special few days.

Bonnie sits alone at a table set for four. She glances up as I enter.

'Ava.' She beckons me over with a pleading look in her eyes. 'I'm so sorry for what I said last night. I wasn't thinking and I just blurted it out and I've been berating myself up about it ever since.'

'It's okay.' I slip into the seat opposite her.

'Is it? Did Cillian freak out like you thought he would?' I nod.

A waitress stops by our table. 'Tea or coffee.'

'Coffee, please. Can you just leave the pot?'

She places it on the brilliant white tablecloth between us.

'What happened?' Bonnie stretches across the table, her voice low and urgent.

'He panicked that history was repeating itself. Then he panicked because I told him I loved him.'

'And where is he now?'

'Somewhere over the Atlantic.'

'Oh shit, Ava, I'm so sorry.' Bonnie bites her nail. 'I can't believe I opened my big mouth.'

'It's okay. It's not even about that, not really. It was more like he felt out of control. My parents insisting it'll be us next at the altar definitely didn't help the situation.'

'What are you going to do?' Bonnie asks.

'Nothing. He wants to feel in control, so I'm leaving it to him. He knows what I want. What he doesn't know is if he's ever going to be brave enough to try to give it to me. And that's something only he can work out.'

It's a bit like what I said to Phoebe when her mother left. Some people's problems come from the inside. And Cillian has his fair share of them, but only he can fix them.

'Things were going so well between you.' Bonnie sighs.

'It's easy for things to go well when the path is smooth and straight, and you know the road. Better I find out now how he handles the bumps and twists that you can't see.'

I know what I want out of life. I've always known what I

want, the kind of relationship my parents have. A love that will last a lifetime. If Cillian isn't capable of that, it's better I find out now than spend another year of my life chasing yet another man who is unavailable.

'There you are!' My mother bulldozes into the conversation. 'What a wedding! Wasn't it the most fabulous day ever? Just so magical.' She clasps her hands together wistfully. 'It'll be you next, mark my words.'

Bonnie and I exchange a glance over the table. No wonder Cillian bolted.

'Where's Cillian? Wear him out, did you?' Dad saunters in, slipping into the seat beside me.

'He had to go home. Between work, and Phoebe, it was hard enough for him to get away for yesterday.'

'Of course.' Mam nods sympathetically.

The thought of Phoebe causes my chest to constrict. Whatever Cillian decides, whether he's man enough to try to work things out between us or not, I promised him I'd always be Phoebe's friend, and that's one promise I'm determined to keep.

A flashback of the FaceTime call winds me like whiplash. *'Love you.'*

All that she's been through and she's not afraid to love others.

I just hope Cillian finds it in himself to feel the same.

'What's the plan for the day?' I change the subject, sounding breezier than I feel.

'I'm going to check out the golf course,' my dad says.

'Spa and bar,' Mam says, helping herself to the coffee pot.

'Sounds like a plan.' Bonnie agrees.

Yep, I'm going to need something stronger than coffee to get through the next twenty-four hours without Cillian, wondering if I'm enough for him to take a chance on.

Or if I've just given my heart to another unavailable man.

CILLIAN

Thursday 21st December

'Hello boss.' Alex greets me with a single arched eyebrow as I pass through the main floor to my office. He fiddles with the button of his suit jacket. 'Or should I call you brother?'

'Don't even joke.' Given what our parents have been up to, it's a distinct possibility. Somewhere deep down, I already know it's true. I even wrote it on my HeartSync sign-up form.

My father is tucked up in a private room at the St Vincent's hospital, receiving the best treatment available for a wounded heart, while my poor mother fights to deal with her broken one alone.

'Perhaps we could be one happy blended family?' My voice drips sarcasm.

Alex blows out a long heavy breath. 'I can't believe it.'

'Huh. The sad thing is, I can.' I nod towards a small meeting room and follow Alex when he steps inside. 'Is this going to make things awkward, you working here knowing my father did what he did?'

'No. Just make sure when it goes to court, that bastard pays for what he did to your mother, and mine. I know she's far from innocent in this but she's stupidly naive. Your father'– he clears his throat – 'is a womanising bastard.'

The fact that Alex is uncannily similar lingers unspoken in the air between us.

Will this change him? Calm him down? Or send him even further off the rails when it comes to playing around?

'I've been waiting for this day for years. I'm sorry you're caught up in it.'

'Me too.' He shrugs. 'My father's gone to Switzerland for the rest of the ski season. He'd rather bury his head in ten feet of snow than face Christmas without my mother. Poor fucker.'

I run a palm across my two-day-old stubble and nod. I've been waiting for years to take him to court. To make my dad pay for the way he's treated my mother. I always thought it would be the ultimate accomplishment. He's the sole reason I chose to specialise in family law. But now the time has finally come, I feel nothing but sorrow.

There are no winners here, not really. My mother gave her entire life to him, and he gave her only a sliver of his.

'How's Phoebe?' Alex asks with genuine concern.

'Blissfully ignorant. Thank goodness.'

'And Ava?'

'Also blissfully ignorant.' Though truthfully, it's me that's the ignorant one.

With everything that's been going on, I haven't called her, despite saying I would. Though, she hasn't called me either.

'We've been friends a long time.' Alex slaps my back. 'I've never seen you look at a woman the way you look at her. You two have something special, you know. I mean, you must do when she turned the chance to dance with me down.' He jokes, trying to lighten the mood.

My spine stiffens at the memory of Huxley Castle. 'You

might want to get a DNA test. You're uncannily like my father.'

'Worryingly, I thought the same.' He tilts his head to the side and rubs a thumb over his chin. 'The difference is, if it transpires that we are related, I'd move mountains for you, not leave you buried beneath them.'

The thing is, I know he means it. We've locked horns often over the years, but we've always had each other's backs.

'Thanks buddy. That means a lot.'

Could this week get any weirder?

'What are you doing here?' Beth demands, her neat eyebrows pinching together with suspicion.

'I came in for the Secret Santa. You know I love all that shit.'

'Clearly.' She scoffs. 'Seriously, you weren't due back until Monday. I know Phoebe's nativity play is tomorrow, but I thought you were on the island until today.'

'I came home early.' I try to nudge past my PA to reach the quiet sanctuary of my office, but she's having none of it.

'You came home early?' She folds her arms across her blouse. 'Or you and Ava came home early?'

'I came home early.' I admit, beckoning her into my office.

She follows me and shuts the door behind her. 'What happened? Is it because of your dad? Alex told me everything last night. I would say I'm sorry, but I know you hoped your mam would leave him years ago. You've been dreaming of taking his slimy ass to court for years.'

'Careful what you wish for, right?' Good thing I wasn't expecting any sympathy from my PA. 'And no, Ava isn't with me.'

'Trouble in paradise?'

'She's been stalking me for an entire year.' My back slams against my leather chair with a thwack.

Beth tips her head back and laughs. 'In your dreams. She's way out of your league.' Her cackle catches in her throat as her eyes rake over my stony expression. 'You're serious.'

'Deadly. Apparently, she and her friend used to watch me walk to Steamy Fix most mornings. They gave me a stupid nickname and everything. It reminded me of what Teagan did.'

Beth scoffs. 'That's different Cillian, and you know it. Teagan took a job here specifically to get close to you. She had access to your calendar. She knew which functions you'd be at. She deliberately got pregnant to keep you, for goodness sake. You're telling me Ava had noticed you around before you met properly, and it's a problem? You should be flattered, you floundering eejit. What's this really about?'

This is the problem with having the same PA since forever. She knows me too well. 'At the wedding Ava's parents were teasing us about marriage and babies and, fucking hell, Beth' – I rub my palm across my stubble – 'I panicked. Then when Bonnie said Ava had been stalking me for a year, I freaked out.'

Beth perches on my desk in front of me and crosses her legs. 'Look, I know your parents' marriage is fucked-up. I know you deal with other people's fucked-up marriages every day. But real relationships go the distance. Look at Carly and me. We're together fourteen years and still going strong. We both came from broken families. Neither believed in true love. Then wham bam, one day we both end up in the same animal shelter fighting over a pussy.' She shoots a smirk. 'And the rest is history, as they say.' She throws her hands in the air.

'That's a lovely story.' I roll my eyes.

'Seriously Cillian. Grow a pair. Take a chance on a relationship with Ava. She's perfect for you. Even a blind person could see it. These last few weeks you've been walking around here grinning like a lovesick fool. So much so that the staff who normally scuttle around here trying to avoid you felt brave enough to ask if you want to be part of this year's Secret Santa.'

'But I have more than a cat to consider. What about Phoebe? What if it doesn't last with Ava, and she leaves Phoebe?'

'It will last, Cillian, if you're willing to make it last. To work through issues instead of hopping on the first ferry when you encounter something that throws you.' Beth pushes herself from my desk and into a standing position. 'But what you need to decide is if you're willing to put that work in. And to take the risk.'

And that's exactly what it boils down to.

Risk.

Because it's not just my heart I'm risking, it's Phoebe's too.

Friday 22nd December

I pull up outside the gates of St. Jude's.

'You won't be late now, Dad, will you?' Phoebe eyeballs me from the back of the car. 'It starts at twelve. Don't get caught up at work and forget, will you?'

I turn to face her and pat her bouncing knee. 'I promise, princess, I'll be sitting in the front row waiting for you to step onto that stage. You're going to be the best Mary that ever was.'

'And you'll save Ava the seat next to you, right?' Her optimistic tone tears my heart in two.

'I think she has to work, princess, I'm sorry.'

I still haven't heard from Ava. I half expected her to

breeze into my office yesterday and kick my ass for bailing on the second day of her brother's wedding, but what did I expect?

I asked her for space and I'm getting it.

In fact, all I see is empty space.

The empty space on my couch where she sat the night before we went to Huxley.

The empty space in my car where she sat next to me, telling me how she was going to get married at the castle.

The empty space across my dinner table where she ate with Phoebe and me the night that Teagan left.

The empty space in my bed where I can't stop imagining her beautiful body sprawled out for me.

I'm beginning to think space is overrated.

Yes, it's a risk letting someone else into our lives, but the reward of having Ava's stunning face and sunny personality around is worth it.

'She said she'd be here,' Phoebe insists, jutting her jaw out with a familiar determination. 'Save her a seat.'

I unstrap my daughter and help her out the car. 'She'll be here, Dad.' Soft grey eyes gaze up at me overflowing with hope and trust.

I need to take a leaf out of my daughter's book. If she can let another woman into her heart after her own mother left, then so can I.

I nod. 'She'll be here.'

I know she will, because I'm going to do what I should have done the second she got home last night. I'm going to go and get her.

She wants the fairy tales and forever.

I'm going to give it to her. Or die trying.

But I'm going to need a bit of help.

Chapter Forty-One

AVA

The apartment has never seemed bigger, colder, or lonelier. Every time I pass the damn Christmas tree, the desire to tear it down rises like a spring tide. It's a perpetual reminder of Cillian, of the time we spent together, of when things were perfect. Of when the future bloomed with hope.

I spent the last two days swigging way too much champagne and pretending to my family that my heart isn't in ribbons. Thankfully they were too preoccupied with Nate, Holly, and Harriet to pay much attention.

The radio silence is killing me. The need to know if Cillian wants to at least try and work things out is eating me alive, but with each hour that passes I'm beginning to get the feeling this case is already closed.

He asked for space. If I don't give it to him, it might push him over the edge.

Though, what's that well-known saying? Something about setting a bird free and if it doesn't come back, it was never yours in the first place?

If Cillian wasn't mine, why did every fibre of my body scream that he was?

We belong together, I've never been surer of anything in my life. I just wish he'd find the courage to give us a chance.

I stare at myself in the bathroom mirror. Panda-like rings circle my eyes. My vagina isn't the only one missing its post-orgasmic glow, my complexion is ashen. I'm going to need a crate full of concealer to get through this morning. And an even larger number of tissues.

Cillian might have asked for space, but Phoebe asked for security. I promised Cillian that whatever happened between us, I'd always be there for his daughter. It's a promise I intend to keep, which is why I'm going to her nativity play, even though it means coming face to face with the man who has my heart and doesn't know if he can handle it.

Because that's what this boils down to.

He couldn't stand the heat, so he legged it out of the kitchen.

I get to work with brushes and liquids and powders until I look half human, run a brush through my unruly hair and apply my trademark Plum Passion lipstick.

I opt for a simple belted dress and boots.

Grabbing my bag, I shove in my phone and a wad of Kleenex.

A horn sounds from outside of the window, long and low. And again. And again.

Someone's got a serious case of road rage. I put my empty coffee cup in the dishwasher, scramble around for my coat, and spray on an extra couple of squirts of Chanel for good measure.

The horn continues to blare from outside.

Jesus Christ. Ballsbridge is supposed to be one of the quieter areas in the city.

I stalk towards the balcony. The morning traffic is at a complete standstill, backed up as far as the eye can see.

I blink hard.

And again.

A white convertible blocks the road below. In the driver's seat is a white-haired man who looks suspiciously like Giles.

Cillian Callaghan is standing on the passenger seat clutching an embarrassingly large bouquet of crimson velvety roses, Richard Gere style. His face is angled up to my window, that square jawline taut with tension.

His silver eyes search upwards, those full lips moving like he's willing me outside.

I unlock the sliding door and step out onto the frost-covered balcony. Horns continue to beep from every direction. 'Get a move on!' an irate driver calls.

Everyone else fades away apart from the man in front of me. The man who exudes strength and vulnerability in equal measures.

'It's no Cadillac limo,' I shout down to the ground, wishing my brother had bought me any other apartment but the penthouse. Laughter bursts from my chest. I can't believe my eyes.

My grumpy divorce lawyer boyfriend seems to be hell bent on making his very own romcom-worthy grand gesture. I'm half embarrassed, half ecstatic, and one hundred percent emotional. Thank God he's not blasting classical music. The horn is attracting enough attention as it is.

'You could have just called. All this is pointless just for me. Please don't even think about attempting to scale the building!' I shout down. 'You already know I love you.' Thank God Dublin's penthouses are a fraction of a size of the ones in the movies, or else I'd have to call him to have this conversation.

'I told you before baby, nothing is pointless "just for you".' He places a hand humbly over his chest. 'You wanted fairy tales and forevers ... I figured it's only fair I deliver.'

Huge swirling eyes lock with mine with a smouldering

intensity that makes my knees weak, and my knickers wet. 'I love you. I'm a silly, scared, cynical fool, but I really do love you and I'm hoping you're going to give me a chance to show you exactly how much.'

Passers-by stop to stare, watching our exchange like it's a movie scene, which I suppose is exactly what it is.

My pulse pounds in my ears. I'm dizzy from looking down, and dizzy with love. I lean on the cold metallic railing, gripping it for support. 'I don't need a grand gesture. I just need you.'

'Well, now you have both, if you still want me that is,' he shouts, cupping his mouth.

'Of course I want you, you mad fecker! I wanted you for an entire year before you even knew who I was. And if that scares you, you should sit down and drive away right now, because I'm about to get started on the really terrifying stuff, like telling you, and all the poor unfortunate people you're holding up with your Richard Gere impersonation, that I want to spend the rest of my life proving to you that love can last.'

Several bystanders begin to clap, a few of them take out their phones. Oh God.

'Also, just to clarify ... I am not a prostitute!' Cillian sniggers and Giles puts his fingers in his mouth and releases a toe-curling wolf whistle.

'That's good to know but can you carry on this *Pretty Woman* re-enactment indoors? Or at least tell Edward Lewis here to stop holding up the traffic!' a woman shouts from the driver's side of a Qashqai. 'I'm trying to get to my kid's nativity play.'

'Speaking of which ...' Cillian beckons me down.

He's ridiculously far away, yet he's never felt more within reach.

'On the way.'

I take the stairs two at a time, way too impatient to even contemplate waiting for the lift. My heels clack against the floor as I run across the lobby and straight into Cillian's open arms. Sharp thorns of the roses graze my back as his mouth crashes over mine, capturing, commanding, and claiming. His tongue sweeps, probes, and delivers an unspoken promise that sets shivers stealing over my spine. Hungry hands trail over my torso as our bodies anchor to each other.

This is it. This is what I've been waiting for my entire life.

And now I have him, I'm going to hang on to him forever. He is my happy ever after. He's my everything. And I'm going to spend the rest of my life loving him so hard he won't ever doubt it'll last.

'Ahem.' Giles clears his throat loudly from the revolving door and we jump apart guiltily. The white convertible, an Audi R8 no less, is double-parked on the street outside, surrounded by an increasing number of applauding onlookers.

'Will you come to Phoebe's nativity play with me?' Cillian asks breathily.

'I was going anyway, with or without you.'

'You were?' Surprise rings in his tone.

'Of course. I promised Phoebe I'd be there. And I promised you whatever happened between us, I'll always be there for her. And I intend to be. I'll always show up for her. For both of you.'

'Did I mention I love you?' He plants a kiss on my cheek.

'You might have, but I'm not averse to hearing it again.' I grab his hand and tug him towards the exit for the underground parking. 'Giles?' I call over my shoulder. 'Will you park that poor excuse for a limo in my space?'

'Absolutely.' He raises his hand in a salute. 'I told you, this is how it starts ... next he'll be leaving his toothbrush here ...'

'Oh no.' Cillian shakes his head vehemently. 'Next you'll be leaving one at mine.' 'Is that right?'

His hand falls to the base of my spine as he ushers me out the back door. 'Nothing's ever felt so right.'

'But who will bring me chips after a night out?' Giles calls, pretending to look horrified.

'Where did you get the car?' I ask Cillian as he hold an upturned palm out and signals for me to hand over my car keys.

'I borrowed it from a brother I never knew I had.' He opens the passenger door for me, and I slide in. 'It's a long story, but first, let's talk about us.'

He hops into the driver's side and adjusts the car seat.

'I'm sorry, I didn't tell you I had the hots for you for a year before we met, Cillian. I didn't want to look creepy, but by not admitting it, things look way worse than they are. I'm not trying to trap you. I'd never do that to you.' I rest a hand on his thigh, revelling in the feel of its thickness beneath my fingers. 'The truth is, knowing how you felt about fairy tales and forevers, I didn't want to scare you off. And in my romantic head, I thought it might have been fate that brought us together.'

'I know, baby. I'm sorry I accused you of trying to trap me.' He takes my hand across the centre console and raises it to his lips, kissing it repeatedly. The car jerks forward but I'm not worried about his ability to multitask – I already know he can control his mouth and fingers simultaneously.

'You're nothing like Teagan. You're nothing like any woman I've ever met before. I'm sorry I wobbled. Bonnie's comment, the wedding, and everyone assuming we were a done deal freaked me out. But the second I left I missed you. Just so you know, that's not why I snuck out in the dark.'

'No?' I assumed space meant mileage but maybe I was wrong.

'I told you, it's a long story, and in the short term, it

doesn't have a happy ending like ours, but in the long term, I'm sure it's going to work out just fine.'

'Spoken like a true believer in fairy tales and forevers ...'

Chapter Forty-Two

CILLIAN

Back at St Jude's the car park is thronged. We abandon Ava's Porsche in the first available spot and nudge our way through the gangs of gossiping mothers. Majella and Stanley Howard fall into step beside us.

'Cillian, how are you?' I didn't see you at ballet this week.' Majella paws my arm. Stanley doesn't bat an eyelid. Yep, that's one party I still don't want to be part of.

'I was with Ava at a family wedding.' I place a hand on the small of Ava's back pointedly.

Majella stills in her tracks and does a double take. 'Aren't you Nate Jackson's sister?'

'I am.' Ava offers a trademark sunny smile.

Majella shoots a sideways glance at Stanley. 'Oh how wonderful, you two must come over for a playdate one day. I'll cook for you ...'

Stanley's eyes gleam.

'Not going to happen, Majella.' I prod Ava forwards.

'She seemed nice.'

'Trust me, that's one "play date" you don't want to be part of.' I blow out a breath.

'Oh.' Realisation sparks in her iris. 'I could give them my parents' number ...'

'Don't even joke.'

There are two free seats in the front row on the left and I tug Ava towards them. 'I'm not a parent,' she protests. 'I should sit at the back.'

'You're not a parent, yet.' I nudge her in front of me and pinch her firm buttcheek. As much as I'm desperate to see my daughter on stage, I'm equally as desperate to see her step off it. The need to make up with Ava properly is overwhelming. Though, it looks like we have the rest of our lives to do that.

We sit side by side on cheap plastic chairs, our thighs touching, our fingers entwined. I glance at Ava from my periphery, she really is stunning. She's everything I ever wanted and everything I was too chicken shit to chase. But I'm here for it now. For the long haul. If she's willing to take a chance on me and Phoebe, I'm willing to take a chance on whatever life throws at us.

'Hey, I thought it was you two.' Savannah Kingsley slides into the seat beside Ava. Dressed in a cream faux fur coat and matching beret, she's channelling Claudia Schiffer in Love Actually (yes, Lillian Callaghan used to watch that on repeat too.)

'Savannah.' Ava greets Dublin's single-mam celebrity like she's her best friend. 'It's so lovely to see you here.'

'Not as lovely as it is to see you here.' Savannah's knowing stare flits between Ava and me with unapologetic glee.

'We'll have to start doing playdates with the girls. Isla and Eden adore Phoebe. We should take them to the nail bar and for ice cream. It would give us the perfect opportunity to catch up. Your sister-in-law is my best friend so that makes us practically related.'

Ava glances to me almost shyly. 'Would that be okay with you?'

'Oh my goodness woman, what part of "I love you" didn't you hear? Of course it's okay with me.' I plant a kiss on her cheek just as the curtains roll back. Phoebe stands in her costume at the front, her silver eyes widening as she takes in me kissing her favourite new friend.

She turns to the twins next to her, hopping from foot to foot with excitement. 'Did you see that? My daddy kissed Ava! It WAS the real Santa at Hollybrooke! He sprinkled his magic! All I need now is a dog!'

'Shh!' Ashley Kearney, St Jude's principal, and Savannah's best friend, appears at the side of the stage and shoots Phoebe a warning look, but even that doesn't diminish the smile stretching Phoebe's lips.

'Is this seat taken?' A burly blonde-haired guy drops into the seat next to Savannah.

Savannah's entire demeanour transforms like the flicking of a switch. 'Yes, it is,' she says at the same time as Ava says, 'of course not.'

He grins and offers a hand. 'I'm Ronan Rivers, one of the teachers here.'

Savannah scoffs as I stretch across her and Ava to shake the guy's hand. 'You're not a real teacher. You shouldn't even be in here.'

Ava raises her eyebrows skywards and sits back in her chair politely pretending to be oblivious to the storm brewing beside us.

'You're right I'm not a "real" teacher. I'm a former Olympic swimmer who was invited by the board of governors to teach here, because St Jude's is the most exclusive school in the country.' He winks in my direction as if to say, watch me wind her up and make her blow.

'Oh, you're a former Olympic swimmer, are you? You

never mentioned that before.' Savannah flicks her hair furiously from her shoulder. 'Much.'

'Sorry sweetheart, I know you thought you were the only celebrity around here.'

'Whatever, dickhead. Sit down the show's about to start,' she mutters, clenching her jaw.

Ava nuzzles into my ear. 'I think it already did.'

I'd have to agree. And if I was still in romcom mode, I'd say this would make the start of a very feisty enemies-to-lovers romance. Or the opening credits of a horror movie.

Thankfully, either way, it has nothing to do with me.

The principal takes to the stage. 'Ladies and gentlemen, mams and dads, welcome to St Jude's nativity. Give a round of applause for all our little stars today, they've worked so hard to put this show together for you all.'

A thunderous round of applause ensues and Phoebe beams and fixes her headdress.

My heart is fuller than I ever thought possible.

My life is complete.

Phoebe remembers every single line and executes them like a pro. She really is the best Mary that ever was, and I'm not biased. Ava agrees, and so does Savannah.

When the curtain falls after the last carol, I'm feeling more festive than I've felt in my life. I'm pretty sure it's because I'm sitting next to my future wife. The mother of the rest of my children.

'Want to go for lunch?' I lean into Ava's ear to be heard over two hundred proud parents' deafening applause.

'Yes! I'm starving! I couldn't stomach a thing the last two days,' Ava confesses, latching on to my bicep. 'Unless you count champagne.'

'Well, I think we ought to have some of that too.' I inhale the jasmine scent of her skin, breathing it deep into my soul. 'I'm sorry for putting you through the mill.'

'Don't be. I told you weeks ago, the wobble is worth it if the grand gesture makes up for it. Stopping the traffic of Ballsbridge was pretty impressive.'

'Why thank you.' I press a kiss against her temple. 'Come on, let's go get Phoebe. School is officially out for Christmas holidays, and I think I know where you'd both like to go.'

An hour later, we're at La Dolce Vita, tucked around the same window table that Ava and I sat at all those weeks ago when she bulldozed into my office and into my life. Maria Romano is clucking around us like a mother hen. We're sipping on another complimentary glass of champagne while Phoebe colours with the complimentary crayons one of the waitresses brought over.

Christmas songs echo through the room. The scent of roasted garlic saturates the air. The lights of Grafton Street glitter in the distance. The waitresses bring over our steaming plates of food, placing them on the table in front of us.

'Cheers.' Ava raises her glass in a toast, and clinks it against Phoebe's lemonade, then mine.

I take the opportunity to grab a slice of pizza from her plate. Her mouth falls open in mock horror.

'What?' I shrug, shoving it into my mouth before she tries to snatch it back. 'You said you only share food with real boyfriends.'

'In that case,' She picks up her fork and stabs it into the centre of my ravioli, helping herself to a mouthful of my second favourite meal.

'At least I know where your mouth has been.' I smirk.

'Yeah, and I know where yours is going,' she whispers, nuzzling into me. 'I mean there are grand gestures, and there are grand gestures ...'

'Is that right?'

'You bet.'

Ava tears off a slice of pizza and hands it to my daughter.

'Can we get a dog?' Phoebe asks.

'Sure.' Ava shrugs. 'One day.'

'This is going to be the best Christmas ever.' Phoebe exclaims, before sinking her teeth into Ava's pizza.

I'd have to agree with her.

Chapter Forty-Three

AVA

Christmas morning

'Merry Christmas, sleepy head.' Cillian's breath tickles my earlobe and grazes my neck. His pillows are on par with the Ritz. I know for a fact, because Nate took us all there for the weekend to celebrate Holly's birthday earlier in the year.

'Merry Christmas to you too.' I snuggle closer, running my fingers through the soft dark hair dusting his chest. He slides a hand under the t-shirt I'm wearing, the red one from the Santa Fun Run, and mirrors my movements.

'Did the big man come?' I prise my eyes open and squint through the dim light spilling from his digital clock. My boyfriend grins down at me. Actually grins. And the effect sets my soul alight.

How did I ever think this man was cold? Fiery flecks spark and ignite those sterling eyes, hot enough to sear anything they land on, including me.

'I've got a feeling he's about to.' He tugs my lower lip with his teeth and tiny tremors shake awake every cell in my body.

'Confident, aren't you?' And why wouldn't he be? The man is perfect. Gifted. Talented. He's the full package and given the day that it is, it would be a crying shame not to unwrap it.

He nudges me flat on my back and eases himself between my thighs. The masculine scent of his skin hijacks my senses. I ought to be creeping out of his bed right about now but he's not making it easy by any stretch.

Warm fingers sweep across my cheeks as he brushes a few loose tendrils of hair from my face. 'I love you, Ava.' His voice is thick with emotion. So is his enormous rock-hard cock, which is digging deliciously through his boxers to chafe the panties I felt obliged to put on in case Phoebe wandered in during the night. Cillian let her stay up way later than usual in the hope she'd sleep in a little this morning. So far, so good.

'I love you too. I've been awake for approximately two minutes, but it's already the best Christmas Day of my life, because I got to wake up with you.'

'Baby, have you been reading those romcoms again?' His hips roll against me in a teasing fashion. 'Because that sounds suspiciously like a line from one.'

'Says the man who went all Richard Gere on me last week.' I buck back. Two can play that game.

'I was hoping you'd go all Julia Roberts and pull out the fishnets for me.' His mouth traces my jaw line, dipping to my collar bone.

A thump sounds from down the corridor. It can only be Phoebe. Tiny feet pitter patter along the hallway at an alarmingly fast rate. Cillian rolls off me and I dive to the floor. For the first time since I woke up, I'm grateful I slept in this god awful t-shirt.

If I can just wait it out on the floor until Cillian leads her out of here.

What kid isn't desperate to check under the tree on Christmas morning?

Through the space under Cillian's King-sized bed, I see Minnie Mouse eared slippers approaching.

'Merry Christmas, princess.' The bed creaks and the slippers, along with two slim little legs are lifted on to the bed.

'Merry Christmas, Daddy.' Excitement oozes from every single syllable.

'Shall we go see if Santa came?' My heart quadruples in my chest. This man. The tenderness he shows his daughter, it makes me want to straddle him every day until I've birthed him five more.

'I already got what I asked for.' Phoebe giggles. 'You can come out from behind the bed Ava. I know you're down there,' she singsongs, and Cillian coughs to mask his shock.

I hesitate for a beat before rocking up from my back to my bum, a sheepish smile playing on my lips. 'I was just checking beneath the bed for any elves.'

Phoebe reaches out and grabs my hand, pulling me onto the bed beside her. 'It's okay. I wanted a second mammy to live with us. And mams and dads share a room, right?' Grey eyes glint with glee, darting between Cillian and me.

'Some mammies and daddies do.' Cillian replies, sounding way calmer than I feel. It's too soon for her to see this, for her to even know these things, but she seems ecstatic about the situation.

Tiny arms wrap around my neck as she tugs me in for a squeeze. 'When are you moving in?'

'Oh, my goodness, sweetie. It's very early for that. We haven't even talked—'

'This time next year.' Cillian cuts over me, running a hand over Phoebe's beautiful blonde locks.

'Really?' That gappy megawatt grin makes it impossible to burst her bubble.

'We'll see.' I cross my legs and pull her into my lap. 'Shall we go and see if Santa left anything for you?'

'Honestly, I have everything I want.' Her back rests against my chest for a split second before she bolts up into the air like thunder. 'Unless he left a puppy down there for me? Do you think he did, Dad?'

I pull back the cover and tug on the leggings Cillian tore off me last night. 'Maybe he left you a practice one in preparation for a real one next year?'

He did – a metre tall, battery-operated, fluffy golden retriever, complete with a pink diamanté studded collar and matching lead. The damn thing even barks. Cillian will be delighted.

'Come on, princesses, let's go investigate.' Cillian holds out a hand to each of us and the three of us venture down the wide staircase together.

My eyes well with happy tears.

I always wanted a love like Frank and Penny, and I've finally found it. Phoebe is an unexpected bonus. That girl has my heart. And I have her back. No matter what.

The pink and white Christmas tree twinkles from the sitting room, luring us over. Neatly wrapped presents punctuate the floor below it, tied with pink bows and silky ribbons.

'Oh. My. God.' Phoebe flies across the room, picking up presents and searching for labels.

'This one is for you!' She squeals, pointing her index finger at me.

'Me?' I glance at Cillian uncertainly. The smirk on his face gives nothing away.

'Go on, open it.' Phoebe urges, shoving it at my stomach.

Shaky fingers pull the ribbon. 'We weren't supposed to be doing gifts. I didn't get you one.' Truly, any spare time we'd had the past few days we spent tucked up here.

'You are the gift. You're everything I never knew I needed in my life.' He presses a kiss to my temple.

Tearing open the paper, I stare down at the gift in my hands. A first edition Bronte. My mouth drops open. Raising it to my face, I open the thick musty pages and inhale deeply.

'I love it. Thank you.'

'It's for your collection.' He tugs me towards the huge floor to ceiling bookcase in his hall. There are two empty shelves.

'I made some space for you.' His Adam's apple bobs. 'For when you're ready.'

I throw myself into his arms, just as Lillian Callaghan drifts down the stairs in a crimson silk kimono. 'Merry Christmas.'

Did his mother's presence delay our Christmas Eve shagfest?

Slightly.

Was I bothered?

Not in the slightest.

Lillian's shrewd eyes take in Cillian's arm around my shoulder, the gift in my hand and the empty space on the bookshelves. Her thin lips stretch into a heartfelt smile.

'This looks promising for more grandchildren.'

'We're certainly practicing for that, anyway,' Cillian sniggers.

Clearly, he's been spending too much time with his future in-laws. I'm not sure Lillian is ready for the force that is Frank and Penny Jackson, but I'm pretty sure nothing could shock her after what she's been through. Frank and Penny Jackson will welcome her with open arms and copious amounts of wine. I just hope they don't offer her a threesome. I wouldn't put anything past them.

Lillian might be relieved to finally know the truth, but it has to hurt. She's shown nothing but grace, humility, and strength the past few days, but now our families are blended, she'll have more support than she ever imagined possible.

Alex is also going to pop in to my parents' house too. He

hasn't sought a DNA test yet, but it's top of his to do list in January. Not that it truly matters. His daily phone calls to both Cillian and Lillian have proved himself family ten times over if you ask me.

'Ahhhh! I got a dog!' Phoebe screams excitedly, ripping the cardboard open like a superhero on speed.

'It barks.' Cillian arches a wry eyebrow. 'Who's for chocolate pancakes?'

'Me.' Lillian, Phoebe and I squeal at the same time.

'With a side order of champagne.' Lillian winks at me. 'I'm starting this Christmas the way I mean to go on – my way.'

I pull her into a hug, Penny Jackson style. 'Good for you.'

Only when every present in the house has been opened, and the floor is barely visible through the shreds of hastily discarded wrapping paper, does Phoebe sit at the table and devour two golden crepes slathered in Nutella.

Her eyes dart between Cillian and me, a question flickering in her all too astute stare. The kid is way ahead of her time.

'You okay, sweetie?' I pat her hand across the table.

'Yes. I'm so happy you're here.' Her gaze falls to the floor, and I sense a but coming.

'Me too, darling. Me too.'

She misses her mother. It's obvious. And it's natural. I'm never going to fill that role, even if Cillian and I do get married, but I'll do whatever I can to plug it for her, so it doesn't hurt quite as much.

'Your mammy texted,' Cillian says gently. 'She's going to pop in for hour before we go to see Ava's parents, okay?'

'Really?' Phoebe bounces in her seat, bright eyed once again.

'Yes. She's bought an apartment in Dublin, and she promises she'll be in at least two weekends every month so you can go and see her and maybe even sleep over some-times.' Cillian stands, flanks her back, and places a reassuring palm on her shoulder.

'This is the best Christmas ever.' Phoebe wipes the corners of her mouth with the back of her hand. 'Wonder what Sarah Snowden got for Christmas.'

'You'll soon find out. You're going for a playdate in a few days.' Dark eyebrows wiggle suggestively at me.

'And so are you.' Cillian murmurs into my ear as he passes behind me.

I push my chair back and follow him over to the sink. 'Really? Where?'

'Paris. The city of love.'

'Seriously?' My boyfriend is turning into one of those romantics he used to scoff at. 'Phoebe's right. This really is the best Christmas ever.'

'Only until next year.' He shoots me that devilishly devas-tating smile again. 'I won't be happy until you're bare foot and pregnant in this kitchen.'

'I can't wait.'

EPILOGUE

Six months later

Cillian

Neither of us could wait until next Christmas, which is why the house that once seemed too big is now cramped with half-unpacked cardboard boxes. Ava spends every night here anyway. It seemed ridiculous not to just bite the bullet and ask her to move in.

My views on marriage and lasting love have been well and truly reformed. I have the black velvet box in my suit pocket to prove it.

'What time is everyone coming?' We invited her parents, siblings, my mother, and my brother – yes, you heard me right – as suspected, Alex is my brother. They're coming over for housewarming celebratory drinks tonight.

My mother apparently has someone she wants to introduce us to, a neighbour of Ava's parents. It's been a tough few months for her, but Alex and I made sure she didn't have to leave the family home, which coincidently, is more like a family home than it ever was when we lived there as a family. The place is overflowing with friends, and laughter and even animals these days. My mother is happy. And it only makes my own happiness so much sweeter.

Dad sold the family business and retired to Portugal with Irene. He had no choice given that neither of his sons wanted anything to do with it.

Alex's relationship with his mother is fragile to say the least, but he remains close with Cyril, the man who was a better father to him than our father could ever have been.

I drop the last box on the varnished hall floor and drag the back of my hand over the sweat beading my forehead. My eyes are drawn to Ava's stunning ass, sculpted by a pair of indecently decent cut off shorts.

'Not until six. Phoebe will be back by then too.'

True to her word, Teagan takes Phoebe two weekends out of every month, which works well for all of us. I get to ravage my beautiful girlfriend – soon-to-be fiancée – in every room in the house.

I debated waiting for our family to arrive, before deciding that I wanted this moment just for the two of us.

Ava's loading books onto the shelf I cleared out for her last Christmas.

She turns around the same second I drop to my knees.

Our eyes meet and her mouth parts into a tiny O.

I reach into my pocket and produce the box, flicking it open with my thumb to reveal the stunning solitaire nestled between the silk lining.

'Ava Jackson, you are the best thing that ever happened to me. You waltzed into my office and waltzed into my life, turning the whole thing upside down with your huge heart, sunny smile, and stunning legs.

You're everything I never knew I needed. You make me a better man.

Will you do me the enormous honour of becoming my wife?'

Her hands fly over her mouth, and she squeals, 'Yes.'

HeartSync Follow Up Form

Congratulations on securing your love match. Please answer the following questions in as much detail as possible for us to help other couples like you. This form is strictly confidential, and for research purposes only.

Name: *Cillian Callaghan*
D.O.B: *Old enough to have a bit of sense now...*
Email Address: *divorcedaddy@gmail.com*
Phone Number: *0876665238 dick picks for my fiancée's eye only*
Occupation: *Lawyer*

I. **Describe your partner in as much detail as possible.**

She's the most stunning woman I've ever met in my life. Inside and out. Her sunny rays have illuminated the darkest corners of my life and turned me in to a walking, talking fanny— I mean believer!

2. Describe your relationship in as much detail as possible.
Transcendent. Tantalising. Tender. Traditional (in the best possible way).

. . .

3. Describe your first date with your HeartSync love match.

She kissed my neck, and I was done.

4. Have you been on holiday together?

Every day we spend together feels like a holiday. You get back what you put in.

5. Have you found your life partner?

She's wearing my ring ... need I say more?

6. Have you ever been unfaithful?

Never. Why go out for a burger when there's steak at home?

7. Provide a brief description of your relationship with your parents.

My mother's a dote. My father is still a dog. At least he lives in a different country now.

8. Do you have any siblings?

A wonderful brother. Every cloud has a silver lining ...

9. How important is marriage to you?

Very important. I can't wait to lock my fiancée into letting me love her forever.

10. Would you recommend HeartSync to a friend?

Abso-fucking-lutely.

THE END

Want a sneak peak of Savannah's epic enemies to lovers romance? Come hang out with me in my reader group Lyndsey Book Lushes https://www.facebook.com/groups/530398645913222

Or turn over the page for the blurb and cover reveal!

Or if you're looking for Nate & Holly's epic romance- The Christmas Crush- click here to learn more:

https://mybook.to/The_Christmas_Crush

ALSO BY LYNDSEY GALLAGHER

DATING IN THE DEEP END

She's treading water with the one man that could sink her...

Savannah:

When He-Who-Has-Never-Been-Named knocked me up and ceremoniously knocked me down with the revelation, "I'm actually married," I fled back to Dublin. There, I dusted off my big girl (maternity) pants and launched my blog, chronicling my life as "Single Sav."

Fast forward six years, and I've built a lucrative empire on that premise. Which is precisely why I haven't so much as looked at the opposite sex for over half a decade. Well, apart from slyly perving on my twin daughters' swimming coach, Ronan Rivers, a former Olympic gold medalist.

The man is ridiculously easy on the eyes but unfortunately not on the ears, for he's the most arrogant man I've ever had the misfortune to meet.

Regrettably, he's also the best swimming instructor in Dublin.

When Coral Chic, Ireland's hottest new Swimwear brand, offers me a million euros to represent their new swimwear range, it's impossible to turn down. Becoming the face and body of that campaign has the potential to take my Single Sav brand global.

But there's one tiny problem... I can't swim and the photo shoots are in the sea.

When Ronan offers to give me a crash course in the deep end, the only thing I'm drowning in is his mesmerising baby blues.

Even if I could get over the fact that I loathe him, I've built my entire brand on being single.

The one man who can save me is also the same man who can sink me...

https://mybook.to/DatingInTheDeepEnd

FALLING FOR THE ROCKSTAR AT CHRISTMAS
SASHA

Ten years ago, I inherited our family castle and sole care of my youngest sister. More Cinderella, than Sleeping Beauty, at the mere age of twenty-eight I have a teenager to raise and a hotel to run. If the hotel is to survive past Christmas, I need a lottery win, a miracle, or Prince Charming himself to sweep in with a humongous... wad of cash.

When my super successful middle sister announces she's coming home for the holiday season, I'm determined to put my problems aside and make this the most fabulous Christmas ever. Especially as it might just be the last one in our family home.

I didn't factor in the return of my first love, **Ryan Cooper**. Back then he was the boy next door. Now, he's a world famous singer/song writer. We were supposed to go the States together. He left without me. Now he's back. Rumour is he has writers block. Apparently this is a last-ditch attempt to find inspiration before his record label pulls the plug permanently.

And guess where he wants to stay? You have it in one- the most inspiring castle hotel in Dublin's fair city.

Every woman in the city wants to pull this Hollywood Christmas cracker. Except me.I'm going to avoid him at all costs.

Easier said than done when he's parading around under my roof, with enough heat exuding from his molten eyes to melt every square inch of snow from the peaks of the Dublin mountains...

FALLING FOR THE ROCKSTAR AT CHRISTMAS- click to learn more

THE COLDEST HOLIDAY OF THE YEAR
JUST GOT HOT...

Lyndsey Gallagher

FALLING FOR MY FORBIDDEN FLING
CHLOE

Even the name **Jayden Cooper** sends a hot flush of irritation through my veins. His rockstar brother might be about to marry my darling sister, but that does **NOT** make us family.

Thankfully, there's a continent separating me from his ridiculously attractive but super-smug face. And his arrogant tongue.

I'm rapidly carving my name in the glittering world of celebrity event management... and what better event to manage than the final farewell tour of my sister's fiancé, Ryan Cooper.

It's the biggest gig of my career.

Eight cities.

Eight concerts.

Eight opportunities to propel my business to a global level.

I couldn't turn it down if I wanted to.

The catch?

It involves working with closely with Ryan's agent- his brother, Jayden-Super-Smug-Cooper.

Going on tour with Jayden is almost as inconvenient as the hate-fuelled lust that steals the air straight from my lungs every time he's near.

Someone somewhere is testing me, but I've survived worse. And I'll survive him.

As long as I don't melt under the intensity of his smug but admittedly smouldering stare ...or fall foul of the talents of the aforementioned arrogant tongue...

Especially when technically...like it or not, we're about to be related.

JAYDEN

I've been through hell to get to where I am today.

I'm *the* best agent in Hollywood's cut-throat industry because I clawed and dragged myself there inch by excruciating inch.

Which is why I refuse to be bossed around by a pushy, Prada-wearing princess when it comes to organising my Rockstar brother's farewell tour. I've got bigger fish to fry, starting with upholding a promise I made a lifetime ago...

But Chloe is about to find out the hard way, what goes on tour stays on tour.

FALLING FOR MY FORBIDDEN FLING- click to learn more

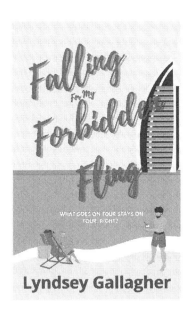

FALLING FOR MY BODYGUARD

VICTORIA

As a student doctor, I deal with bullet wounds on a regular basis, but one teeny nightclub shooting is all it takes for my sister and her rock star husband to send me a new bodyguard/ babysitter.

The last person I expect to turn up is Archie "can't-bear-to-look-you-in-the-eye" Mason.

Now we're roommates until graduation. I can't turn around without tripping over him. If only I could trip underneath him. Because he is every bit as alluring as he was five years ago. And equally as unavailable.

But when my night terrors result in us sharing the same bed, our situation sparks a brand new danger.

One that could hurt both of us irreparably...

ARCHIE

I've been *obsessed* with Victoria Sexton for years.

If my boss and friend, Ryan Cooper, had any idea how bad I have it for his wife's little sister, he'd sack me on the spot.

Living with her is testing every inch of willpower I possess.

How can I watch her back when I can't stop imagining her on it?

FALLING FOR MY BODYGUARD- click to learn more

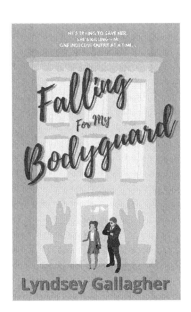

HE'S TRYING TO SAVE HER.
SHE'S KILLING HIM
ONE INDECENT OUTFIT AT A TIME...

Falling
For My
Bodyguard

Lyndsey Gallagher

LOVE & OTHER MUSHY STUFF

ABBY

I need a man. Not in my bed, but for my radio show. I'm an eternally single agony aunt responsible for dishing out romantic advice to the nation. It would be funny if it weren't so tragic. I desperately need to up my ratings.

What better way than to employ one of the country's hottest rugby players to offer his take on love and other mushy stuff to the frenzied females of the nation?

Callum Connolly is the classic example of male perfection.

He's everything I need for my show and everything I don't need in my life...

CALLUM

I'm not looking for *the one,* merely for *the next one.* That is, until my teammates bet I can't keep the same woman long enough to bring to my best friend's wedding.

How hard can it be to date the same woman for three months?

When I bump into a beautiful DJ in a hotel spa, we strike an unlikely but alluring deal. I'll feature on her show and help up her ratings, if she fake dates me until after the wedding.

I don't bank on falling for her.

Especially when nailing her proves harder than nailing the most elusive touchdown ever...

https://mybook.to/Love_OtherMushyStuff

LOVE

& Other Mushy Stuff

LYNDSEY GALLAGHER

LOVE & OTHER GAMES

EMMA

I spent one mind-blowing night with the country's hottest rugby hooker.

It was the best night of my life.

Transcendent, in fact.

And foolishly, I believed **Eddie Harrington** when he swore the feeling was mutual.

But it turns out, the man is a notorious player off the pitch, as well as on it.

They don't call him "Hooker Harrington" for nothing.

One year later, I board a flight to my best friends beach wedding, dreaming of sun, sea and sangria. The last person I expect to find in the seat next to mine is Eddie "love-them-and-leave-them" Harrington.

His best friend is about to marry mine.

I *hate* the ground he walks on, but to keep the peace, I'll play nicely.

Even when a mad twist of fate forces us to share a romantic, idyllic honeymoon suite, complete with only one ginormous, rose petal-covered bed.

Eddie is certain his practiced tactics will earn him a replay, but this time around, I'm sticking firmly to my game plan.

Even if the chemistry between us is hotter than the Croatian sun...

https://mybook.to/Love_

LOVE & OTHER LIES
<u>KERRY</u>

Who's unlucky enough to get sacked and evicted in the same week?
Me. That's who. But a chance phone call with a witty, velvet-voiced
stranger provides a stunning solution to both my problems.

Nathan's looking for a live-in nanny for his sunny five-year-old
daughter and as fate has it, I have a degree in childcare, even though
I swore I'd never use it.

Taking this job will force me to face demons I've been hiding from
for a long time, but I have no choice but to accept.

It's only when I reach the magnificent Georgian house, my new
home for the summer, I realise Nathan "the velvet-voiced stranger"
is actually Nathan Kennedy, Ireland's most successful rugby player,
and the only man I ever kissed when my boyfriend and I were on a
break.

I can only pray one tiny (hot as hell) blip in my past doesn't ruin my
future.

I need this job more than I've ever needed anything.

And worryingly, now I'm here, I want it more than I ever wanted
anything too.

As the summer heats up, so does the escalating chemistry with my
new boss.

Nathan's advances are becoming harder to resist.

And this time round, he swears he's playing for keeps...

https://mybook.to/love_and_other_lies

LOVE
& Other Lies

LYNDSEY GALLAGHER

LOVE & OTHER FORBIDDEN THINGS

<u>AMY</u>

I've always been a good girl, but for the first time in my life, I'm ready to do something bad...

Hot, half-naked men lurk everywhere I turn. But the one whose soul screams to mine wears the number six jersey, along with a look of sheer uninhibited desire.

Six has always been my lucky number, but it's hard to see how this will end auspiciously for either of us.

Ollie Quinn is my brother's teammate. And thanks to my recent appointment as the team's physiotherapist, he's now my patient too. He might be newly single and ready to mingle, but he is utterly off-limits.

Does that stop me?

Of course not.

Chemistry crackles like an invisible circuit between us but when sparks fly, one us will get burned...

<u>OLLIE</u>

Injuries sustained on the pitch seem minimal compared to what Eddie Harrington might do if he finds out I'm sleeping with his little sister. But Amy is everything I never knew I needed and I couldn't give her up if I tried.

Is it simply the temptation of tasting the forbidden fruit?

Or will forbidden turn into forever?

Love & Other Forbidden Things

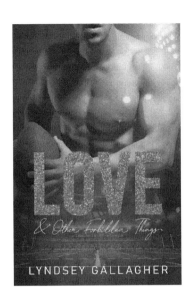

LOVE

& Other Forbidden Things

LYNDSEY GALLAGHER

LOVE & OTHER VOWS

MARCUS

Once upon a time, I was the captain of the national rugby team, surrounded by the loyalty and laughter of my teammates, basking in the glory each winning match brought our country.

Now, I'm a stay-at-home-dad to my two beautiful, bubbly, busy girls while my stunning wife, Shelly, slides, shakes and shimmies her pert little ass all over national television as part of the newest, sexiest, celebrity dance show.

I don't resent her.

She's my world.

But if I tell you I'm struggling to adjust, it's an understatement.

SHELLY

After years of flying solo with the kids while my husband travelled the world with his teammates, the light has finally emerged at the end of a long and lonely tunnel.

Living in Marcus's shadow has been hard but now, I'm finally getting my chance to shine.

I never dreamed I'd be offered a place on the hottest new dance show around.

Nor did I dream I'd be paired up with Marcus's oldest rival either, though. And they weren't just rivals on the pitch.

We have a whole lot of history. And history has an awful habit of repeating itself.

Marcus and I vowed to stay together through sickness and health, but can we survive the pressure brought by fame and wealth?

https://mybook.to/love_and_other_vows

THE SEVEN YEAR ITCH

Twenty-seven-year-old **Lucy O'Connor** has been asked to be her future sister-in-law's bridesmaid despite the fact they don't see eye to eye. The last thing she expected was to fall in love with a complete stranger at the hen weekend. Which wouldn't be a problem, apart from the teeny tiny fact that she's already married to somebody else...

Is it a case of the **Seven-Year-Itch**? Or could it be the real deal?

Lucy needs to decide if she's going to leave the security of her stale marriage in order to find out if the grass is indeed greener on the other side, or whether it's worth having one more go at watering her own garden.

Could this party-loving, city girl really leave the country she loves for a farmer from the west of Ireland?

Is there such a thing as fate?

What about karma?

Is John Kelly all that he seems?

★★★★★ *Love can be insane, gut-wrenching, and dizzying*

https://mybook.to/The_Seven_Year_Itch

ABOUT THE AUTHOR

Lyndsey Gallagher lives in the west of Ireland with her endlessly patient husband, two crazy kids, and and an even crazier boxer puppy. When she's not dreaming up the next boyfriend, she's circuit training, sea swimming, or eating more chocolate than is healthy.

Hang out with her in her private reader group, Lyndsey's Book Lushes. https://www.facebook.com/groups/530398645913222
Or subscribe to her newsletter @ www.lyndseygallagherauthor.com

ACKNOWLEDGMENTS

Thank you dear reader for choosing Dating For December when there are so many amazing books on the market. I hope you enjoyed Cillian and Ava's love story! This one flew out of me. When I read it back during edits, I made myself cackle. Supersoaker 3000?? Where do I even come up with these lines???! :)

A huge thank you to my author friends especially Sara Madderson, Margaret Amatt and Evie Alexander. I value you all more than you'll ever know.

And a massive thank you to the members of my reader group Lyndsey's Book Lushes. The daily check-in's, friendship, support and shout outs fill my heart. Knowing I have all of you cheering me on, and sharing my books and characters across all of Romancelandia is a dream come true. You're the extended family I never knew I needed! Thank you!

Last but not least.. the hubby always gets a mention. He's the reason I write romance. He taught me that no matter what happens in the third act, everything will always work out in the end. Love you GG xxx

MEET MY ALTER EGO...

If you're still with me... well done! ;)

I've recently started writing under L. A. Gallagher in addition to publishing under Lyndsey Gallagher. Spice and sass levels are similar but a different branding attracts a different audience, some readers simply don't like the cute covers, while others won't buy the male model ones, so I decided to do both.

Introducing **The Beckett Brothers Series**

WRECK ME

I am James Beckett, heir to the world's most lucrative distillery empire, that is if I can prove to my overbearing father that I've shed my playboy ways both in the boardroom and the bedroom.

The last thing I need is an uptight trophy wife, especially when I'm surreptitiously obsessed with a stripper.

Day after day, I endure dull dates with Dublin's aspiring elite, searching for a suitable fit.

Night after night, I endure Scarlet baring her body on stage, while she strips my soul bare behind the confines of our private booth, refusing to let me touch her, no matter what I offer her.

Turns out, she's saving herself for marriage.

How ironic.

It feels like fate. Which is precisely why I sign over my heart, and my life in an intimate Italian ceremony.

But it turns out my little stripper wife isn't as innocent as it seems.

She's been keeping a secret.

One that could wreck me...

https://mybook.to/Wreck_Me

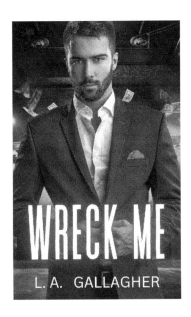

Printed in Great Britain
by Amazon

36143356R00191